THE WOLFGANG PIERCE SERIES

VOLUME 1: BOOKS 1-3

LOGAN RYLES

RYKER
MORGAN
PUBLISHING

ISBN:

Library of Congress Control Number:

Published by Ryker Morgan Publishing.

Cover design by German Creative.

Book 7: *Sundown*

For Abby and Naomi, my original super fans, and two of the coolest people I know.

Thanks for keeping me inspired.

THAT TIME IN PARIS

BOOK 1 OF THE WOLFGANG PIERCE SERIES

————

"Paris is not a city; it's a world."
— *King Francis I*

————

[1]

June, 2011

Horace Artemus Hawthorn IV stumbled down the sidewalk fifteen yards ahead of Wolfgang. In spite of the stiff breeze that ripped through the city, sweat streamed down the polished face of the fourth-generation Chicago aristocrat, outlining his red-rimmed eyes. Every few steps, Hawthorn caught himself against the glass face of a high-dollar storefront. He dropped his briefcase and wiped his forehead, dislodging the eight-hundred-dollar Gucci eyeglasses he wore as he struggled for balance.

Wolfgang stopped on the sidewalk and passed his own briefcase to his free hand, giving Hawthorn a moment to collect himself. The briefcase was identical to the one

Hawthorn carried, albeit empty, and Wolfgang felt a little conspicuous carrying it.

Who even uses briefcases anymore?

Crowds of bustling Chicagoans surged around them, passing Hawthorn with no more notice than if he had been a panhandler. Wolfgang adjusted the light jacket he wore, feeling the weight of the package strapped to his lower back. It bit into his skin and chafed with every stride, but the close proximity to his body kept the package invisible to the naked eye. That was lucky, because if any one of the half dozen cops he had passed in the last half hour detected the package, Wolfgang would have earned a one-way ticket to prison faster than he could sneeze.

Hawthorn swabbed his forehead with a handkerchief—something Wolfgang figured only truly rich people carried—and then adjusted his glasses. He recovered his briefcase from the sidewalk and started forward again. His shoulders were squared in the resolute stature of a man who believed himself to be self-made, regardless of the silver spoon he was born clutching. With each stride, he stared directly over the heads of the meaningless worker bees that surged past him—mere pawns in the game of empire of which he was a key player. But in spite of Hawthorn's confident stride and condescending glare, there was a tremor in his knees and an uncertainty to his steps that couldn't be hidden. It was an odd dichotomy to the strange and unexpected euphoria that

Wolfgang knew Hawthorn had experienced over the past three weeks.

Heroin is a hell of a drug. Especially when you don't know you're taking it.

Wolfgang hurried after Hawthorn, checking his watch as he slipped among the bustling pedestrians.

It had been seven minutes since Hawthorn left the coffee shop. Each morning, he left his thirtieth-story condo in the Millennium Centre tower and took a private car to his favorite coffee shop, where a dark roast with two creams and one sugar awaited him. He sat near the window, where all the peasants of the world could stare longingly at his sculpted jawline and premium Armani-clad physique, and made a show of reading the *Chicago Tribune*.

Wolfgang doubted whether Hawthorn could read at all, but for a rising star in the powerhouse world of business, appearance was everything.

After consuming the coffee, Hawthorn trashed the paper and walked two blocks to the office suite of Hawthorn and Company, a multi-billion-dollar real estate firm founded by his great-grandfather over a century before, now located on the eightieth floor of the Willis Tower.

And there, encased in an oak panel office, sitting behind the Rolls Royce of desks, the young master of the universe planned the development and destruction of a real estate empire worth more than a small country.

That was a typical day for Hawthorn, but today was

anything save typical. Today Hawthorn was destined to spearhead his very first major deal—the eight-hundred-million-dollar acquisition of a rival firm based out of Houston. It was young Hawthorn's first foray into the serious business usually managed exclusively by his father, Hawthorn III, and it marked his initiation as the future CEO of the company.

This was why Hawthorn plowed on toward the Willis Tower, in spite of the chills that racked his body and the dizziness that sent him stumbling into walls. After all, heroin *is* a hell of a drug, and you can't just blindly ingest it for three weeks and then cut yourself off two days before the biggest meeting of your life.

Too bad Hawthorn didn't know he'd been ingesting it. The doses had been small—just frequent and powerful enough to give him a jolt of jollies, yet innocent enough to be dismissed as the thrill of impending corporate stardom. When Wolfgang cut off the supply a little over forty hours before, the loss hadn't been noticed. Not until now, anyway. Now, the rages of withdrawal were in full effect, clouding Hawthorn's mind and jeopardizing his entire future.

Wolfgang remained close enough to keep Hawthorn in sight, but far enough that nobody would take note. The cold sidewalks of downtown Chicago passed beneath him amid a clamor of car horns and shouting voices, but it was easy to keep Hawthorn in sight all the way up to the front steps of the mighty Willis Tower.

Formerly the Sears Building, the Willis Tower was the tallest building in Chicago and the third tallest building in America. Jutting almost fifteen hundred feet into the sky, it loomed over downtown Chicago like a domineering emphasis dedicated to the gods of the corporate universe— which it pretty much was.

Hawthorn stumbled up the front steps toward the glass canopy entrance of the tower. Tourists from around the world were already crowding toward the building, eager to experience the breathtaking view from the tower's observation deck. Hawthorn ignored them, pausing at the door and suddenly clutching one hand over his stomach.

Wolfgang checked his watch. Nine minutes and eighteen seconds had elapsed since Hawthorn left the coffee shop, which meant that his present gut distress was right on schedule. Wolfgang closed the distance between them as Hawthorn pushed through the door and stepped into the massive lobby. More tourists and suit-clad businessmen hid Wolfgang from view as he followed Hawthorn toward the elevator.

But Hawthorn never made it to the elevator. He came within two paces, then doubled over, gripping his stomach. A moment later, he spun on his heel and bolted toward the lobby bathrooms, waddling like an old man with stiff knees —because a laxative is also a hell of a drug and virtually undetectable when mixed in a dark roast with two creams and one sugar.

Wolfgang turned to follow, his shoulders loosening as his stress level began to subside. The operation was all but over now. Hawthorn blasted through the door into the lobby-level bathrooms, and Wolfgang followed two strides behind. The bathroom was bright, with light gleaming off of porcelain sinks and polished mirrors. Banks of bathroom stalls lined the right-hand wall, and Hawthorn made for the first one, sliding through the door like a baseball player skidding onto home plate. The door smacked shut, the briefcase hit the floor, and then Hawthorn hit the throne.

Wolfgang winced at the sounds erupting from the stall. He dug beneath the collar of his dress shirt and produced a stretchy neck gaiter, passing it across his mouth and nose to help block out the smell as he slipped into the stall adjacent to Hawthorn's. Wolfgang kicked the seat cover down over the toilet and sat down as Hawthorn grunted and groaned like a cow giving birth. His hand smacked against the side of the wall as though he were retching, and then another wave of bodily ejections erupted inside Hawthorn's stall.

Wolfgang grimaced and tried to hold his breath. He dug a pair of rubber surgical gloves from his pocket and tugged them on, wishing he could pull them over his head instead. Then he peeked beneath the edge of the stall. Hawthorn's briefcase was visible, standing next to the toilet, only inches from Wolfgang's fingers. He waited until Hawthorn retched and groaned again, then quickly swapped his briefcase for Hawthorn's.

Wolfgang produced a small case from his pocket and snapped it open over his knees. Two electronic plates were inside, connected by wires. The plates featured tiny LED screens on the top sides, with three rubber wheels and a rubber thumb on the bottom side. Wolfgang lifted the plates out of the case and fitted them over the locking dials on the briefcase. The rubber wheels landed perfectly over the metal dials of the briefcase's combination lock, sucking tight against it with magnetic force, and the rubber thumb pressed against the lock switch. He checked to ensure that the device was properly aligned, then hit the only button on either plate.

A soft whirring began a moment later, and numbers flashed across the LED screens as the device began to spin the dials while the rubber thumbs maintained pressure on the lock switches. It checked twenty-eight possible combinations every second as the right-hand device worked backward from 999 and the left worked upward from 000.

It was almost certain that both combinations were the same, so as soon as one device found a winning number, the second device would cease its search and attempt the same number on the opposite side. Most people set the combinations of both sides to the same number, and Hawthorn was anything but a security genius.

Wolfgang leaned back and crossed his arms, waiting and trying not to breathe. Seconds ticked by, and then the left-hand lock popped open with a soft click. 317. Wolfgang tried not to roll his eyes. He should have guessed that number. It was Hawthorn's birthday.

The right-hand plate attempted the same combination a second later, and the lock popped open. He pocketed the device, his fingers moving in a blur as he reached into his coat and unclipped the package from his lower back.

The pod that he produced from beneath his coat wasn't much bigger than a cell phone, but about four times as thick and worth infinitely more. Wolfgang opened it at the same time he opened the briefcase, and carefully deposited its contents inside. Heroin. A lot of heroin. Enough to get Hawthorn slapped with an intent-to-distribute charge.

Wolfgang clicked the briefcase shut amid another round of groans from Hawthorn, and then swapped it with his own again. Then he straightened, flushed the toilet in case anybody was observing him, and exited the stall. After conducting a perfunctory wash of his hands, he walked back through the lobby and into the crisp Chicago air, drawing his phone and punching in a number from memory. The phone rang twice before an elderly male voice answered.

"Hello?"

Wolfgang would have known he was talking to an old WASP by the tone of that word alone.

"Mr. Dudley, my name is Richard Greeley. I'm with the *Wall Street Journal*."

"How the hell did you get this number?"

"I'm working on a story involving your company's merger with Hawthorn and Co and was wondering if you had a comment on Horace Hawthorn's drug problem. Will it be a consideration in the final negotiations?"

"Drug problem? I don't know what you're talking about."

"*The Daily* reported on it just this morning, Mr. Dudley. You *are* involved in final negotiations, are you not?"

The phone clicked off, and Wolfgang lowered it from his ear, shooting off a quick message to a contact labeled only as "E."

OPERATION COMPLETE.

Less than a minute passed before a reply lit up the screen.

B&B. 3.

———

THE BAKER and Bean Café and Coffee Shop sat on the edge of downtown, close enough to Lake Michigan that the waterfront wind wafted away the smell of coffee and pastries, replacing it with an odor a lot more fishy and a lot less appetizing. Somebody probably thought it was a great idea to put a cutesy coffee joint this close to the water, but like most contrived attempts at "old-fashioned simplicity," it didn't really work.

Wolfgang was okay with that. He drank little coffee,

and he wasn't hungry anyway, so he didn't have an appetite to be spoiled by the acrid odor of diesel fumes and fish guts. Nonetheless, he ordered a water because a man sitting alone in a coffee shop with no drink drew more attention than he wanted.

Edric arrived seventeen minutes late, which Wolfgang expected. Edric had probably been on scene for the better part of an hour but was willing to let Wolfgang sit by himself—exposed—long enough to flush out any possible assassins.

"It's Chicago, Eddie," Wolfgang said as the older man slipped up to the table with an oversized jacket draped over one shoulder. "Nobody is waiting to kill us."

Edric sat down, allowing the coat to slide off his shoulder and into his lap, exposing a white cast encasing his right arm from his shoulder to his wrist. Wolfgang sat up, but Edric held up a cautioning finger.

"What have I told you about that?"

Wolfgang sighed and rolled his eyes. "Act. Never react."

"That's right. It should've been a red flag when I walked in here wearing a coat in early June. Why wasn't it?"

"Because you're my boss," Wolfgang said. "And because I'm wearing a coat. Because people wear coats in Chicago all times of the year, and because I really don't care. What happened to you, anyway?"

Edric waved his good arm dismissively as the server approached.

"What can I get you?" she asked, barely glancing at Edric as her gaze swept Wolfgang from ankle to forehead.

Wolfgang winked at her, a grin creeping across his face.

"Dark house roast," Edric said, shooting Wolfgang a glare. "Black."

She walked off, her hips swaying beneath her apron. Wolfgang followed those hips with his eyes until they disappeared behind the counter.

Edric snapped the fingers on his good hand. "What the hell is wrong with you?"

Wolfgang shrugged, leaned back, and interlaced his fingers behind his head. "Based on my physiological reaction to that ass, I'd say all systems are fully operational. What's wrong with *you*?"

Edric leaned back, rubbing his chin as his bandaged arm rested on his thigh. He stared Wolfgang down for a long moment, then sighed. "Debrief."

Wolfgang closed his eyes and cocked his head until his neck cracked. "Hawthorn is a heroin addict, but he doesn't know it, and he's currently enjoying some aggressive withdrawals. I phoned a tip to the lead partner of the company out of Houston. When he sees Hawthorn sweating bullets today, he'll connect the dots. At some point, the heroin in Hawthorn's briefcase will be discovered, and the deal will collapse. Mission accomplished." Wolfgang rattled off the answer in relaxed monotone, his gaze drifting back to the server about halfway through.

She set the coffee on the table and smiled at Wolfgang with a little scrunch of her nose—some kind of cutesy gesture, he supposed—then disappeared again.

Edric ignored the coffee and stared Wolfgang down. "Why heroin?"

"What?"

"Why did you select heroin?"

"Oh, you know. I'm using cocaine now, but I had some heroin in my sock drawer. Does it matter?"

Edric made a production of rubbing his eyes with his good hand. "Yes, it matters. Depending on the drug and how you sourced it, that could be a weakness in the operation—a hole that could be exploited if somebody started poking around. Unless, of course, you actually *are* taking drugs. . ."

"Are you kidding me? I'm not on drugs. What's wrong with you? I bought the heroin off a dealer in Detroit. It's not traceable. Hawthorn is a walking idiot, and nobody is going to question his addiction. Frankly, I'm surprised he wasn't already using. My god, Edric. You get more suspicious all the time."

Edric slowly tapped his finger on the table, still staring Wolfgang down. "What's up with you, Wolf?"

"What are you talking about?"

"You're not . . . sharp. You're not focused."

"Sure I am."

"No, you're not."

"Prove it."

"Today, you took the bus to Hawthorn's coffee shop. I was sitting two benches back, dressed as an old man with a cane, reading a novel. You never saw me."

Wolfgang laughed. "The old man reading the novel was Asian. You should know that because you were sitting at the bus stop where he boarded, feeding pigeons out of a bread bag. Seriously, Edric. Maybe *you're* losing focus."

Edric continued tapping his finger, his stare unbroken.

Wolfgang sighed and threw up one hand. "What?"

"You're bored, aren't you?"

Wolfgang shook his head, then hesitated and shrugged. "Maybe a little."

"You're getting sloppy. Have been for weeks."

"Maybe," Wolfgang admitted.

"Why?"

Wolfgang searched for the server, then sighed. "It's been three years, Edric. I guess . . . I don't know. I just thought the work would be more exciting."

"When I recruited you for SPIRE, I promised you travel, money, and danger. Have I not delivered?"

"You have," Wolfgang said. "Maybe I just need a little more of each."

Wolfgang thought back to Edric's recruitment speech three years before, when he talked with animation about the mysterious company he worked for. SPIRE: a private espionage service specializing in subterfuge, procurement, infiltration, retaliation, and entrapment. At the time, Wolfgang was eighteen, and it all sounded very thrilling, but dumping a laxative in a business executive's coffee felt more junior high than espionage elite, regardless of how effective the strategy was.

"A little more of each," Edric repeated, his voice trailing. "Drugs or no drugs, you have to admit, that's something an addict would say."

Wolfgang didn't dispute the accusation. Excitement was its own form of drug, and like any high, everything dulled after a while. "I don't know, Edric. Just give me another op. Something tropical. I need a tan."

Seconds ticked into minutes while Edric continued to stare, then he seemed to reach a decision. "Does the name 'Charlie Team' mean anything to you?"

Wolfgang shook his head. "Video game?"

"No, it's one of SPIRE's elite team units."

Wolfgang frowned. "What do you mean, team units? SPIRE only hires individual operators."

Edric shrugged. "For petty corporate ops like the Hawthorn job, sure. But sometimes those operators turn out to be exemplary. And sometimes a job is too big for one man."

"What are you telling me?"

"In addition to being your handler, I'm the operation commander of Charlie Team. We execute covert operations on behalf of SPIRE around the world. Next-level stuff. Stuff with a lot more risk and a lot more reward."

Wolfgang remained relaxed, trying to disguise the twitch he felt in his stomach.

Edric held his gaze, then picked up the coffee and took a long sip. "Charlie Team is fully operational, with five members—myself, a techie, and three ground-level operators. Three weeks ago, we conducted an operation in Damascus and things went sideways. One of my guys was killed, and I was thrown off a building. Hence the cast."

Wolfgang sat forward involuntarily. He could tell where this conversation was headed, and he was already sold.

"I received a call from the director this morning. He's got a special job that he wants Charlie Team to take. I can lead from behind, given the cast, but I can't get by without three operators on the ground. I need somebody new. Somebody . . . exemplary."

Wolfgang flipped a twenty-dollar bill out of his pocket and pinned it beneath his water.

"Lucky you. I'm free this weekend."

[2]

THE SETTING SUN gleamed against The Gateway Arch as Wolfgang stepped out of the cab and passed the driver a fifty. The driver fumbled for change, and Wolfgang waved him off, taking a moment to admire the old monument. A haze of pollution clouded it, and shabby buildings blocked part of his view, but it was still something worth admiring.

Wolfgang had never been to St. Louis before. He wasn't sure if this was SPIRE's headquarters or if Edric simply deemed it to be the most convenient location for Charlie Team's next rendezvous. The cryptic, encoded text message from the previous night directed him to fly into St. Louis and meet on the fourteenth floor of the Bank of America Plaza at seven p.m. It was now barely five-thirty, but Wolfgang believed in arriving early. It gave him an advantage over whatever kind of initiation awaited him.

He had the cab drop him off six blocks north of Eighth and Market Street, choosing to walk the final stretch to acclimate himself to the city. There wasn't much to see on a Saturday afternoon—apparently, most of the St. Louis downtown action orbited around business, not tourism. Only a few people bustled past him on the dirty sidewalks, although he counted at least thirty panhandlers, along with two distant gunshots.

St. Louis—not exactly a family town.

Wolfgang arrived at the Bank of America Plaza without breaking a sweat, but still appreciated the air conditioning inside. His shoes clicked against marble floors, echoing inside an empty lobby as he moved toward the elevator. There was a security guard at the front desk watching Netflix on an iPad, and he made no effort to stop or question Wolfgang before the elevator door closed.

Wolfgang pressed the button for the sixteenth floor and stuck his hands into his pockets, contemplating all the things that could happen. Prior to the previous day, he really had no idea that SPIRE operated multi-person units, but it shouldn't have surprised him. His three-year tenure with the peculiar, independent espionage service had led him all over North America, mostly conducting petty sabotage and intellectual theft jobs against corporations, not governments. The prior day's operation was a prime example—somebody didn't want the Hawthorn and Company deal to close, and they were willing to pay handsomely to have it sabotaged. So they hired SPIRE, and SPIRE deployed Wolfgang, and Wolfgang got creative and made it happen. Boring, really.

When Edric recruited Wolfgang to work for SPIRE just months prior to his eighteenth birthday, Wolfgang had dreamed of fast jets, flying bullets, and exotic locales. So far, his average mission was more likely to land him in Cleveland than Bangladesh. Hardly the stuff of James Bond movies.

The elevator dinged to a stop on the sixteenth floor, and Wolfgang stepped into the lobby. Offices for a construction firm lay to his right, and more elevators to his left. The entire floor was dark and silent, fast asleep after a busy week.

He stepped out of the elevator and slipped his hand into his coat, feeling for the Beretta 92X Compact handgun held in a shoulder holster beneath his left armpit. Wolfgang kept his hand on the gun as he stepped to the stairwell and eased the door open, listening for any sounds from two floors beneath him.

As he expected, all was silent. He really didn't foresee any games from Edric; he wasn't the game-playing type. But then again, twenty-four hours before, Wolfgang hadn't expected to be recruited to an unknown team, either. He wasn't about to walk in with his pants down.

He took a cautious step into the stairwell, then crept down two flights of stairs and into the lobby of the fourteenth floor. All was silent, and Wolfgang adjusted his grip on the pistol, then took a cautious step down the hallway.

"Hey, moron! Over here."

Wolfgang jumped and whirled around.

An office door, half-hidden behind a decorative tree at the corner of the lobby, swung open, and Edric leaned out. He shot Wolfgang a glare, then jerked his head toward the room behind him. "You're early," Edric said as Wolfgang sheepishly withdrew his hand from his coat.

"Early is alive," Wolfgang said.

It was one of Edric's favorite quips, and Wolfgang hoped it would win him some points for being caught with his back turned.

Edric didn't seem to care. He just stepped back, allowing Wolfgang to slide into the room, then the door smacked shut.

The office suite was laid out like a penthouse, minus the fancy trappings or expensive furniture. A wall of windows stared out over the Mississippi River and the Gateway Arch, while a hodgepodge of folding chairs, a cheap futon, and a beanbag were strewn over the industrial carpet.

On one wall was a massive marker board, currently festooned with a series of completed tic-tac-toe games, and in the middle of the room was a folding table with a few chairs gathered around it. The only light in the room shone in from the windows, growing gradually dimmer as the sun faded behind the tower.

Three people looked up as Wolfgang shuffled in. First was a tall man with broad shoulders and the kind of buzzed haircut that only an ex-military guy would subject himself to. He had milky blue eyes, and from the moment Wolfgang caught his gaze, he felt unwelcome. Buzzcut stood next to the windows and raised one eyebrow in condescending dismissal.

A second man was short and wiry, with long fingers and round glasses that sat on a sharp nose. His black T-shirt was covered with bleach stains, and he leaned over a laptop computer as though it were his child, not even looking up as Wolfgang entered.

Then there was the petite woman sitting in a corner. Wolfgang didn't notice her at first. She leaned back against the wall with her legs crossed and a cocktail glass in one hand. Shadows played across her face, obscuring her features, but it was impossible to miss the bright red of her hair, which was held back in a ponytail and laid over one shoulder. Eyes closed, she looked perfectly relaxed, as if the world around her either existed or it didn't, and either way, she wasn't going to move.

Wolfgang felt Buzzcut's glare and realized he'd been staring. Somehow, the irritation of the big man only made him want to stare longer.

Edric cleared his throat. "Drink?"

"Sprite," Wolfgang said.

Edric retrieved a beer and a can of Sprite from a mini-fridge, then hit a switch on the wall. The room flooded with bright LED light from overhead, and Wolfgang could now see the woman in perfect clarity.

She was attractive. She kept her eyes closed, apparently undisturbed by the glare. Her face reminded him of a china doll, with rounded cheeks and a nose that was more of the button variety than the supermodel shape, but suited her perfectly.

She was cute more than hot. Pretty more than runway gorgeous. The kind of woman you might just as soon meet in Iowa as you would Los Angeles, but she'd draw eyes either way. Wolfgang liked that for some reason. Something about the way she gently pulled herself to her feet and turned to the window, stretching and running a hand through her hair was confident but weary, as if she hadn't slept much lately or had something heavy on her mind.

Whatever it was, it kept him staring far longer than was polite.

"Hey, shitface. Shut your mouth before I stick a brick in it."

Wolfgang turned toward Buzzcut, whose eyes blazed somewhere between disgust and irritation.

Wolfgang smirked, a retort already wavering on his lips as Edric pressed the Sprite into his hand.

"Ease up, Kev," Edric said. "Let's be friendly." He snapped his fingers and motioned to the table.

Wolfgang glanced back in time to see the woman take

one more look out the window before turning to the table, and then he saw her eyes. They were large and grey, a little brighter than stone, and crystal clear, but sad. As she brushed hair away from her face and scrunched her nose, he saw a deep pain accentuated by a slight redness in her cheeks. Their gazes met, and in an instant, the sadness vanished, replaced by a block wall. Her back stiffened, and she looked away, proceeding to the table without giving him a second look.

"Have a seat, Wolf," Edric said. He motioned to the end of the table as the woman and Buzzcut found their seats.

Wolfgang slid into the end chair and took a long pull of the Sprite, suddenly feeling very awkward and self-conscious.

"All right, everybody," Edric said. He stepped behind Wolfgang and gave him a slap on the shoulder. "This is Wolfgang Pierce. He's been with the company for three years, and he's now joining Charlie Team."

The woman picked at her fingernails, and the wiry man behind the computer continued to stare at his screen. Only Buzzcut faced Wolfgang, his eyes as cold as death.

Man, what's up this guy's ass?

Edric walked around the table and smacked the laptop shut without ceremony. The wiry man opened his mouth to object, but Edric continued.

"Wolfgang, welcome to Charlie Team. On your left is Kevin Jones. Besides being a three-time world champion of the Resting Bitch Face Olympics, Kevin is our primary driver and combat specialist. When we need the big guns, Kevin's our man."

Wolfgang nodded once at Kevin but received nothing more than a continued glare.

Edric moved around the table. "Center stage is Lyle Tillman. Lyle is our tech wizard. Phones, computers, security, communications, high-tech gadgets . . . Lyle makes it happen."

Wolfgang offered the nod to Lyle and was gratified to have the wiry man return it, even if he wouldn't meet Wolfgang's gaze. Edric moved toward the woman, and Wolfgang felt self-conscious again.

"Last but not least is Megan Rudolph. Megan is our senior operator and Charlie Team's second-in-command. Her specialties include interrogation, infiltration, and operations coordination. Prior to working for SPIRE, she worked for the FBI. If Megan says jump, you say how high. Got it?"

Wolfgang flashed what he hoped was a friendly smile. "Pleasure to meet you."

Kevin stiffened, but Megan looked up. She appraised Wolfgang with a quick sweep of those brilliant grey eyes, her lips lifting in a perfunctory smile, and Wolfgang adjusted his assessment again. Megan was more than cute; she was beautiful. Not in an ordinary way, certainly, but that smile, however brief and stiff, lit up the room like a flare.

She returned her gaze to her fingernails, and the smile faded as quickly as it had come. Wolfgang swallowed and chugged his Sprite.

"Okay, then," Edric said. "I realize the circumstances around Wolfgang's recruitment are rushed and unusual, but—"

"We don't need him," Kevin growled. "It's a liability having somebody we don't know. I don't like it."

Edric's tone remained calm. "I hear you, Kev, but we do need him. I'm out of the field until my arm heals, and you and Megan can't operate alone."

"Is he trained?" Lyle's voice was as mousy as his appearance—little more than a squeak.

"Yes," Edric said. "Like I said, he's a three-year veteran of SPIRE's corporate espionage division."

"So, he's got no experience with a team," Kevin said. "He shouldn't be here."

Edric set his beer down and leaned over the table, wrapping his fingers over the back of a chair.

"Look. I hear you. But this is happening. If you're not comfortable with it, you can leave. Okay?"

Kevin shot Wolfgang a long glower, then looked at Megan. She was still busy picking her fingernails, but she looked up and swept another passive gaze over Wolfgang, every bit as quick as she had the first time. He felt her look in his bones—sharp and penetrating—and he had the distinct impression that she was evaluating him on a molecular level, like an X-ray that searched for weaknesses in his body language. The experience was maddening, but something about her attention was addictive, too.

Megan nodded once, and Kevin grunted and folded his arms.

"Okay, then." Edric wiped away the tic-tac-toe games from the marker board, then selected a red marker and began to write.

"We're going to Paris. Bravo Team was originally tasked, but the director reassigned the operation last minute. So, the pressure's on . . . got me?"

Edric wrote *Paris* across the top of the board, then turned to the table. "Our primary objective is an unknown male, code-named Spider. He's an anarchist suspected of running a complex, multi-national terrorist organization. His ethnicity, background, and true identity are all unknown. The CIA has been tracking him for the past six months and believe that his organization is preparing a terrorist attack for someplace in Western Europe."

"Why?" Kevin asked.

Edric wrote "Spider - ID unknown" on the whiteboard. "Why what?"

"Why the attack?" Kevin said. "What's his motive?"

"He's an anarchist," Edric said with a little shrug, as if that explained it. "Captured manifestos from his organization call for the dismantlement of all governments around the world. Basically, anarchists want chaos. They believe it will 'restore natural balance' to the planet. Whatever that means."

"So, we're gonna take him out?" Kevin asked. There was a hint of a smile on the edge of his lips that sent a chill down Wolfgang's spine.

Edric shook his head. "Negative. In fact, our mission is to protect him."

"What the hell?" Kevin's eyebrows furrowed, but Wolfgang's mind was spinning, already unraveling the puzzle.

"The CIA is in contact with him," Wolfgang said. "They need intel."

Edric pointed the marker toward Wolfgang. "Bingo. The CIA has an operator, code-named Raven, who has established contact with Spider and is slowly gaining his trust. Spider is meeting Raven in Paris thirty-six hours from now. The CIA hopes this meeting will provide critical intel about Spider's identity, his operations, and the attack he's planning."

Edric returned to the whiteboard and wrote "CIA" on it, with an arrow connecting "CIA" and "Spider."

"Wait . . . You said we were protecting Spider, though," Kevin said. "From who?"

Wolfgang wondered the same thing.

Edric wrote another word on the whiteboard, completing a triangle with lines connecting the new word. "Russia," he said, stepping back from the board. "The Russian Foreign Intelligence Service has been tracking

Spider also, and they've obtained his plans to meet a foreign operator in Paris. As far as we know, the Russians are clueless as to the CIA operation, and we need to keep it that way. However, if we know anything about our friends from Moscow, they aren't likely to ask questions. We suspect they've already deployed a hit team to eliminate Spider and prevent his planned attack."

"But if they succeed, we'll never know where the attack was planned to take place, or who else was behind it," Wolfgang said. He leaned forward, his mind racing as he connected the dots. "We need more than Spider. We need the people behind him. The financing, the foot soldiers, the weapons suppliers."

"Cha-ching. Exactly," Edric said. "The CIA needs intel from Spider, and they'll never get it if Moscow guns him down. So, we have to protect Spider—at least until the CIA is finished with him."

"Why can't the CIA protect him themselves?" Kevin asked.

"Plausible deniability," Wolfgang said. "Spider is a global terrorist, and the US isn't on great terms with Russia. If they discovered the CIA protecting a known anarchist, Russia could easily spin their hit squad as a policing team sent to detain Spider, and then frame the CIA as collaborating with him. It would be an international scandal. The CIA needs a third party to shield Spider. Somebody they can disavow."

The room fell quiet, and Wolfgang noticed that every-body seemed to be waiting on Megan to speak. She sat still, staring at him with piercing, unblinking eyes. Then she nodded once, and the gesture sent a strange jolt of elation shooting through Wolfgang.

Edric replaced the cap on his marker. "Right again. The CIA needs distance. Also, France is a sovereign nation. The CIA can't deploy an armed commando force into down-town Paris uninvited. That's a serious breach of international ethics."

"The Russians are doing it," Lyle said.

Kevin snorted. "The Russians don't give a shit about international ethics."

"They really don't," Edric said. "Which is why we can expect a fight if things go sideways." He set the marker down and scratched his injured arm beneath the edge of the cast.

Wolfgang drained the rest of the Sprite. *Paris. Russian hit teams. Intriguing teammates.* Charlie Team was looking like a heck of a good idea, regardless of Kevin and his RBF.

"Okay, then." Edric smacked his cast with his good hand. "Our mission is to fly to Paris and find Spider before the Russians do, then protect him until he completes his rendezvous with Raven. We'll be armed, but ideally, we pull this off without any fireworks. I'm setting operational protocols at Code Orange."

Wolfgang raised a finger, and Kevin rolled his eyes.

"Oh, for heaven's sake. He doesn't even know the protocol codes."

"Calm down, Kevin," Edric said. He turned to Wolfgang. "We have three levels of engagement: yellow, orange, and red. Yellow means we're unarmed. Orange means we carry guns, but we don't shoot unless we're shot at."

"And red?" Wolfgang asked.

Edric laughed a little. "Red means Kevin takes over."

Lyle and Kevin joined in on the laugh.

Edric rested his hands on the back of the nearest chair. "When we reach Paris, Kevin, Megan, and Wolfgang will be on the ground. Lyle and I will remain in the rear, running communications and surveillance. Questions?"

Nobody said a word.

Edric grinned. "All right, then. Let's go save a terrorist."

[3]

"HOLY COW," Wolfgang whispered. "Am I getting a pay raise with this job?"

Hot summer wind whipped across his face as he shut the door of the taxi and stared out across the tarmac. A Gulfstream G550 jet sat on the private runway outside of St. Louis, the engine already running at idle, with the door open and the steps resting on the concrete.

"Private espionage is high-paying work," Edric said. "When you're the best, you get the best toys."

He tossed Wolfgang a duffle bag loaded with what felt like bricks and started toward the plane. Wolfgang followed as Kevin and Megan ran up the steps carrying similar backpacks. Lyle struggled behind them, wheeling two heavy cases full of what Wolfgang assumed to be computer equipment.

Wolfgang shouldered the duffle and turned back, holding out his hand. "Here. Let me help."

Lyle blinked up at him from behind smudged glasses. He reluctantly surrendered one of his precious cases, and the two started toward the plane.

"Thanks," Lyle said. "Nobody ever helps with my gear."

"I don't mind," Wolfgang said. "What have you got here, anyway?"

Lyle's eyes flashed, and Wolfgang wondered if he'd regret asking.

"Everything we need," Lyle said. "Communications, surveillance, infiltration equipment. It's just like the movies. I've got all the gadgets."

Wolfgang laughed. "Got any X-ray glasses?"

Lyle stopped mid-stride and squinted up at Wolfgang. "X-ray glasses?"

Wolfgang grinned. "You know. Glasses that let you see through stuff. Walls . . . doors . . . clothes . . ." He winked and tilted his head toward the plane.

Lyle wrinkled his nose before his gaze turned cold, and he snatched the second case from Wolfgang's grasp. Without a word, he set off in a quick march, wheeling both cases behind him.

"Hey!" Wolfgang said. "What did I say? It was just a joke, man."

Wolfgang hurried up the steps as Lyle clattered ahead, dragging his cases and disappearing into the plane. The cabin of the aircraft smelled faintly of an ocean breeze air freshener. Wolfgang had to duck to step inside, and he stared down an interior featuring plush leather chairs, a minibar, and a door at the back that he guessed led to bunks.

The others were already gathered around the middle of the cabin, pivoting their chairs to face each other.

"Wolf, hurry it up," Edric said, waving his cast-frozen arm.

Wolfgang slid into the nearest chair, casting a casual glance around the cabin. He'd never flown first class, let alone private. The aircraft was small, but with only five of them on board, it felt like Air Force One.

Lyle took a seat in the back, pushing his glasses up his nose. Kevin sat in the middle, dressed in cargo pants and a black shirt that was two sizes too small, accentuating a six-pack that would make Chuck Norris envious. He glared at Wolfgang, then looked away as if the newcomer wasn't worth his attention.

Megan, next to a window, had a closed sketchpad and a stick of charcoal in her lap. She stared out the window absently, her scarlet hair swept behind one ear.

Wolfgang watched her a moment and wondered what was in the sketchpad. He knew next to nothing about art but was intrigued by the idea that Megan might be an artist.

"Hey! New guy!" Kevin's chunky fingers snapped in front of Wolfgang's face. "Are you retarded or what? Stop gawking."

Wolfgang felt a vague irritation and brushed Kevin's hand away but said nothing. He was still thinking about Megan. Still wondering what lay behind those grey eyes.

"Don't say *retard*, Kevin," Megan said in a soft voice with just a hint of rasp. "It's not acceptable anymore."

Wolfgang realized it was the first time she'd said anything in his presence.

Kevin flushed and leaned back, his glare darkening to a scowl.

"That's enough, all of you." Edric settled into his seat as the plane's door hissed shut and the aircraft began to move. He held a glass with a pool of liquor swimming in the bottom, his broken arm held close to his side.

Wolfgang noticed him wincing as he settled into the plush seat and took a sip.

"All right. Eyes front, everybody."

Wolfgang tore his focus away from Megan and sat up. He felt the blistering wrath of Kevin directed his way and shot the bigger man a wink and a grin. Kevin looked ready to explode.

Edric produced a file from the seat next to him, opened it, and passed photos around the circle. They were black-and-white distance shots of a tall man in a business suit with black hair and a bold jaw. He appeared to be Caucasian but sported a tan so dark he may have been of Italian or Greek descent.

"This is Raven," Edric said. "He's currently in the air on

the way to rendezvous with Spider. Our communication with Raven will be highly limited on the ground. The CIA doesn't want him to wear any direct communications equipment in case Spider searches him."

Wolfgang stared at the face as the plane gained speed and the wheels left the ground. The deep eyes of the man in the photograph were penetrating, but not uncomfortably so. If Wolfgang had to guess, he wouldn't have said that this man was a CIA operative, but maybe that was part of the job description—you had to blend in.

"We also don't know where the meeting is going to take place," Edric continued. "Spider will communicate that information to Raven at the last moment, for security purposes."

Kevin said, "We can't talk to Raven, we don't know where Spider is, and we don't know what he looks like. How the hell are we supposed to pull this off?"

Edric nodded at Megan, who was fixated on the photograph.

"We know when Raven lands, right?" Megan asked.

"Yes," Edric said.

"So, we pick him up at the airport," she said. "Trail him from there to the meeting spot. Stay in the shadows and look out for both Spider and the Russians. It's not ideal. It leaves us at the vulnerability of whatever terrain Spider chooses. But if we can't communicate with Raven, it'll have to do."

Megan leaned toward the file, her relaxed and disengaged posture of only moments before melting away. Her voice was clear and strong, carrying a hint of command that Wolfgang hadn't noticed before.

Edric smiled. "Very good. That's the plan."

"What about an SDR?" Wolfgang asked, eager to contribute. "Won't Raven run one?"

"SDR?" Kevin said.

"Surveillance detection route," Wolfgang said. "It's a tactic used by covert operatives to shake away anybody trailing them—"

"I know what an SDR is, moron," Kevin said. "Did you miss the part where this guy is working *with* us? He's not trying to shake us."

Megan ran a hand over her eyes. "Don't say *moron*, Kevin."

"Of course Raven doesn't *want* to shake us," Wolfgang said. "But if he's in communication with Spider, and Spider is worried about security, don't you think he might order Raven to conduct an SDR? Raven wouldn't have a choice."

"Wolfgang's right," Edric said. "It's a possibility we have to consider. Raven will do everything he can to keep us with him, but he doesn't know what we look like, and he can't appear to be working with anyone. Unfortunately, we can't put a tracker on him for the same reason we can't put communications on him. So, it's up to us to stick on him like a flea on a dog. We *cannot* lose him. Understood?"

A chorus of grunts passed around the room.

Edric drained the glass. "Good. Everybody familiarize yourselves with some Parisian maps. Lyle and I will be positioned in a van as close to the action as possible. I'll drive and maintain operational control of the mission while Lyle hacks into the Parisian traffic camera network. That should give us an edge on keeping track of Raven. Megan will take point on following him while Wolfgang and Kevin provide direct support. Megan, did you work out some transportation?"

"Yeah. Got us set up with some bikes."

"That should do it. Questions?"

Wolfgang looked back at the photo of Raven, absorbing the facial features staring back at him—the face he couldn't afford to forget.

Edric stood. "Okay, then. Make sure you guys get some sleep." He reached into his coat and produced a glossy travel brochure, then flipped it to Wolfgang with a smirk. "Welcome to Paris, Wolf."

He disappeared into the back of the plane, and Wolfgang studied the brochure. It was an English travel guide to Paris, prominently featuring the Eiffel Tower. He flipped through it, surveying a few paragraphs of tourist lore. He'd never been to Paris before. "The City of Lights," the brochure said, and a city of romance. He glanced over the top of the brochure at Megan. With her notebook now open, her hand moved in gentle arcs across the page, scraping charcoal against the paper.

Kevin snapped his fingers again. "Hey, dum-dum."

Wolfgang looked up and sighed. "Don't do that."

"Do what?"

"Snap your fingers at me. It's really irritating."

"Oh yeah? What you gonna do about it?"

Wolfgang held his gaze, then grinned, lifting his lip just enough to expose some teeth. It was a tactic he'd used before. He called it his "crazy stare," and it never failed him.

Kevin broke after less than twenty seconds, standing up and stomping to the minibar while muttering curses.

Wolfgang stood up also, tapping the brochure against his fingers, and stepped across the cabin toward Megan. His stomach felt suddenly unstable, as if an ocean were swimming inside. "What are you drawing?" he asked.

Megan continued to sketch, her body language tensed and focused.

Wolfgang fiddled with the brochure. "I mean, I don't want to pry. I just like art. Maybe when we get to Paris we'll have some time to see some paintings. Have you ever been to the Louvre?"

Without looking up, Megan drew a slow breath and swept a stray strand of hair behind her ear. "Do you have questions?" Her voice was calm but all business.

He frowned. "Questions? I just thought we could get to know—"

"About the operation. Do you have questions about the operation?"

"Oh." The ocean in his stomach froze over instantly. "No. I think I'm good."

"That's great. You should probably get some sleep. This is gonna be a high-energy job."

Wolfgang could feel Lyle's and Kevin's eyes on him. "Right. Of course." He turned toward the tail of the plane.

The engines roared outside, reduced to a loud hum by the thick insulation of the premium fuselage.

Kevin sat at the rear of the cabin, a glass of whiskey in one hand, his lips gleaming with residue from the drink. He grinned as Wolfgang stepped toward the door to the bunks. "Why don't you pour yourself a drink, Wolf? We can get to know each other." The sarcasm in his tone cut like a blade.

Wolfgang stopped at the door and dug his fingernails into the travel brochure before reaching for the handle. "No, thanks. I don't drink."

[4]

THE PLANE TOUCHED down a little over ten hours later, the tires squealing against a private airport someplace outside of Paris. Wolfgang slept six or seven hours and spent the rest of the flight studying maps of the big city. It was impossible for him to really absorb so many streets in such a brief period. Paris was huge, sprawling over an area of almost forty-one square miles, packed with over two million people. Finding one man in that mix and keeping track of him through the busy streets for an indefinite period was daunting, to say the least.

Wolfgang changed into a pair of jeans, a T-shirt and a loose leather jacket that allowed for plenty of room to conceal the Beretta in a shoulder holster. Handguns in Paris were highly restricted items, and being caught with one was sure to be a nightmare. But being caught without one while hunting an elusive terrorist amid a team of Russian assassins seemed the greater risk.

Wolfgang stepped out of the plane and shielded his eyes against the bright sunlight that was just breaking over the eastern horizon. There wasn't much around them other than rolling green farmland. The plane sat at the edge of the tarmac near a row of low hangars, and Wolfgang realized he had yet to see or interact with the pilots. He glanced up at the cockpit, then shrugged and hurried to follow the others toward the nearest hangar.

Dusty and dimly lit inside, the cavernous space was empty except for four vehicles—a white Mercedes panel van and three identical motorcycles parked in a neat row, their front wheels all canted to the left.

Lyle headed straight for the van, trailing his cases, and Wolfgang hurried to follow him. He still wasn't sure what he had done to offend the tech wizard, but he didn't want to leave the issue unresolved. If Lyle had all the gadgets and ran all the communications, he wanted to be friends.

Lyle opened the rear door of the van and started to lift the case. Wolfgang grabbed it first and slid it inside, and Lyle squinted up at him from behind his dirty glasses.

"Hey," Wolfgang said. "About last night . . . I just want to say, I meant nothing by it. Bad joke. I appreciate the work you're doing." He offered his hand.

Lyle's gaze switched from Wolfgang's face to his hand, then back again. He chewed his lip a moment, then accepted the offered hand with a surprisingly strong grip. "Come here. I've got something for you," Lyle said. He ducked into the van, and Wolfgang followed. Lyle flipped a hard plastic case open and produced a tiny earpiece, flicking a switch on before passing it to Wolfgang. "This is your comm. Signal is great, and the mic is sensitive. No need to speak in louder than a conversational tone. Only thing is, the battery life isn't great. Remember to charge it between use."

Wolfgang fit the little device into his right ear canal. It slid in without resistance and was almost comfortable.

Lyle dug into the case and produced another box, sliding the lid off with obvious care and exposing a watch nested inside. At least, it was on a band like a watch, but instead of a round face it had a square face with a black screen. Wolfgang had never seen anything like it.

"And this . . ." Lyle indulged in a brief smile, the first Wolfgang had seen. "This is truly special. I've only got one of them. You can try it out."

"What is it?" Wolfgang asked. "Some kind of watch?"

Lyle lifted the device from the case and passed it to Wolfgang. "It's not a watch. It's a fully purposed spy gadget. I ripped the design off some Apple blueprints. Apparently, they're designing something like it for release in a few years, but I couldn't wait that long. Took me months to perfect it. There's a camera built into the outside of the case, and anything you direct that camera at, I can see. So if you need intel on something, you just show it to me, and I can look it up for you."

"Sweet, man." Wolfgang lifted the watch and wrapped it around his left wrist. It felt great. A little heavy, but not unbearable.

"The true benefit, though," Lyle said, "is in its detection ability. I call it a sniffer. The watch can detect all kinds of poisonous gasses and chemical agents, and it'll give you an alert if there's anything you should be worried about. It even has a built-in Geiger counter."

"Like, for nuclear?" Wolfgang raised one eyebrow, and Lyle nodded eagerly.

"Absolutely. It's not perfect, but it's pretty reliable. Let me know how it works in the field."

Edric's voice boomed from someplace in the hangar. "Hey, Wolf. Get out here!"

Wolfgang slapped Lyle on the shoulder, then piled out of the van. The others were gathered around the bikes, Megan already astride hers. She sat with the easy confidence of a woman who was familiar with fast motorcycles, and Wolfgang couldn't help but stare again.

"Get your comm?" Edric asked.

He scratched his cast again, and Wolfgang realized Edric was probably nervous. This was his first mission since breaking his arm and his first mission with a new operator . . . and without an old one.

Wolfgang tapped his ear. "Right here."

"Very good. We only use radio tags, for extra security. I'm Charlie Lead. Lyle is Charlie Eye, Megan is Charlie One, Kevin is Charlie Two."

Edric paused a moment, and his tone softened. "You're Charlie Three."

Wolfgang saw Megan glance down, and for just a moment, he thought she winced. It was such a small reaction he couldn't be sure, but he thought it corresponded with Edric's mention of Charlie Three.

That was his call sign . . . The guy who died on the last mission.

Wolfgang didn't know what to say, so he just nodded.

"While you're on the ground, you take operational orders from Megan, unless and until I override them. Is that clear?"

Wolfgang nodded again.

"Great. Let's roll."

Edric shuffled to the van, and Wolfgang moved to the bike at the end of the line.

"Can you ride, dum-dum?" Kevin asked.

Wolfgang looked down at the bike, taking a moment to trace his finger down the fuel tank's smooth curve. It was a Triumph Street Triple RS, brand-new, shadow grey with red accidents. Identical to the others. He'd never driven a Triumph before but assumed it operated pretty much the same as his Kawasaki back home. "I can ride," he said.

Kevin snorted, then slid his helmet on and flipped up

the visor. He turned to Megan. "You good?" His tone was softer but still gruff and condescending.

Megan slapped her visor down without a word and kicked the starter. The bike roared to life, and a second later, she shot out of the hangar like a bullet.

Wolfgang hit the starter and gunned the motor as a shot of adrenaline raced into his blood. This was something new. Something different.

And it was starting right now.

––––––––

CHARLES DE GAULLE AIRPORT, better known as Roissy Airport, sat twenty miles northeast of downtown Paris. It took them twenty minutes to get there, roaring amid tightly packed morning commuters as they circled the eastern side of the city and approached the airport.

Megan was difficult to keep up with. She pushed the Triumph hard, cutting in and out of trucks and taxis as if she were on a racetrack. Wolfgang was surprised—he would have assumed they would want to avoid attention, not attract it. But there were a lot of motorcycles on the road, many more than in America, and they all drove aggressively. He pushed himself to keep up, taking moderate gratification in Kevin's obvious hesitation to push himself as hard. Apparently, his bark was worse than his bite. At least on a bike.

After reaching the airport, they deposited the Triumphs in short-term parking, leaving the helmets and venturing into the nearest terminal.

Megan spoke over the comm. "Charlie One, I'm taking over ground control. Comm check."

"Charlie Lead, roger ground control assumption. Comms clear."

"Charlie Eye, I have you on satellite." Lyle's voice was squeaky over the earpiece, but at least Wolfgang could hear him clearly.

"Charlie Two, loud and clear."

To Wolfgang's surprise, the arrogance had left Kevin's tone. He spoke with calm focus. Wolfgang shot him a look as he radioed in his own confirmation, and Kevin sneered at him.

"Moving into the terminal now," Megan said. "Charlie Two, take international arrivals from Europe. Charlie Three, you've got North America."

"Copy that." Wolfgang resisted the urge to scratch his ear. Talking made the earpiece move, and it itched now. He feigned a yawn to adjust it, but it only helped a little.

The airport was nothing short of massive. Tourists and business travelers pressed in on all sides, dragging roll-around suitcases and shouting to each other over their own clamor. There was no dominant nationality. Wolfgang saw Asians, Arabs, South Americans, and Africans as frequently as Europeans. They crushed in on every side, frequently slamming into his shoulders.

How the hell was he supposed to find a single man in this melting pot? He couldn't even see Kevin anymore. His fellow operator had faded like a ghost.

"Dammit, Charlie Three," Megan said. "You're sticking out like a clown. Relax and move to North America."

Wolfgang cast a glance around him, but he couldn't see her. She, too, had faded into the crowd and was now lost from view. He drew a deep breath, which morphed naturally into another yawn. He pretended to pop his neck, then shoved his hands into his pockets and followed the signs toward international arrivals from North America. Everything was written in English as well as French, making navigation easier than he expected.

Dozens of airlines lined up next to each other, pressed together with travelers flooding out of boarding tunnels. Wolfgang assumed a position at the edge of the room, then slid onto a bench and pulled out his phone, retrieving his digital copy of Raven's image. He stared at it a moment, then scanned the room.

"Get me out of your pocket, Charlie Three," Lyle said. "Let me have a look."

Wolfgang frowned in confusion, then recalled the wristwatch. His left hand was still jammed in his pocket. He withdrew it and casually rested his hand against the armrest, exposing the undetectable camera lens to the main lobby of the terminal.

"That's better," Lyle said.

Wolfgang made a mental note to pay specific attention to the position of his left hand next time he went to take a piss, then returned to his surveillance of the lobby. Minutes dragged into half an hour, but he didn't mind. He was used to operations like this. In three years as a lone operator, he'd spent hundreds of hours simply sitting and watching, waiting for something to happen or somebody to show up. It wasn't difficult. It just took practice to remain alert for that long.

The comms remained silent, and Wolfgang twisted his left arm from time to time, panning the watch's camera around the room and giving Lyle an opportunity to detect anything he might have missed. A flight attendant in a form-fitting skirt walked past, and Wolfgang had the momentary, immature urge to follow her with the camera. He recalled Lyle's poor reaction to his last joke and decided against it.

What's up with that, anyway? Why is he so stiff?

Maybe Lyle wasn't stiff. Maybe he was just defensive of Megan. Everybody on the team seemed oddly defensive of Megan. Kevin obviously had a thing for her, which was fine. Wolfgang wasn't threatened. But deeper than that, it was almost as if . . .

Wolfgang's thoughts were interrupted by a new flood of travelers exiting a nearby gate. A tall man walking in the middle of the crowd, dressed in a black suit with a black overcoat and carrying a briefcase, caught his eye. Wolfgang checked the face against the image on his phone, then cleared his throat. "Charlie One, I have a possible match."

He twisted his left wrist to give Lyle an unobstructed view. "Charlie Eye, can you confirm?"

There was a pause, then Lyle's excited, nasally tone filled the comm. "Positive confirmation. That's Raven."

Wolfgang stood slowly, stretching his back and keeping Raven in his peripheral vision. "Charlie One, I have Raven exiting Delta Flight 7067, direct from New York. Moving to customs."

"Copy that, Charlie Three. I have him."

Edric broke over the comms. "Charlie Lead assuming operation control. Charlie One, stay on him. Charlie Two, Charlie Three, return to transport and stand by."

Wolfgang slid his phone back into his pocket and broke away from the crowds, stepping back through the terminal and into the bright sunlight of the French morning. By the time he made it to his bike, Kevin was already there, his helmet on and his visor up as the motor rumbled beneath him. Wolfgang slid the helmet over his head and gunned the motor to life, then yawned to adjust the earpiece again.

"Raven is through customs," Megan said. "Staying with him . . ."

Wolfgang felt his heart rate rise, and he twisted his hand around the accelerator, suddenly wishing he'd thought to bring gloves. Even in June, it was cooler in Paris than he expected, and the biting wind on the highway made it worse.

"Raven has taken a black Citroën C5 taxicab," Megan said. "Plate number Lima, Bravo, two, six, five, Lima, Alpha. I've affixed a beacon to the car. Breaking contact now."

Wolfgang felt a buzz in his pocket and withdrew his phone to see an alert flashing on the screen. The GPS link from the beacon had already connected directly to his navigation app. He clipped the phone into the mount between the handlebars and reached for his visor.

"Hey, dum-dum," Kevin said.

Wolfgang shot him an irritated look and detected no sarcasm—just pure disgust.

"Don't screw this up." Kevin smacked his visor shut and shot out of the garage.

Wolfgang dropped the bike into first gear and raced to follow.

[5]

Wolfgang couldn't think of a better way to explore Paris than astride the Triumph. The motor was powerful, if not oversized, providing plenty of juice to launch him between the lines of stalled cars filling the streets along his path to the highway.

Kevin drove like a brute, apparently deciding to overcompensate for his previous timidity. He gunned the bike at random and charged ahead at every available opening, but still lacked the skill to effectively navigate the traffic. Wolfgang quickly overtook him and was the first to slide down the ramp and onto France's A1 highway, stretching southwest toward the city.

Raven's cab driver was good. He'd already circumvented the bulk of the congested traffic and led Wolfgang by almost a kilometer. Wolfgang gunned the motor and swerved around a line of trucks laden with fresh produce. The food's fragrant odor mixed with the stench of petrol fumes and tire smog, but it wasn't an unpleasant smell. It smelled like adventure. Like something new.

Wolfgang held back a grin and whipped the bike between two cabs, lane splitting and gaining another two hundred meters on Raven's cab.

"Charlie Three, ease the hell up!" Edric barked over the radio. "You're drawing attention."

Wolfgang reluctantly relaxed on the throttle and glanced in his mirror. Kevin was a half klick back, riding easily behind the produce trucks with a clear view of Wolfgang.

He snitched on me. That rat.

Wolfgang rolled his eyes, then forgot about Kevin as Megan appeared a moment later, gently swerving between cars with the ease and grace of somebody who was accustomed to riding a bike. Her scarlet hair rode the wind over her shoulder blades, snapping against a denim jacket. She leaned close to the handlebars, her legs bent at the knee to mold her body next to the bike.

"Charlie Three, heads up!" Lyle said.

Wolfgang snapped his gaze away from the rearview mirror just in time to slam on the brake and swerve around the rear bumper of a bus stopped in the highway. His heart lurched toward his throat, and he hit the clutch, down-shifting and twisting the throttle just in time to avoid being flattened by a horn-blaring truck behind him.

"Dammit, Charlie Three," Edric said. "What the hell are you doing?"

Wolfgang panted, feeling suddenly like crawling under a rock.

"Are you watching me?" he demanded.

Lyle's laugh was dry but still the most emotion Wolfgang had witnessed him express. "Why do you think they call me Charlie Eye? I've got you on satellite, Charlie Three."

Great.

Wolfgang flipped his visor up and sucked down a breath of smoggy air. He glanced to his left to see Megan riding with one hand on her hip, glaring at him from behind her visor. Then she turned away and rocketed ahead.

Wolfgang felt a rock in his stomach and smacked his visor shut.

————

RAVEN LED them straight into the heart of Paris, circling the north section of downtown before his cab left the highway, and the three operators followed. The traffic began to slow, and Wolfgang looked up to see the sun break over the Arc de Triomphe directly ahead. Napoleon's Arch rose in majestic glory, dominating the center of a roundabout as the orderly highway became a hurricane of honking cars and squealing tires. At any other time, Wolfgang would have pulled off the road to admire the national landmark, but after almost kissing the backside of a bus, he forced himself to focus on the road and zipped right around it.

"Raven is two klicks ahead," Megan reported. "Charlie Two, Charlie Three, close ranks."

Wolfgang swerved amongst the slower-moving cars, drawing closer to Megan but still keeping her a few cars away. He was aware of Kevin on his left side but resisted the urge to look.

"I have Raven's cab stopping at the intersection of Saint-Germain and Rue Bonaparte," Megan said. "Intel, Charlie Eye?"

Wolfgang ran his tongue over dry lips as he felt the thrill of impending action wash over his mind. Be it Paris or Cleveland, at the end of the day, he was an operator. And he was about to operate.

"Confirmed, Charlie One," Lyle said. "I have him on satellite. Raven is exiting the cab and approaching Café Les Deux Magots."

"This could be it," Edric said. "Park the bikes and move in. Eyes on the street."

"Copy that, Charlie Lead. Moving in."

The highway rumbled beneath the tires of Wolfgang's bike as the buildings fell away and the road rose onto a bridge. Sunlight blazed down, warming his back and glistening off the glassy surface of the river Seine, stretching out to either side. Wolfgang stole a glance to his left and caught sight of France's famed Grand Palais, rising like a football stadium to the left of the highway. The structure's glass roof reflected the light back toward the water, and everything around him gleamed in pure gold.

The City of Lights . . . even in broad daylight.

Megan led the way past Grand Palais and back into the tangle of city streets. Five minutes later, Wolfgang's bike ground to a halt in a narrow parking space next to Megan's and Kevin's. He cut the motor and lifted his helmet. Megan and Kevin were already gone, splitting off in different directions as predetermined by Edric.

"Charlie Three, hurry it up," Edric snapped. "Eyes open!"

Wolfgang ran his hand through his hair to straighten it, then adjusted his jacket and hurried toward the café.

All around him, bustling Parisians collided with clueless tourists, laughing and shouting, pressing each other to the side and waving for cabs. In that respect, at least, Paris was no different than any big city. Lots of people crammed in a small place, all hurried and animated, and fully consumed by the human experience. Except that today, unbeknownst to the tourists and locals alike, one CIA agent, a team of armed operators, and maybe a couple of Russian assassins, were lost in the mix.

A police car rolled by, and Wolfgang resisted the urge to

look at it. His stomach twisted, and he pressed his arm closer to his side, feeling the gun against his ribcage. What would happen if he were caught in Paris, armed and undocumented? Would Edric bail him out?

"Charlie Lead, I have a visual on Raven," Megan said, jarring Wolfgang back to the job at hand. "He's taken a seat inside the café, near a window."

"Copy that, Charlie One. Any sign of our Russian friends?"

"Negative. But I'm still fifty yards out."

"Move into the café and assume a surveillance position. Charlie Two, move one block down Saint-Germain. Charlie Three, take up surveillance opposite the café."

Wolfgang quickened his walk as the café appeared at the next street corner. The building was six stories tall, triangular in shape, and dressed in stunning French scrollwork, with the café built into the bottom floor. Tourists and Parisians crowded around the entrance, and every table visible on the other side of the glass was occupied.

"Shouldn't I remain close to the café?" Kevin barked across the comm. "Charlie Three can take distance. I need to be closer to the target—"

"Assume your assigned position, Charlie Two," Edric said.

Wolfgang saw Kevin fifty yards ahead, moving away from the café. His posture radiated irritation, and the bigger man cast frequent glances over his shoulder.

That's why Edric wants you in the shadows. You're too obvious.

Wolfgang stepped onto the sidewalk, opposite the café, and shoved his hands in his pockets, pretending to admire the building's decorative stonework as he surveyed the block, one angle at a time.

"Charlie Three in position," he whispered.

"Charlie One in position."

Wolfgang glanced across the café's entrance, hoping to catch sight of Megan. He couldn't see her, and he briefly wondered how the hell she'd gotten inside the café at all. It was packed to the brim.

"Charlie Two?" Edric asked.

Kevin's voice was curt. "In position."

"Great. Eyes sharp, now," Edric said. "Any sign of Spider?"

All three of them radioed back in the negative, and for a while, the comms went silent. Wolfgang stood next to the curb amid the throng of pedestrians and surveyed the block, doing his best to look like just another tourist, starstruck by the Parisian fairytale around him.

Raven sat next to the window. Seeing him in person did little to alter Wolfgang's impressions of him based on the photograph. He was tall, with hair as black as night—hence the call sign, perhaps. Late forties, maybe early fifties, depending on how his genetic dice had fallen. Raven ordered a drink in a white china cup and sipped it while pretending to read a book. Wolfgang could tell by the angle of the man's face that he was reading the crowd outside the café rather than anything on the page.

Wolfgang switched his attention to the faces that passed along the sidewalk, searching for a Russian assassin. What did Russian assassins look like, anyway? Not like the movies, surely. Not dressed in black, with pale eyes and silenced pistols. No, these people would be professionals, trained to blend in, just like he was. And in this environment, crowded with noisy people and honking cars, it would be as easy for an assassin to vanish as it was for Wolfgang or for Spider.

Which means I'll never find them in this crowd.

Not only would he not find them, it would also be impossible to protect Spider if he took a seat with Raven directly in front of a window, fully exposed. Wolfgang needed to put himself in the shoes of an assassin. If he were here to kill Spider, and Spider was going to meet with Raven next to that window, where would he be?

Wolfgang's attention switched from the thronging crowds to the buildings that surrounded the café. The block was wide, with five streets intersecting together in a sort of knot, right in front of the building. On every corner were other buildings, apartments, and offices, with little shops and bakeries on the ground floors, all full of windows and facing the street. People churned in and out of those build-

ings, hailing cabs and shoving past each other as cars and
buses whirred past.

The windows.

There were so many windows, but not all of them had
an unobstructed view of Raven's position. Wolfgang
squinted into the sun and scanned first one building, then
the next, running his eyes along each floor, searching for
irregularities.

Kevin's voice broke across the radio. "I have a target
moving south along Saint-Germain! Matches Spider's
description. Charlie Eye, do you have him?"

"Hold, Charlie Three . . ." Lyle said.

Wolfgang ignored the exchange and continued to scan
the windows. His stomach tightened with an increasing
unease—a practiced instinct he'd learned to follow over
years of mishaps and near-death mistakes.

Their position was far too exposed. Raven's position
was far too exposed. A lone sniper, nestled in an elevated
position less than fifty yards from Raven's seat next to the
window, wouldn't need a high-powered rifle. He could take
both Raven and Spider out with two quick shots from a
silenced .17 HMR, or even a high-powered air gun. There
would be no sound—just two men crashing forward over a
coffee table, with blood spraying from their skulls.

"I can't confirm identity. The satellite is lagging," Lyle
said. "Charlie Two, can you confirm physical attributes?"

"He's short," Kevin said. "Five-seven, five-eight. Round

glasses. European complexion. I can't determine any more without closing in. Should I proceed?"

"Negative, Charlie Two," Edric said. "Do not approach. Maintain cover."

Wolfgang shot a glance back up Saint-Germain. He saw the man immediately, working his way toward the café with a briefcase in one hand, the other hand jammed in his pocket. Was it Spider, or was it an assassin armed with a silenced pistol?

What would I do if I were the assassin?

Wolfgang chewed his lip, then turned back to the surrounding buildings. He wouldn't use a pistol. He wouldn't get that close.

"Working the satellite now. I think I have an image," Lyle whispered over the headset.

Wolfgang saw movement from the fourth floor of an apartment building across the street from the café. A Juliet balcony was mounted to the wall, directly in front of an open window. He could have sworn that window was closed only five seconds before. Now it was open, and while darkness shrouded the apartment's interior, he knew he'd seen something move.

"Charlie Lead," Wolfgang said, keeping his eyes fixed on the window. "I have movement. Fourth floor apartment building, across from the café."

"Monitor, Charlie Three. Hold position."

Wolfgang squinted into the sun. He would have held

his hand up, shielding his eyes, but the gesture would draw attention. Instead, he ignored the discomfort and focused on the window.

There it was. Another movement. A shadow in the apartment.

"I have the image!" Lyle said. "Running facial recognition now. I think this is Spider."

"Where is he?" Megan asked from inside the café.

"One hundred yards from the café and closing," Kevin said.

"Stay on him, Charlie Two," Edric said.

Wolfgang pressed his finger against his ear, adjusting the earpiece. "Charlie Lead, I have movement in this apartment. Open window with clear line of sight to Spider's route."

"Hold your position until we confirm identity," Edric said.

Then Wolfgang saw it—a hard outline running perpendicular to the spindles of the Juliet balcony, pointed toward the café.

"Gun!" Wolfgang snapped. "I'm moving in!"

6

WOLFGANG BROKE INTO A RUN, launching himself off the sidewalk and into the street as horns blared and Edric barked over the radio.

"Negative, Charlie Three! Hold your position. Do not engage!"

Wolfgang ignored the order, keeping one eye on the window as he ran. He could still see the outline of the rifle muzzle pointed at the café.

Tires shrieked, and Wolfgang twisted, his hip glancing off the front corner of a car as an irate motorist screamed at him in French. He jumped back onto the sidewalk and crashed toward the first door he saw, his breath whistling through his teeth as he smacked his elbow against the gun beneath his jacket. All his second thoughts about carrying the weapon were gone now. He was about to take down a

Russian sniper, right in the heart of a European city, and he was likely to need all the firepower he could get.

A glass door with a reception desk guarded the side entrance to the apartment complex. Wolfgang skidded past the desk and took the first hallway that led to the edge of the building. He instinctively knew that a stairwell would be located there, providing the most efficient method of escape in the event of a fire.

Edric continued to shout over the earpiece, but he wasn't shouting at Wolfgang any longer. The commands were directed at Kevin and Megan, ordering them to reposition to cover Wolfgang's vacancy.

"Target has stopped!" Kevin shouted. "He saw Charlie Three moving. He's backing away."

"Charlie Two, stay on him," Edric ordered. "Charlie One, stay with Raven!"

Wolfgang reached into his ear and dug the earpiece out, cramming it into his pocket as he bounded up the stairwell. He took the steps three at a time and launched himself around the corner of each landing. His heart pounded, and in his mind he counted the number of windows from the corner of the building to the window he'd seen overlooking the café. Was it six? Or seven? He wasn't sure, and it mattered.

He reached the fourth floor and slid to a halt, catching his breath and laying his hand gently on the door handle. Quiet, now. Not too fast. He didn't want that rifle redirected at him. The fourth-floor hallway was quiet and still. Each door, made of wood and painted in different shades of bright pastels, was shut and bolted, with glistening Roman numerals to mark the apartment number.

Wolfgang slid his hand beneath his jacket and felt the comforting weight of the Beretta. He closed his eyes momentarily and envisioned the window again. It was the seventh window from the corner; he was sure of it now. He *had* to be sure.

He opened his eyes and hurried down the hall, bending low and keeping the gun inside his jacket. He would try the knob first, and if it was unlocked, he would ease inside before drawing the gun.

The door was unlocked, and he held his breath as he pushed it open, mentally pleading for it not to squeak. The apartment on the other side was dark, quiet, and empty, with wooden floors that were polished but dusty. There was a kitchen on his right, and from someplace on the other side of the dining room, soft light drifted toward him. Light from the open window.

Wolfgang eased the handgun out of his jacket as he pressed the door shut and held his breath. He heard the distant blast of horns and a chorus of voices from the streets below. He could smell coffee in the air and pastries from the café. It was the smell of Paris, and it shielded the scent of a Russian assassin in the room.

Wolfgang held the gun up, bracing his shooting hand

and slipping into the dining room. It was empty also, but light spilled over the hardwood from the sitting room on the other side of the door. He drew a half breath through dry lips, then crouched and stepped into the next room. It was empty, like the rest. An open window looked over the Juliet balcony, with a white silk curtain flapping in the breeze. But on the floor were marks in the dust—twin scrapes about ten inches apart, just inside the window.

A rifle's bipod sat there. I was right.

Wolfgang took a cautious step forward, then glanced around the room. Nobody was visible, but there was only one entrance to the apartment. The Russian had to be inside. He had to be close. He had to be—

Wolfgang heard the soft creak of the hardwood only a millisecond before the first blow hit him between the shoulder blades like a baseball bat, sending him rocketing forward and crashing face-first onto the floor. The Beretta spun out of his hand, and he rolled over, kicking out with both legs for the shins of his attacker. His desperate attempts at defense were useless. The shadow of a man in all black encircled him with deft agility, moving toward his head. Wolfgang instinctively shielded his head with both arms as he tried to roll out of the way, but his attacker's movements were a ploy. The Russian stepped backward like a cat, landing on one foot and sending the other smashing into Wolfgang's stomach.

The air rushed from Wolfgang's lungs, and his arms

flew toward his middle, bracing for another blow and leaving his head exposed. The butt of the rifle crashed toward his temple only a moment before his head erupted in pain and everything went black.

———

THE TRIUMPH's motor died with a gentle rumble, and Wolfgang deployed the kickstand but didn't dismount. He looked at the other two Triumphs parked twenty yards farther down the hotel parking lot, and then the white panel van parked next to the dumpster in the back.

Edric had booked them a two-room suite at the Hilton near the airport, which was large enough to provide a reliable safe house with multiple routes of approach. The team hadn't planned on using it. The plan was to be back in the air by now, popping champagne and collecting paychecks.

Wolfgang winced. His head pounded from the impact of the rifle butt on his temple, and it still hurt to breathe. But mostly, it hurt to be him, to be sitting there knowing he had to face the team.

They're going to blame me. Maybe they should.

Wolfgang slid off the bike, hung his helmet on the handlebar, and walked into the hotel's lobby. He picked up his keycard at the main desk, using the fake passport Edric provided—John Altman, a Canadian businessman traveling for pleasure—and then took the elevator to the eighth floor.

His stomach didn't churn anymore, but that was probably because the muscles were so bruised by the impact of the Russian's boot on his abdomen.

What was he thinking? He should have waited in the apartment's hallway or just inside the door. After all, where was the Russian going to go? He was boxed in.

Wolfgang stopped outside the suite and ran a hand through his hair. He wasn't sure if his face was bruised, but there was dirt all over his T-shirt, and his leather jacket was scratched. He looked like a fool.

Nothing for it.

He opened the door and was unsurprised to find the lights off. Two steps in, and he heard heavy footfalls coming toward him from the main room.

"You moron! You tryin' to get us all killed?"

Kevin barreled forward like a charging bulldog, his eyes blazing hatred. He grabbed Wolfgang by the collar and slammed him against the wall. "Are you working for the Russians?" Kevin snarled, his face only inches away.

Wolfgang snapped. He grabbed Kevin's elbow with one hand and shoved it inward, slicing Kevin's leverage in half before plowing his left knee into his groin. Wolfgang slid out of his grip, spinning him by the arm and driving him onto the floor. Wolfgang landed on his lower back, twisting Kevin's right arm toward his shoulder blades.

Kevin shouted, and Wolfgang drove the heel of his palm into his neck, shoving his face into the carpet and completely disabling him. "Don't you *ever* question my loyalty, you overgrown, arrogant piece of meat! I've met dogs who are smarter than you!"

Kevin wriggled and grunted in pain as Wolfgang applied more pressure to his arm, knowing he was only an inch away from snapping it. Then he felt powerful hands dig into his coat from behind, and before he could resist, he was slung to the left, farther down the hallway. Megan stood behind him, her eyes blazing. "Stop it, you idiots! Are you out of your minds? We've got work to do!"

Wolfgang lay on the floor, propped on one elbow. He shot his nemesis a sideways glare, then picked himself up and stumbled into the suite.

Edric stood next to the window, cradling a whiskey glass in his good hand and watching Wolfgang in stoic silence. Wolfgang avoided his gaze and crashed onto the nearest couch, wiping sweat from his forehead.

Kevin barreled in a moment later. His bottom lip bled from a cut, and he looked ready to commit murder. "He blew it!" Kevin shouted, spitting blood and saliva and pointing at Wolfgang. "We should never have brought him. He's a liability!"

"Get a drink, Kevin," Edric said. His voice was calm, but there was an edge of restrained anger just beneath the surface.

Kevin stumbled to the minibar and poured himself three shots of bourbon. Megan, with cheeks flushed, settled into a chair across from Wolfgang and dusted off her pants.

Edric turned to Wolfgang, took a sip of his drink, and cleared his throat. "What the hell happened, Wolf?"

"I told you. I saw a sniper on the fourth floor of the apartment building across from the café. He had a clear shot down Saint-Germain and of the window where Raven was sitting. I made a call."

"You made a call?" Kevin said. "Are you kidding me?" He slammed his glass down and barreled across the room, making it halfway before Megan shot her foot out. Kevin almost tripped, catching himself on the edge of a chair.

"Sit down, Kevin," Edric said. He turned back to Wolfgang. "What do you mean, you made a call?"

"The sniper was gonna have a clean shot if I didn't move in. It was a calculated risk, and I made a call. I moved in."

"Right. Only you're not *paid* to make calls, are you? *I'm* paid to make calls. You're paid to obey them."

"Come on, Edric." Wolfgang rolled his eyes. "You trained me to use my head."

"I did. But I also trained you to follow orders, and what you did today not only had the potential to blow the entire operation, it also endangered the lives of every person on this team. Have you considered that?"

"If I didn't move, he could've made the shot."

"I'm aware of that," Edric said, his tone boiling with

growing tension. "Let me tell you what else I was aware of. I was aware that Lyle was having difficulties with the satellite but was only moments away from obtaining a clear image of the target. Do you know how valuable it would've been to confirm identity on Spider? We never got the chance because *you* spooked him before Lyle got the image."

"The Russian was gonna shoot."

"Probably not. Most likely he would have waited for Spider to sit down with Raven because the Russians aren't clear on this guy's identity, either. Even if he did plan to take Spider out on Saint-Germain, Kevin knew where the sniper was, which means he knew how much time we had before the Russian had a clear shot, and we *needed* that time to get the satellite working. You didn't know that because it's not your job to know that. It's my job."

Wolfgang swallowed and glanced around the room. He noticed Lyle for the first time. The wiz sat in the far corner behind the lunch table, nestled behind computers. His beady eyes overlooked a laptop screen, watching Wolfgang.

Wolfgang looked away. "You're right," he mumbled. "I was out of line. I'm sorry."

"Sorry," Kevin snarled. "Lot of good that does."

Edric turned to Kevin. "I'm not happy with you, either, hotshot. I told you to stay on Spider. Where is he?"

Kevin's gaze dropped to the floor, and his cheeks flushed.

"You lost him," Edric said. "So now Spider is gone, the

Russians know what Wolfgang looks like, and the CIA is raising hell. This entire operation is teetering on the edge of collapse for one reason—this team failed to maintain discipline. I've never seen such a shit show in my life. We were all over the place!"

Edric's voice rose in intensity as he spoke, ripping through the room like a hail of bullets. Wolfgang winced and looked down at the floor. He wasn't angry or defensive anymore. He just felt like a fool.

Edric drained his glass and slammed it down on the counter. "Let me be clear. If any of you ever leave your post, or violate this or any future mission in any way, you're done. No excuses, no conversations. You'll never work for SPIRE again." Without another word, he stomped across the room and disappeared into a bedroom, slamming the door behind him.

7

THE HOURS DRAGGED by as the sun rose over Paris, then descended toward the ocean. Edric remained in his bedroom, leaving the four others to occupy themselves however they chose. Kevin drank until Megan cut him off, then he sat at the table next to Lyle and made a show of cleaning his firearms. He'd brought quite a few, and Wolfgang was impressed to see that they were already spotless.

Lyle remained behind the computer, still fussing with the satellite. It clearly bothered him that his technical issues had threatened the mission's success. He didn't speak to anyone but toiled at the computer for hours on end without moving.

Wolfgang rubbed his sore stomach and watched Megan. From his angle in the corner, he could see the bright flash of her eyes as she pored over maps of Paris and scratched notes on a pad. The sun that leaked between the blinds shone against her scarlet hair, turning golden over smooth skin. All the distance and weariness he'd noticed when they first met was gone. She worked with an intensity and a focus that would rival a professional scientist, ignoring the world around her as completely as Lyle.

He looked down at his battered hands. The Russian in the apartment had left Wolfgang's Beretta, and Wolfgang recovered it before returning to the hotel. It now rode in the shoulder holster again, but when he had crashed to the floor, his knuckles, propelled by the heavy gun, slammed into the hardwood.

I failed the team. I failed Edric. I failed Megan.

Wolfgang shoved his hands into his pockets and stood up, shuffling toward Megan. He could feel Kevin's stormy glower on him the entire way.

Wolfgang cleared his throat. "Hey, Megan?"

"What?" she said.

"I just . . . I just wanted to say I'm sorry about today."

"You should be." Her tone remained cold and uninviting.

Wolfgang sat in the chair next to her and dusted off his knees. "What are you working on?"

She turned back to the maps. With practiced twists of her elegant fingers, she left another line of neat handwriting on the pad. It was feminine and strong, written with confidence and command.

"Listen," he said. "I know I messed up today. There's no excuse. But you can count on me, all right? I really am good at my job, and I can contribute, too. Maybe if we talked more ahead of time, I could really add to the discussion and be an asset."

"An asset?" Megan's lips were set in hard lines, but he saw a vein flex in her temple. "I don't need an asset, Wolfgang. I need somebody who follows orders. We're not a family. We're not friends. We're a team, and all I need from you is for you to get the job done. Are we clear on that?"

Wolfgang felt like he'd been kicked in the gut again. He winced, feeling his cheeks flush. Megan looked back at her maps, and Wolfgang stood up, catching sight of Kevin smirking at him from the corner.

Is she always this cold?

Wolfgang found his way to the minibar and sifted through the alcohol until he found an unopened can of seltzer. It was warm, but the carbonation still helped to clear his throat. He felt Kevin's glare on him, and a bubbling wave of rage began to boil inside of him again.

What the heck is wrong with this guy? I've not done a thing to him.

Wolfgang turned to Kevin, ready to resolve the issue head-on, but the bedroom door swung open, and Edric appeared, a notebook in one hand. "Gather up! We've got another shot at Spider." He flipped the overhead lights on and motioned everybody to the table. "Megan, bring the maps."

The group crowded around the table as Lyle reluctantly shifted his computers to one side. Megan spread out the map, and Edric traced it with the tip of a pen. He stopped at a point in the heart of Paris, just northeast of the Arc de Triomphe.

"The Hôtel Salomon de Rothschild. An exclusive, invite-only art gala is taking place there later tonight. Spider has reached out to Raven and rescheduled their meeting for during the event."

"So, he hasn't gone to ground," Megan said.

Edric let out a tired sigh. "Thankfully, no. He must've seen Wolfgang running, and it rattled him enough to cancel the rendezvous, but apparently, he's willing to reschedule."

"Not only that," Megan said, "he gave Raven the rendezvous point hours ahead of time. He wouldn't before."

"That's true," Edric said, "and it gives us more time to plan. But we have to assume that the Russians have obtained the same intelligence, and they also have time to prepare. They still want this guy dead, and we can only assume they're willing to shoot up a gala to get the job done."

"So, what's the play?" Kevin said. "Do we establish a perimeter and monitor for intruders?"

Edric shook his head. "No. Spider chose the gala as a rendezvous because he believes it'll be safe. I can only assume that hotel security is already pretty tight, and like I mentioned, it's an invitation-only party. Spider provided Raven with a fake invite. They will each enter the party posing as VIPs, and I'm sure the Russians will do the same, which means . . ." Edric looked at Megan.

She began shaking her head almost immediately. "No. I told you, I don't play dress-up."

Edric smiled disarmingly. "Come on, Megan. I wouldn't ask if I didn't really need it. Raven provided a copy of the invite so we can doctor and duplicate it for you and an escort. Then Lyle can hack the hotel computer systems and add your pseudonyms to the electronic guest list."

"I told you, I'm not a Barbie doll. We can infiltrate the hotel via the roof and provide protection from the shadows. Armed."

"No go," Edric said. "That drastically increases the complexity of the mission. Megan, I need this. I need you to play ball."

Megan scowled but nodded once.

"Thank you." Edric turned back to the map. "Lyle and I will park the van two blocks away. We'll provide central control, and hopefully, satellite surveillance."

Lyle nodded quickly. "I've almost regained access. Shouldn't be a problem."

Wolfgang held up a hand. "Wait. *Regained* access? Does that mean what I think it means?"

Edric waved the comment off, but Lyle blushed. "Look, it's not like we can afford our own satellite."

"So, when you said earlier that you were having trouble with the satellite, what you meant was . . ."

"I was kicked off, yes. But no worries. I've just about hacked my way back in. We'll be good to go."

Edric waved his hand again. "Let Lyle take care of the satellite. Wolfgang, you've got other things to worry about. What's your tux size?"

"Wait, you're sending *him*?" Kevin lurched out of his chair, his fists balled. "He's an incompetent moron!"

"Sit down, Kevin." Edric snapped his fingers, but Kevin didn't budge.

"I don't like it, boss. I should go. Megan and I have worked together for years. We know each other!"

"You're right," Megan said. "And we both know you have the acting skills of a pop star on cameo. You'll blow our cover before we make it past the front door."

Kevin fumed. "Are you serious? Meg, come on. We did the London job together."

"It was a corporate board meeting, and you played my bodyguard. Completely different scenario."

"You don't trust me."

"It's not about trust, Kevin. It's about skill set. Don't make this personal."

Kevin folded his arms. "James trusted me."

The room fell deathly silent, and Wolfgang noticed Lyle's gaze drop to the floor as darkness crossed Megan's eyes.

Edric spoke between gritted teeth. "Sit down, Kevin."

Kevin slumped into his chair, his cheeks dark red.

Megan turned away, facing the wall.

"I'm sorry," Kevin said. "I shouldn't have said that."

Wolfgang opened his mouth, but then thought better of saying anything. A hundred questions boiled into his mind, but this didn't seem like the right time to ask them or press an advantage over Kevin.

"Meg?" Edric said.

She turned around. "What's my identity?"

"Rebecca and Paul Listener, from Toronto." Edric produced a pair of fake Canadian passports from his coat and passed them to Wolfgang and Megan. "You've been married for three years. Paul teaches humanities at Centennial College, and Rebecca is a full-time art critic. You're traveling to Paris on vacation, and your invite was courtesy of a friend in the art world. Be vague about that."

Wolfgang admired the passport, feeling the smooth perfection of the laminated pages, and tilted the primary ID page in the light to examine the inlaid Canadian seal. The passport was a perfect fake—or very close to it.

"The mission is simple," Edric said. "Kevin will drive you in and remain on standby for exfiltration, and if it comes to it, additional firepower. Once you're inside the gala, make your way around the party until you locate Raven. Stay with him until he meets with Spider. Wolfgang, we'll need a full facial image. Use the watch."

Wolfgang nodded. "What about the Russians?"

"Protecting Spider is still our primary objective—at least until he completes his rendezvous with Raven. After that, the CIA has requested we forestall any sort of fireworks until Raven has left Paris. Remember, they're looking for plausible deniability here. So, ideally, we'll shield Spider until the end of the gala. Then we'll withdraw, and what happens, happens."

"What about Wolfgang?" Kevin asked. His voice was still sulky but less hostile. "The Russians will recognize him."

Edric nodded. "Unfortunately, that's true. Wolfgang, were you able to identify the sniper?"

Wolfgang shook his head. There was no point in lying about it. "No, I never saw his face."

"Okay. In that case, he'll identify you before you identify him. That's not ideal, but it could put the Russians on guard. They know you aren't actually a humanities professor, but it's not like they'll set off any alarms. After all, they're working under false identities, also. The most important thing is for you to pick them out as soon as possible. Feed Lyle as many facial images as you can, and look out for the usual signals—body language, people who look out of place, people who are checking out faces more than they're checking out paintings."

"No problem," Wolfgang said. "What happens after I find them?"

"Hopefully, nothing. Stay between them and Spider, and stall for time. As soon as Raven and Spider complete their rendezvous, Raven will leave, and Spider probably will, also."

"What if the Russians . . . you know . . ." Wolfgang trailed off, unsure if he was playing up a movie stereotype.

"Go full Ivan and light the place up?" Edric leaned against the wall, rubbing his chin with one hand. "There's not a lot we can do about that. Kevin will be on standby in case you need additional muscle. If you're confident the Russians are about to turn up the heat, I guess I'd rather you disable them. Quietly, of course."

Wolfgang exchanged a glance with Megan. "I understand."

The room was silent for a minute as Kevin's brooding darkness hung over them like a black cloud. Wolfgang knew they were all thinking the same thing.

He cleared his throat. "Look, I screwed up today. I realize you guys are taking a risk by working with somebody you don't know. And I just want to say . . . I've got your backs. You can trust me."

There was a hint of a smile on Edric's face, too vague to call, but it still gave Wolfgang some reassurance.

"Everything that happened this morning is behind us," Edric said. "We move as a team, now. Charlie gets it done."

Megan grunted. "Charlie gets it done, but Charlie's gonna need shopping money."

[8]

WOLFGANG STOOD in the main sitting room of the hotel suite and fidgeted with his cuff links. Following the brief, Megan had left the hotel and returned two hours later with a couple of shopping bags and two shoeboxes. She produced a brand-new tux from one bag, complete with a black bow tie, a pressed shirt, and silver cuff links. Wolfgang wasn't sure if a professor from a liberal arts college would wear cuff links, but he wasn't about to question her.

Megan disappeared into one bedroom, and Wolfgang dressed. Kevin left to rent a car that could pass as a private taxi, and Edric took a shower. Wolfgang wondered how you showered with a full-arm cast, and decided he probably didn't want to know.

"How do I look?"

Wolfgang turned to Lyle, flexing his arms and wiggling

his shoulders beneath the jacket. Lyle looked over his computer screen, squinting through his smudged glasses. Then, to Wolfgang's surprise, he stood up and stepped around the table, approaching Wolfgang and inspecting him from head to toe.

The tux fit well. It wasn't a custom garment by any stretch, but Wolfgang felt good in it. He just wished it left room for his gun. There was no chance of squeezing the Beretta into the confines of the form-fitting jacket, and he felt a little naked.

Lyle nodded once, then reached up and adjusted Wolfgang's bow tie. "Almost good enough," Lyle said.

"Good enough?" Wolfgang laughed. "Good enough for what?"

Lyle pointed toward the bedroom as the door clicked open. "To stand next to her."

Wolfgang turned, and the breath caught in his throat. Megan wore a jet-black evening gown, long enough to trail the floor, with a slit that ran up her right leg to just inches below her waist. The gown hugged her hips and was suspended by a single shoulder strap that rode just to the left of her neck.

Her hair was pinned back on one side, while the majority of her locks flowed loosely over her shoulders and down her exposed back. Her crimson lipstick matched her hair in a darker shade of red, but the whole ensemble was offset by an awkwardness in her posture that Wolfgang hadn't seen before.

Wolfgang swallowed, and Lyle laughed.

"What?" Megan snapped, avoiding his gaze.

"Nothing," Wolfgang mumbled. "You . . . you look nice."

"Great. Are you ready?"

———

KEVIN ACQUIRED a black Mercedes sedan to ferry them to the gala. He drove without a word, chewing gum and glancing from time to time into the rearview mirror.

Wolfgang ignored him, sinking into the back seat and watching Paris flash by. The city was alive now, with lights within each building glimmering like a million stars as the Mercedes bounced through the streets and whizzed down the highway.

As they topped a hill and turned south toward downtown, Megan tapped on her window. "Look."

Wolfgang leaned over, peering through the glass. In the distance, he made out the elegant, curving outline of the Eiffel Tower, shooting up from the Parisian skyline like a giant in the night. It was so much taller than he expected, framed against the black skyline with just a couple of marker lights.

"Have you ever been?" he asked.

"I've been someplace a lot like it, once," Megan said, her voice a little wistful. "Never here. I thought it was usually illuminated at night."

"Maintenance," Wolfgang said. "I read about it in a travel brochure."

Megan said nothing, and Wolfgang sat back, his focus drawn away from the distant tower and back to her legs, crossed over each other with casual elegance. She leaned back and closed her eyes, and for a moment, Wolfgang just stared. He was conscious of Kevin glaring at him through the rearview mirror, but he didn't care.

Screw this guy. I'm done worrying about him.

After another ten minutes, Kevin turned onto a quiet street, and Wolfgang saw other cars lined along it: Mercedes, Bentleys, Rolls-Royces, and a smattering of supercars purred in neat lines, all gently circling through the hotel's main entrance. Wolfgang leaned close to the window, admiring the display of opulence and wealth, his attention settling on a bright-red Ferrari with gloss-black wheels. Wolfgang knew very little about cars beyond basic brands, but this car was beautiful in every sense of the word, hugging the ground and rumbling with the restrained power of its massive Italian engine.

Wolfgang pictured himself behind the wheel of a car like that, rocketing up the California coast. He imagined riding with the windows down, the radio playing, and somebody special sitting next to him.

Focus, fool. You don't have time for this.

Wolfgang shelved the daydream and turned his attention to the people gathered around the cars. A small crowd of men in tuxedos and women in evening gowns stood in knots, laughing and migrating inside.

Megan pressed her earpiece into her right ear, then turned to Wolfgang. "Got yours?"

Wolfgang nodded, slipping the earpiece out of his pocket and into his ear.

"Keep it in your ear this time," she said.

A valet approached Megan's door, bowing and opening it in one smooth motion. In a flash, Megan's icy expression melted, replaced by a smile both warm and austere. Wolfgang felt his heart lurch, and he hesitated a moment in the car, watching her walk.

"If she gets hurt," Kevin said, "I'll kill you."

Wolfgang cocked his head, almost willing to let the threat go, then he smacked Kevin on the arm. "Kev, you couldn't kill me if I was tied to an electric chair. Keep the motor warm, will you?" He slid out of the car, adjusting his tie.

Megan waited at the bottom of the steps, glancing back at him. To his surprise, she reached out for his arm, and he accepted while trying to disguise his satisfaction.

Act or no act, it still felt great for her not to be glaring daggers at everybody.

They ascended the red-carpet stairs, arriving at the admissions guard at the top.

"Mr. and Mrs. Listener, Toronto," Wolfgang said.

The guard smiled and bobbed his head, then checked his iPad.

Wolfgang stiffened a moment, suddenly realizing he'd never received confirmation from Lyle that the hack was successful.

"Welcome to the gala, monsieur, madame."

The guard nodded them in, and Wolfgang relaxed a little. So far, so good.

"Charlie Lead, all systems, check."

"Charlie Eye, I'm live. Satellite is back online."

"Charlie One, we're in."

"Charlie Two, on standby."

Wolfgang started to speak, but Megan just shook her head. "Relax, hot stuff," she said. "You're as tense as Kevin."

Wolfgang flushed, following Megan through the hotel's double doors and into a stunning lobby. Bright lights glistened from chandeliers, reflecting off marble flagstone flooring and illuminating rows of oil paintings that lined every side of the lobby and proceeded into the halls. Everywhere, people in expensive evening attire gathered, admiring paintings and murmuring as they sipped champagne. White-gloved servers scurried in and out of the main lobby, replacing champagne flutes and serving hors d'oeuvres.

"Just like the movies," Wolfgang whispered.

Megan rolled her eyes. "Why do you think I didn't want to come?"

"I'm not sure, actually. I was wondering about that."

Megan shot a sunbeam smile at a server bright enough to blind him, and accepted a champagne flute.

Wolfgang waved the server off with a polite smile.

"You should drink," Megan said. "You'll stick out if you don't."

"I don't drink alcohol."

"Why the hell not? Are you sober?"

They drifted closer to a row of paintings as Wolfgang scanned the room for any sign of Raven. The American was nowhere to be seen.

"I'm not sober. I just don't drink. Why didn't you want to come to the party?"

They settled in front of an obscure art piece that may have depicted a battle, or a sunrise, or a circus—Wolfgang really had no idea—and continued to scan the room.

"Let's just say I'm not much for tropes," Megan said.

"Tropes?"

"You know. The hot spy girl dressing up for a party to catch the bad guys."

"So, you admit to being hot. I'm relieved. I was starting to think I was seeing visions."

Megan stared at him a moment, and he almost thought she'd slap him. A smirk played at the corner of her mouth, and she took a sip of her champagne, leaving a lipstick smudge on the flute. "That's *almost* funny."

"Kind of my move," Wolfgang said with a self-deprecating shrug. "Why don't you like tropes?"

"Hypothetically?"

"If you like."

"Okay. Hypothetically, dressing up like this makes me feel a touch objectified."

"Hmm. I can respect that. But can I offer an alternative interpretation?"

Megan pretended to study the painting and took another sip of her champagne, and Wolfgang took her silence as permission to proceed.

"Everybody on the team respects you. Kevin waits on you like a freaking lap dog. You're the only person whose opinion Edric blindly accepts. You've got me ready to jump off a building, if that's your call."

Megan rotated the flute in her fingers. "Your point?"

Wolfgang shrugged. "Doesn't sound much like objectification to me. Sounds more like . . . a pedestal."

Megan lifted one eyebrow, and he thought he saw that smirk playing at her lips again. She finished the champagne and turned away. Wolfgang followed her, casting casual looks at the passing art and settling on a painting that was most definitely a nude of some kind of princess. He twisted his arm until his watch camera captured the canvas, and Lyle uttered an involuntary snicker over the earpiece.

Megan jabbed him in the ribs. "You're a child. Focus on your job for a change."

A sudden rustle from the crowd brought a stillness to the room, and then everybody started moving toward another set of double doors at the end of the hallway. Wolfgang and Megan moved with them, checking every face they passed. There were lots of old, overweight men in tuxedos—one of whom actually wore a monocle—but no sign of the trim, dark Raven. Wolfgang felt uneasy again. In this crowd, it shouldn't have been hard to spot the Russians. He needed only to look for men who weren't twenty pounds overweight and guzzling booze. But that also meant there would be no confusion for the Russians in identifying Raven, or Spider, or himself, for that matter.

"Sitrep," Edric said.

"We're moving into the ballroom," Megan said. "I think there's gonna be a speech."

They passed through the double doors and into a massive square room. More appetizers lined one wall, while a string quartet in the corner sat stiff and upright on their stools. The center of the room was left open.

Wolfgang felt a twist in his stomach. *Dancing.* He didn't dance. In fact, he'd never danced, unless you counted a quick movement of the feet to dodge a bullet. Wasn't this supposed to be an art gala?

There shouldn't be dancing.

A soft clinking sound rang off a champagne flute, and

the crowd grew quiet. Then a short man with tiny glasses and a bald head appeared at the front of the room, standing on a low platform. He held a mic, smiled, and then launched into a quick salutation in French. Wolfgang couldn't understand a word of it.

Megan stood attentively, appearing to watch the speaker while her eyes darted almost imperceptibly, scanning the room. Wolfgang followed suit but still didn't see Raven.

Raven should be here by now.

The speaker concluded his monologue with a clap of his hands and a big smile, and then the quartet began to play. Everybody in the room turned to their partner and, almost in unison, started dancing.

Megan sighed, then twisted and offered her hand with the enthusiasm of a janitor approaching a soiled toilet.

"I can't dance," Wolfgang mouthed, feeling his face flush.

"What's that? You can't dance?" Megan was loud enough for at least a few people standing nearby to hear, not to mention the entire team.

Wolfgang's blush deepened, and Megan offered a slight smirk. "Relax, dude. Just follow me, and don't step on my feet."

He took her hand reluctantly, and they swung into a smooth side-step, followed by a turn, then a backstop. Wolfgang struggled to keep up, even though Megan moved decidedly slower than the rest of the crowd. His face flushed again, and Megan actually laughed. It was a dull sound, but it still brought to life that warmth in his chest again.

"Relax," she said. "Pull me a little closer . . . that's it. Now, move like the wind. Smooth . . . easy. Feel the music."

Wolfgang did feel the music. He focused on the violin's gentle hum, matched by the deep throb of the upright bass and the rich gravity of the cellos. The beautiful, haunting sound made him momentarily forget about the mission, and he lost himself in the reality of where he was standing. In Paris, the City of Lights, the city of love, dancing with a beautiful woman at a beautiful gala.

Her grey eyes flashed fire as she ducked and twisted, challenging his ability to keep up. Wolfgang was certain he looked like a waddling duck next to the rich and accomplished art connoisseurs around him, but he didn't care anymore. He pretended he knew what he was doing, and it seemed to help.

The music wound down, and they stopped. Wolfgang wobbled on his feet a minute, suddenly feeling a little dizzy. He steadied himself and offered his best imitation of the bows the men around him performed.

"You're pretty good," he said.

Megan released him and stepped back. To his surprise, she offered another smile—softer this time.

"You're not half-bad yourself."

She led him to the edge of the room and selected two flutes of champagne from a server. She passed him one and held up hers. "You don't have to drink, but at least pretend."

Wolfgang returned her smile and lifted the flute, but Megan's gaze darted over his shoulder to the far side of the room.

"Charlie Lead, I have eyes on Raven."

Wolfgang started to turn, but Megan stopped him.

"Don't look now. You'll draw attention. He's in the corner, near the hors d'oeuvres."

"Charlie One, close on target," Edric said. "Charlie Three, maintain surveillance."

Megan drained her flute and set it down, then set off casually across the room without a second glance at Wolfgang. He felt a tug of longing watching her go, but he shrank back against the wall and scanned the room until he saw Raven.

The American stood alone in the corner, dressed in a white tux, sipping champagne. The string quartet had started up again, but nobody danced. The crowd milled about, enjoying the food and drifting in and out of the art galleries. Raven seemed to ignore them all, but to Wolfgang's trained eye, the American was looking for something. Or someone.

"No sign of Spider," Wolfgang whispered. "Charlie Two, do you see anything outside?"

The line remained silent.

Wolfgang licked his lips and scanned the room again. "Charlie Two, anything from outside?"

Still, Kevin said nothing. Then Wolfgang felt a powerful hand descend on his arm from behind and yank him into the hallway.

[9]

Wolfgang slid backward into the shadows before he could reach for the pistol that wasn't even there. He grunted and felt his shoulder blades collide with the wall as his attacker stepped in front of him. Wolfgang braced his knee for a groin shot and twisted to break free of the hold, then he looked up and faced his attacker for the first time.

Kevin shoved a meaty hand against Wolfgang's throat, half choking him while his free hand descended over Wolfgang's ear, cutting off the mic built into the earpiece.

"What the hell are you doing?" Kevin snarled.

Wolfgang wheezed and tried to break free, but Kevin owned all the leverage. His forearm pinned Wolfgang's neck against the wall, held just beneath his chin, while Kevin continued to block off the earpiece.

Wolfgang choked and tried to kick. Kevin blocked the

attack and then drove the toe of his shoe into Wolfgang's shin. Pain shot up Wolfgang's leg and his eyes watered. He gasped for breath, and Kevin leaned closer.

"You greasy weasel!" Kevin snarled. "You think I'm gonna let you poach Meg like this?"

Wolfgang's vision blurred, and Kevin relaxed his forearm just a little. Precious oxygen flowed in, and Wolfgang gasped it down. "What's wrong with you?" His voice sounded distorted in his own head with Kevin's palm still clamped over his ear.

"I'm watching you, you rat. Back off. She's not a piece of meat!"

Wolfgang gritted his teeth and smacked Kevin's hand away from his ear. Then he dug out the earpiece and flicked the power switch off.

"You wanna do this? Right here and now? I'll *wreck* you." He stepped forward, his fists balling up, ready to fight. Then he caught sight of something out of the corner of his eye and turned to see a couple walking across the ballroom, approaching the hallway. He relaxed his shoulders and stepped back. The couple passed by, casting each of them a suspicious glance but saying nothing.

As soon as they rounded the corner, Kevin closed the distance. "I'll make this perfectly clear, shithead. Meg is off the market. So back off. I'll kill you, and I won't think twice about it. It wouldn't be the first time."

There was an edge in Kevin's voice that chilled Wolf-

gang to the bone. He saw a blend of self-righteous justifica-
tion and stupidity in his dark eyes—perhaps the most
dangerous cocktail known to man.

Wolfgang's blood boiled, but he rubbed his throat and
slid the earpiece back into his ear. "We've got work to do,"
he snarled. "But don't worry. This isn't over."

Wolfgang flicked the earpiece on and was immediately
flooded with radio chatter.

"Charlie Three! Do you copy? Target inbound, possibly
Spider!"

Wolfgang hurried back into the ballroom, smoothing
out the wrinkles in his jacket. He caught sight of Megan
almost immediately, standing near the wall, her body tense
and ready for action. He followed her line of sight to a
clean-cut man in a tuxedo and black-rimmed glasses. Wolfgang walked with grace and purpose, making a beeline for
Raven, who now stood near an emergency exit door.

"That's him," Kevin whispered from just behind Wolfgang. "That's the guy I saw at the café."

"Charlie Two, is that you?" Edric said.

Wolfgang and Kevin exchanged a glance, and Wolfgang
saw the defeat in Kevin's eyes. He'd been caught away from
his post. Wolfgang wanted to smirk, but he didn't have time.

"Charlie Eye, can you confirm identity of target?" Wolfgang twisted his left arm, aligning his watch's camera with
Spider. He tracked Spider for ten feet, then dropped his
arm to avoid drawing attention.

"Hold one, Charlie Three," Lyle said.

Wolfgang held his breath, counting the seconds as Spider drew closer to Raven.

Lyle's excited voice broke over the comms. "Identity confirmed! Target is Ramone Ortez. He's a Spanish-born physicist specializing in nuclear technology, currently employed by a conglomerate of nuclear power plant owners based in Kiev. No living family or known associates."

Nuclear technology. The blood chilled in Wolfgang's veins. He remembered Edric's briefing back in St. Louis when Edric mentioned that the CIA was attempting to mine information out of Spider about an impending attack. A *nuclear* attack. Was Spider building a bomb?

"Copy that," Edric said. "All right, everybody. This is it. We've got to give Raven time to obtain Spider's plan. Charlie One, close on Raven, but remain undercover. Charlie Two, where the hell are you?"

Wolfgang saw Kevin swallow and heard Edric's threat echo in his mind: *"If any of you ever leave your post . . . you're done."*

Kevin spoke clearly, without hesitation. "I'm with Charlie Three, Charlie Lead."

The line was silent for a moment, and when Edric spoke, his anger was barely contained. "Copy that. Establish a security perimeter. Any sign of our Russian friends?"

"Negative," Kevin said, scanning the room. Then he

paused. "Wait . . . I've got two men entering the room from the north. Black suits, dark hair—"

Wolfgang held up his finger, then pivoted the watch toward the intruders, stepping into the room and searching over the tops of the guests' heads. Even though they wore matching tuxedos, nothing about them said 'art enthusiast,' but Wolfgang could smell 'Russian killer' from across the room.

"Hold on, Charlie Three," Lyle said again.

The seconds ticked past, and Wolfgang held the watch steady.

"I only got a clear image of one of them," Lyle said. "Facial recognition is coming up empty."

Just then, the left-hand man's gaze swept to the left side of the room and collided with Wolfgang's. He was a big man with long black hair and a dominant stance that reeked of military experience and a lifetime of giving orders. A split second passed, and then, like glass shattering on the floor, recognition passed across his face. A soft smirk tugged at his lips, and he lifted two fingers and tapped his temple.

Wolfgang recalled the impact of the rifle butt crashing through the air and colliding with the side of his head . . . right where the man tapped his fingers.

"That's them," Wolfgang snapped, lowering the watch and starting into the ballroom. "They're the Russians."

"How do you know?" Edric said.

"I know. One hundred percent."

"Copy that, Charlie Three. Keep them away from Raven. Watch out for guns. Charlie Two, take his flank."

Kevin stepped out behind Wolfgang, pivoting to the left and sliding his hand into his pocket as Wolfgang walked along the right-hand wall, circling toward the Russians and keeping his sights on them the entire time.

"Raven is on the move," Megan said. "He's approaching the gallery. Spider is with him."

"Stay on him, Charlie One!" Edric said. "Charlie Three, where are the bogies?"

Wolfgang said, "Moving toward the hallway, Charlie Lead. They've identified Spider."

"Copy that. Charlie One, stay in between Raven and the bogies. Charlie Two, Three—close in."

Kevin and Wolfgang quickened their stride, casting wary glances around the crowd of laughing, half-drunk art connoisseurs as they moved toward the main art gallery. The Russians were quicker, splitting up and taking separate hallways that both led to the gallery.

"Bogies have split," Kevin said. "They're closing in."

"Copy that. Stay on them."

Kevin and Wolfgang parted ways without a word, each taking the Russian closest to them as they moved into the hallways. Once more, Wolfgang was bitterly aware of the space beneath his arm where his pistol should have been. Why didn't he have a smaller gun? Or a knife? Or a freaking rock? Something.

The long-haired Russian with the devilish smirk led the way, walking in quiet confidence without glancing over his shoulder, even though he had to know Wolfgang was on his heels. It was Wolfgang's friend from the apartment outside the café.

You won't get me twice, Ivan.

Wolfgang quickened his stride, breaking into the main gallery and squinting under the bright lights. There was art everywhere, lining the walls and suspended on circular stands throughout the room. He caught sight of Raven disappearing down a short hallway and saw Megan stop short and cast an unwilling glance his way.

"Problem, Charlie Lead," Megan said. "Spider and Raven have entered the men's room. I can't follow without breaking cover."

Megan hesitated at the end of the short hallway, but Ivan didn't. He walked quickly across the room and right by her, winking as he passed.

"Move in, Charlie Three," Edric said. "Don't let him near Spider!"

Wolfgang broke into a fast walk, smiling quickly at an old woman he almost ran over on his way to the bathroom. Ivan shoved the bathroom door open and stomped inside like he owned the place, then Wolfgang heard a broken shout from Kevin over the radio.

"Charlie Lead! I'm engaged. Back alley!"

There was a crashing sound, then Kevin's muted scream.

"Charlie One, help him out!" Edric said.

"Copy that!" Megan broke into a run through the middle of the art gallery, breaking for the exit door to the back of the hotel.

"You're on your own, Charlie Three. Stay sharp!"

Wolfgang placed his palm against the bathroom door and shoved inside, ducking instinctively to avoid a surprise blow. But none came. The large bathroom had polished flagstone floor tiles and a line of marble sinks along one wall, with framed mirrors behind them. The door swung shut automatically as Wolfgang stepped inside, his shoes clapping against the flagstones.

Wolfgang crouched and saw Spider and Raven standing in the last stall near a fire exit barred with a red alarm latch. And then there was Ivan, standing at the sink and washing his hands under steaming water while watching Wolfgang in the mirror. Ivan grinned.

Wolfgang drew a slow breath and straightened his jacket. He glanced under the stalls again, but the men hadn't moved. If Raven and Spider were talking, he couldn't hear them. He turned back to Ivan and saw the big Russian's smile grow wider as he continued to rub his hands beneath the piping hot water.

Screw this guy.

Wolfgang stepped across the room, his shoes clicking

like a tap dancer, and selected the sink two slots down. He flipped the water on and stared at his reflection in the mirror, keeping track of Ivan out of the corner of his eye.

"In Mother Russia, we treat bruises with vodka," Ivan said. He spoke softly enough that Spider and Raven wouldn't hear. His English was good, but heavily accented, like a true movie villain.

Wolfgang waited for the water to grow hot, then he ran his wet hands through his hair, finger-combing it into order and gently dodging the spot where Ivan's rifle butt had crashed into his head.

"Hell of a bruise you have, Amerikos," Ivan continued.

"It was a cheap shot," Wolfgang said without taking his eyes off the mirror. "In the Land of the Free, we treat those with a beatdown."

"You haven't got the stones."

"I won't need stones for the likes of you, Ivan. You'll be eating through a straw when I'm finished with you."

Ivan pulled his hands from beneath the water and flipped the faucet off as his wolfish grin reflected toward Wolfgang in the mirror. Then he reached out without looking and tore a length of paper towel from the dispenser.

"Too bad we will never know," he said. "My comrade, Igor, is in alley dealing with your friends. When he is finished, he will join us. Then we will see how big your stones are . . . before we crush them."

"Why wait?" Wolfgang asked, turning the water off.

"Let's get it on, right here, right now." He turned to face the bigger man.

Ivan's smile widened, but he didn't move.

"Oh, that's right. You can't," Wolfgang said. "You can't afford to make a scene. Not here. That's why you need Igor —so you can mop up the blood before the cops show up."

Fire flashed across Ivan's eyes, but he didn't say anything.

Wolfgang tore off a sheet of paper towel and stepped closer, glaring Ivan down as he dried his hands.

Then metal clicked against metal, and a hinge squeaked. Both Ivan and Wolfgang glanced impulsively toward the back of the room and saw Spider appear first. His face was white and sweat dripped down his cheeks as Raven walked just behind him.

Fear crossed Spider's eyes, and Raven appeared calculative as they both saw Wolfgang and Ivan. Moments ticked by in perfect stillness as all four men processed the situation, their minds spinning for the best move in this impossible, deadly game of chess.

Then Raven jumped. He grabbed Spider by his upper arm and spun, ramming his shoulder through the fire door and hurtling outside into the darkness. Only a second later, Ivan roared like a bear and lunged toward Wolfgang as a fire alarm screamed from overhead.

10

WOLFGANG SLIPPED to the left and stuck out his right foot just in time to dodge the charging Russian and trip him up. But Ivan caught Wolfgang by the arm, and they crashed to the floor in a tangled mess of flying legs and flipping coattails.

"Charlie Three, do you copy? What's going on?" Edric's shouts screamed through the earpiece, but Wolfgang didn't have a prayer of answering as he continued to roll.

Ivan landed on top, but before he could brace himself against the floor, Wolfgang delivered a rabbit punch to Ivan's jaw and spun to the right. The Russian's jaw crunched upward as teeth ground and splintered, then Ivan toppled. Wolfgang rammed his elbow against the floor, propelling himself up and on top, already preparing his next combo to Ivan's face.

Wolfgang's next punch landed squarely on Ivan's over-sized nose, flesh meeting flesh, with bony, cartilage-crunching force. Blood spurted across Wolfgang's pressed white shirt, and he raised his fist again.

Ivan glared up with wild, crazy eyes, the grin having never left his face, and he spat blood at Wolfgang. "You punch like Polish bitch, Amerikos!" He bowed his back and rolled abruptly to the right. Wolfgang lost balance and hurtled backward, sliding across the floor and crashing into the first stall. His head snapped back against the polished marble of the stall wall with a dull crack, and his world spun. Ivan rolled to his knees, then jumped to his feet, his teeth dripping blood like a vampire as he hurtled forward.

Wolfgang was vaguely aware of the fire alarm still screaming overhead from the breached fire door, along with panicked voices and pounding feet outside the bathroom. Edric shouted in his ear again, but somehow, the only thing that mattered was the two-hundred-fifty-pound hunk of Siberia hurtling toward him like a pass rusher ready to sack the shit out of a panicking quarterback.

Wolfgang dipped to his right, ducking beneath the bottom edge of the stall wall, and then rolled under it only seconds before Ivan crashed into the marble at full force. Metal screeched, and a bracket tore loose. Wolfgang's head lay next to the toilet, barely shielded from the collapsing marble panel that crashed into the toilet. Porcelain shattered as water sprayed across his face and Ivan continued to roar.

Wolfgang felt a shoe slam into his exposed calf, then heard the sickening *click-click* of a pistol being chambered.

"Where are your stones?" Ivan shouted.

Two sharp pops cracked through the tight bathroom as a silenced pistol fired into the marble wall shielding Wolfgang. He rolled and crawled his way into the next stall as shards of porcelain and flakes of marble exploded behind him. Ivan directed his fire at Wolfgang's kicking legs, and Wolfgang felt a bullet tear through his pants, scraping his skin and barely missing his knee. He winced and jerked his leg inside the next stall as more gunshots rang out.

"This is Russian beatdown!" Ivan cackled, his feet pounding around to the front of the stalls.

Wolfgang's body was alive with adrenaline, his mind flooding with panic. He had to get to his feet. He had to find a weapon.

He rolled to his knees and slapped the lock on the stall door just in time to keep it closed under Ivan's next blow. The Russian swore, and Wolfgang danced backward as two bullets skipped and ricocheted beneath the stall wall.

"Dance, Amerikos! Dance, if you have the stones!"

Wolfgang stumbled backward. His heels hit the toilet, and he sat down with a crash as Ivan pressed the muzzle of his pistol against the crack in the stall door and blew the lock away.

"Now I put your head in toilet and make Russian hurricane!" Ivan plowed his shoulder against the door, and it burst open.

Wolfgang twisted, reaching to his right and lifting the lid off the toilet with both hands as Ivan slid inside, gun first.

The first bullet flew wide, smacking into the wall as Wolfgang ducked and swung with the lid. The leading edge of it crashed against Ivan's hands, hurling the gun aside as Wolfgang launched himself off the toilet. The gun clattered to the floor, and Ivan stumbled back. Wolfgang snatched the lid back, then twisted it and swung upward, piloting the corner of the lid straight into Ivan's nose.

Cartilage collapsed, and fresh blood sprayed from Ivan's face. He stumbled backward again, and Wolfgang pressed forward, driving him out of the stall and into the bathroom. Then Wolfgang delivered a lightning kick with his left shin, straight into Ivan's groin.

The big man grunted and fell forward onto his knees, unable to maintain his balance.

Wolfgang brought the lid down, full force across Ivan's skull, and said, "Where are your stones?"

The porcelain cracked as Ivan's eyes rolled backward, then the big Russian collapsed to the floor.

Wolfgang panted, dropping the lid's shattered half and swabbing his bloody forehead with his sleeve.

Edric's voice was near panic. "Charlie Three! Do you

copy?"

Wolfgang staggered to the sink and splashed water across his face. "I'm here, Charlie Lead . . . I'm here."

"What the hell is going on?"

"The Russian . . ." Wolfgang wiped water from his face. "He was confrontational."

"Not the Russian. Where's Spider?"

Wolfgang's heart lurched. *Spider*. He'd forgotten about him in the heat of the fight.

Wolfgang broke toward the fire door, pausing long enough to scoop up the Russian's fallen pistol. He wasn't sure how many rounds were left, but he wasn't about to crash through another door unarmed.

Biting night wind stung his eyes as he burst into the narrow street behind the hotel. The fire alarms faded behind him, but now he could hear the distant scream of European fire trucks hurtling toward the hotel. Voices shouted from the front of the building, but in the back, all was dark and still.

Wolfgang raised the pistol and turned down the street. It was framed on both sides by tall buildings that blocked out the streetlights and gave shelter to the dumpsters and heating units that lined either side of the road. Beneath the screech of the fire engines, the heaters hummed softly, masking Wolfgang's footfalls as he eased down the alley.

"I'm in pursuit," Wolfgang whispered.

He looked to the end of the alley, then behind him

toward the hotel front. In truth, he had no idea which way to go or where to look. Spider could be anywhere by now. He could be halfway out of the city.

Wolfgang's stomach twisted in knots as he took another two steps into the alley. Maybe their mission was already accomplished. Raven had plenty of time to talk to Spider. Maybe he had already ascertained the date and location of Spider's planned attack, and maybe it didn't matter where Spider was anymore. He was the CIA's problem now.

But no. Something in Wolfgang's gut warned him that this wasn't over. Something was still wrong. Something felt cold and uneasy.

The sharpening breeze that whistled down the street bit through his tuxedo. He took another few steps into the alley and paused when something on the ground beyond the next dumpster caught his eye. He couldn't tell what it was, but by the soft angles and irregular shape, he knew it wasn't made of metal, and probably wasn't man-made at all.

Wolfgang broke into a jog, leading with the gun and closing on the object. His stomach churned as he heard Edric call through the earpiece again. Broken and distorted, his voice was becoming more difficult to discern, but Wolfgang wasn't listening anyway. He approached the dumpster from the back side and held the gun at eye level, then slowly turned the corner.

Spider lay on his back, staring skyward, his throat slit from ear to ear. Blood spilled across the pavement in a growing pool of rapidly cooling crimson. Wolfgang swept the gun left and right, but there was no sign of the killer, or of Raven.

Wolfgang stepped back. "Charlie Lead, I've located Spider. He's dead. Repeat, Spider is terminated."

Wolfgang's earpiece clicked and hissed.

Edric's reply sounded distant. "What is your location, Charlie Three?"

"Behind the hotel, in the street."

"Repeat, Charlie Three. You're breaking up." Edric's voice faded and clicked, then the earpiece beeped.

Wolfgang knelt next to the body, quickly digging through Spider's pockets, searching for anything useful. The pockets were empty, but as Wolfgang moved to search Spider's coat, another beeping filled his ears, this time not from the earpiece. It was from his watch.

He twisted his arm. The watch face blinked red, with a yellow message flashing in the middle of the screen: RADIA-TION DETECTED.

Wolfgang pulled his hand back, almost rolling onto his ass, then looked down at the body again as he remembered Lyle's description of the watch. *"I call it a sniffer . . . It even has a built-in Geiger counter."*

Wolfgang pushed himself to his feet and took another step back as he scanned the length of Spider's body, from his slit throat all the way to his shoes.

His shoes. Wolfgang's gaze stopped on the exposed

soles of Spider's dress shoes. They had leather soles, and the bottoms were stained with bronze-colored patches, from the heel to the toe. Wolfgang knelt down, leaning close to the shoes as the watch buzzed again. He reached out and scraped at the stains. Some of the substance lifted free of the soles in gummy strips. It was half-dried paint.

Wolfgang stood up again and took a step back, his mind racing.

A nuclear scientist, exposed to radiation, walking through paint . . .

The realization hit Wolfgang like a ton of bricks. He turned toward the alley and broke into a run, pressing his hand over his ear. "Edric! Edric, the attack is today! Here in Paris! There's a bomb in Paris!"

The earpiece remained quiet. Wolfgang pulled it out and tapped it against his leg, then jammed it in again and repeated his frantic monologue. Once more, he was answered only by silence, and a lead weight descended into his stomach as he remembered Lyle's other words about his gadgetry. *"The battery life isn't great."*

Wolfgang had neglected to charge the earpiece after the café mission. It was dead now—completely useless. He gritted his teeth and dashed around to the front of the hotel. People were everywhere, crowding around the firetrucks as firefighters dashed into the hotel, towing canvas hoses. Red lights flashed, and alarms screamed. Charlie Team was nowhere in sight.

Wolfgang pressed through the crowd, frantically searching the faces for Megan or Lyle, Edric, or hell, even Kevin.

Somebody. Now.

The breeze on his face intensified, bringing with it an omen of doom. He didn't have time to find the team. He was already out of time. His hands shook, and he scanned the parking lot. He needed a car. Something fast.

A low snarl echoed across the parking lot, and Wolfgang looked to his left. A knot of gala attendees had gathered around a substitute valet stand. They waited in line, shouting for their cars to be brought around as the wives shivered and the men cursed. The sound had come from the race-red Ferrari he'd seen earlier that night. The beast growled as it approached the valet stand, its lights flashing across the faces of the waiting gala attendees. Wolfgang broke into a run, shoving through the crowd as the driver's door of the Ferrari swung open and the valet stepped out. Wolfgang grabbed his arm and jerked him out of the way amid shouts from the crowd, then slid inside, slamming the door and hitting the locks. The valet snatched at the door handle, shouting at him to open it. Wolfgang ignored him and searched for the gear selector. There wasn't one, but there were three buttons built into the console next to his right leg: R, Auto, and LC—probably Launch Control.

Wolfgang hit the auto button and slammed on the gas.

11

PEOPLE SCREAMED, and the Ferrari roared. Wolfgang was hurled into the plush leather seat as the back wheels spun, and then the car launched out of the portico and hurtled toward the street.

Wolfgang slammed on the brakes and cut the wheel to the right, sliding around a corner in the parking lot before hitting the gas again and rocketing into the street. He couldn't hear the screaming pedestrians or fire engines now, only the bellow of the V12 engine filling his ears as the car hit redline and the dash lit up with a warning light. Wolfgang hit the paddle shifter, and the transmission clicked like a fine watch. The Ferrari blasted forward as if a rocket were launching him from behind. He swerved to dodge taxicabs and late-night buses as the blinding lights of Paris filled his view.

He turned to the dash and poked at the navigation screen next to the tachometer. Wolfgang saw what looked like a voice command button, and he smashed it.

"Take me to the Eiffel Tower!" he shouted.

"Bienvenue dans votre Ferrari. Veuillez dire une commande."

"I don't speak French! English!"

"Veuillez dire une commande."

Wolfgang looked up from the nav system just in time to pull the wheel to the right and slide into the roundabout surrounding Napoleon's Arch. Buses, cars, bicycles, and motorbikes surrounded him on all sides as people shouted and horns blared. He narrowly missed colliding with a taxicab as he completed a full circle of the arch, the Ferrari still roaring. A marker appeared on the nav screen, just a mile south of the arch on the other side of the river Seine. It was the Eiffel Tower.

Wolfgang turned back to the left, exiting his hectic orbit of the arch and shooting onto Avenue d'Iéna. Trees leaned over the street on both sides, hugging the bright-red car as he flashed forward at over eighty miles per hour. Shoppes, apartments, tall office buildings, and squat cafés flashed past on both sides, and then he rocketed around another much smaller roundabout.

He could see the tower now, rising out of the cityscape in majestic, semi-illuminated glory, with odd dark patches covering the middle section. Wolfgang slowed the Ferrari as he screeched into Jardins du Trocadéro. Directly ahead, the massive Trocadéro Garden's pool stretched out to either side, with a jet of water shooting out and arcing in graceful glory before falling into the pool halfway down its length. Soft lights illuminated the fountain and the surrounding green space, and directly to his left, the Eiffel Tower shot skyward, just on the other side of the river.

Wolfgang jerked the wheel to the left and slammed on the gas. He wasn't intimidated by the car anymore. He knew what it could do, and he knew he could handle it. He rocketed through the Gardens and then hit the bridge, laying on the horn to alert the handful of late-night pedestrians and lovers who leaned over the water under the light of the Eiffel Tower. They screamed and scattered as the Ferrari screeched across the river and then blew through the next intersection. Directly ahead, the tower's four legs spread out, surrounded by a low metal fence that blocked pedestrians from walking beneath it. Wolfgang hit the gas and burst through the fence at fifty miles an hour. Metal screeched down the sides of the car, and he cut the wheel to the right, spinning to a halt directly beneath Paris's most iconic monument.

Wolfgang threw the door open and rolled out as police sirens wailed in the distance. He tilted his head back and stared up into the interior of the tower, shielding his eyes. The tower was lit all along its frame, stretching up over one thousand feet into the Parisian sky. At odd intervals along the graceful metallic superstructure, tarpaulins blocked off the light, and scaffolding covered the tower. Stacks of barrels rose like a small mountain at the base of the tower, and the main tourist entrance was completely blocked off with yellow construction tape.

The tower was closed for maintenance. Wolfgang remembered reading about it in the travel brochure he picked up on the plane. Every seven years, the entire thing was repainted to preserve the metal from decay. The process took three years and consumed over sixty tons of iconic, bronze-colored paint.

The same paint that Spider's shoes were stained with.

Wolfgang scanned the base of the tower and immediately saw the elevator, the entrance of which was closed off with a metal gate. Faint footprints marked the concrete leading up to the elevator, with parallel tire marks running behind them. Small tires, like you might find on a hand truck. The gate swung open without resistance, but when Wolfgang reached for the keypad, nothing was there. The entire control panel had been smashed in and obliterated. There was no way to call the car.

Wolfgang felt the tension rising in his stomach, and he ran a hand through his hair.

Think. Think!

Spider must have smashed the control panel, which meant he had in fact been here. But there must be another way.

The stairs. The brochure said there were 674 steps between ground level and the second floor of the structure. 674 steps, at one step a second. That was eleven minutes. But there was no way he could travel that fast for that long.

Screw it.

It didn't matter. He had to go, now.

Wolfgang rushed to the nearest leg of the tower and tore aside the construction tape. He started running, clearing the first flight in seconds and turning up the next. Every step clapped beneath his feet as the expensive leather soles of his dress shoes smacked against the metal. He forced himself not to take more than one step at a time—it would be an easy win now that would cost him dearly in the long run.

Not even his daily six-mile runs, weight training, and swimming could have prepared him for the grueling reality of 674 steps as the brisk French wind tore through the open structure and blasted his face. That wind—something he may have enjoyed were it a romantic night under the stars with Megan—now filled him with dread. Spider would've counted on this wind, holding out, biding his time, waiting for the perfect French night when the wind was strong but there was no rain. Because that's how dirty bombs work. They explode with a blast only as strong as whatever ordinary explosives they're packed with—C4, or more likely, plain dynamite.

But the fallout . . . the fallout would be the real killer. Spider would've packed his bomb with pounds of radioactive waste—the kind of thing a man working in nuclear energy could have obtained—exhausted rods from the reactors that fueled power plants, cut into small pieces and packed inside a lead case around the explosives. That package would be so radioactive that even though Spider would've worn protective gear, some of it still would've saturated his skin. Enough to set off Wolfgang's watch when he searched Spider's lifeless body.

Then Spider would've taken that bomb to the top of the tower. It would be heavy, necessitating his use of the elevator. He wouldn't have stopped at the first floor, or even the second. He would've taken the bomb all the way to the top of the tower, almost one thousand feet in the air, where the wind was the strongest.

And that's where he'd set it off. High above a densely populated city, where the dynamite would blast outward in all directions, and the nuclear waste would be carried by the wind over thousands of city blocks, there to rain down on unsuspecting civilians and poison them with a certain death that would take days, if not weeks, to materialize.

It was enough to bring down the city. It was enough to break the French economy, which would topple the European Union's economy and then bring down the world economy. And that would bring chaos. Anarchy. Because Spider was an anarchist, and chaos is a hell of a weapon.

Wolfgang ran, pumping out one step at a time, panting, and not pausing for a second as he reached the first floor of the tower, 187 feet off the ground. He spun to the next set of stairs and ran.

He wasn't sure how many minutes had ticked by, but he knew the wind was growing stronger, blowing out of the west and ripping through the open superstructure of the tower. With every blast in his face, he imagined a sudden detonation high above him. He imagined the tower shuddering as metal blasted outward amid a ball of fire and a boom so loud it would shake the ground.

But then nothing. The noise would fade, and people would stand in shock and stare at the shattered top of their beautiful tower, unaware that death itself was in the wind, only seconds away.

Wolfgang leaned on the rail and heaved, his head spinning. He wasn't sure how much farther he had to go. He hadn't counted steps, but he knew he was at least halfway to the second floor. After that, there was only one way to the top—a final elevator.

Wolfgang pushed himself up the steps, refusing to stop. Megan was someplace in the city, unprotected, unaware. Lyle and Edric and Kevin would all certainly die if he didn't reach the top in time.

The steps blurred, and he heard the scream of police sirens far below. He glanced down to see blue lights flashing near the Ferrari, but he didn't care. He only cared about reaching the top in time.

Another hundred steps rocketed past in a blur. Wolfgang's legs burned, his chest heaved, and his head swam, but he kept going.

The second floor opened around him in a flash. Wolfgang skidded and slid, grabbing a railing and heaving. He looked around the observation deck and blinked in the blast of the wind as it ripped through the tower with a vengeance. Spider had picked a good night.

Wolfgang found the elevator to the top floor surrounded by the tattered remnants of torn construction tape. The control panel was also smashed, like the first elevator. But unlike the first, this panel was built directly into the thick steel of the tower framework, and while the buttons were busted, the housing was still intact. He pressed the top button, smacking and wiggling it a few times until a dim light lit up behind it. The doors rolled open, and Wolfgang lurched inside, then hit the button for the top floor. The doors closed as distant shouts drifted up from someplace farther down the tower. The police.

A dull whine rang from the motor, and the car began moving up the final six hundred feet to the top. Wolfgang closed his eyes and forced himself to breathe evenly. The bomb could detonate at any moment, and if it did, he would certainly die. But if there were just five minutes left before the bomb went off . . .

The car rose, gaining speed. Wolfgang braced himself and suddenly wondered what he was going to do when he reached the top. He didn't know a *thing* about disabling a bomb. Did he cut the red wire or the blue?

The car ground to a halt, then the doors rolled open, and a fresh blast of wind ripped straight through Wolfgang's tux. Only a few feet ahead, the wall of the tower rose to waist-height, with a chain-link fence covering the space from the top of the wall to the tip of the tower. Observation scopes were mounted at intervals along the wall, and the observation deck encircled the top of the tower like a giant donut.

Wolfgang rushed outward, catching himself on the rail and staring straight below toward Paris. His stomach flipped, and he stumbled back, his knees feeling suddenly weak. He wasn't usually afraid of heights, but the vast distance between himself and the ground seemed cataclysmic. He imagined the bomb going off and him being hurtled off the tower and into the dead air beyond. Falling. Falling to his death.

Wolfgang shook his head and began to circle the observation deck, one corner, and then the second. The empty deck was smudged with half-dry paint and mucky footprints. Spider's footprints.

He grabbed the railing to steady himself, then turned the final corner. The bomb lay in the middle of the deck, planted like a forgotten suitcase. But it was much bigger than a suitcase—built into a 55-gallon drum, strapped to a hand truck with a lid pressed over the top.

Wolfgang rushed forward and pressed his fingers into the gap around the lid, then prized it up. The lid wouldn't move, and Wolfgang's fingers slipped off the rim with a pop.

He searched his pockets, but the only things he had left with him were his passport and a small bundle of Euros.

Think. Quickly.

Wolfgang felt around the side of the drum until his fingers found the ratchet of the strap binding it to the hand truck. A quick tug on the ratchet, and a press of the release switch, and the strap came loose. Wolfgang pulled it free of the drum and felt down its length until he found the metal hook tied to the strap's end. It was flat and stiff and fit perfectly into the gap around the drum's lip.

The lid was tightly battered down like the lid of a paint can, but as Wolfgang shoved down on the hook, he felt it give. Just a little at first, then more. A small gap opened at one side, and Wolfgang dropped the hook, shoving his fingers through the gap and jerking upward. The lid flew off, and the dim lights from the spire of the tower shone down inside the barrel.

Dynamite. It was packed in the middle of the barrel with unidentifiable metal cases crammed in all around it, each of them painted yellow with red radioactive labels on them. On top of the dynamite was a mess of multi-colored wires, a couple of circuit boards, and an LCD display counting down from six minutes.

How do I do this? Do I just rip away the wires?

No. Wolfgang had seen movies where people did that and the bomb ending up going off. Was this like the movies? Surely it wasn't that simple.

He wiped his face, and his hands shook. The clock read under five minutes now, ticking down one second at a time. With each flash of the screen, Wolfgang felt the wind at his back and imagined the top of the tower exploding into flames.

No. Think. Think!

Another flash caught his eye, and when he glanced down at the smartwatch on his arm, his heart lurched.

The watch. Lyle can see.

Wolfgang unlocked the watch and cycled through the apps but couldn't find a messenger or texting function. Had Lyle disabled it to make room for the other applications?

Come on . . . give me something!

Suddenly the watch's screen went black, and Wolfgang's stomach sank, thinking for a moment the battery had died. Then the screen flashed green and the whole watch lit up in single colors. Red. Yellow. Purple. The colors changed quickly, and Wolfgang felt the blood surge through him again. Lyle *could* see.

He directed the watch's camera to the top of the barrel as the screen went black again. Slowly, he maneuvered around the edge of the barrel, providing Lyle with different angles of the bomb.

The timer counted down under three minutes.

"Come on, Lyle!"

The screen flashed yellow. Wolfgang peered into the bomb case and dug through the wires until he located a yellow wire. He started to pull it, but then the watch began to flash through the different colors again.

"What?" he shouted. "I don't know what you want!"

The watch stopped flashing, and Wolfgang sucked in a breath. He closed his eyes and forced himself to think. He couldn't panic. Not now.

He opened his eyes and turned the watch until the camera faced him, then he slowly mouthed, "Two blinks . . . yes." He held up two fingers, then a thumbs-up. "Three blinks . . . no." Three fingers, then a thumbs-down. "Understand?"

The watched blinked blue, twice.

"All right, buddy. Let's get it done." Wolfgang leaned over the barrel and fingered the yellow wire. He held the watch to where Lyle could see, and then he waited.

The watch blinked red three times. Wolfgang dropped the wire and wiped his eyes, then dug through the barrel. The watch blinked yellow again, then black.

"That's the only yellow wire, Lyle!"

The clock on the bomb read one minute, twelve seconds. Wolfgang's heart thumped. The watch blinked yellow, then black. Yellow, then black. Wolfgang dug through the wires as the clock flashed rhythmically.

His fingers shuffled through a red wire, then a blue, and

two green, then he touched a black wire. The watch flashed frantically: yellow, black, yellow, black.

Wolfgang twisted the wire and saw a yellow stripe running up its back side. He held the camera close to the wire. "This one?"

The watch flashed green, twice.

He snatched the wire, and it broke free of the mechanism, but the clock didn't stop ticking. Twenty seconds, now. Nineteen.

The watch flashed red. Wolfgang put his fingers on the red wire, and the watch flashed green, twice. Wolfgang snatched the wire.

Nine seconds. Eight seconds.

"Come on, Lyle!"

The watch flashed purple. Wolfgang dug frantically through the mess. Two purple wires ran into the same mechanism—neither with any stripes.

Four seconds. Three seconds.

He didn't have time to confirm with Lyle. He grabbed both wires and snatched them free of the mechanism.

The clock froze over the two-second mark, then went black. Wolfgang stumbled back until his hips hit the wall.

The bomb didn't go off.

He collapsed to the floor of the observation deck, nervous sweat streaming down his face despite the cold. He let out a soft sob and lowered his head into shaking hands.

I did it . . . I did it . . .

The elevator door rolled open on the other side of the tower, and footsteps rang against the deck. Two French police officers darted around the corner, guns drawn. They skidded to a halt only feet away, and Wolfgang leaned back against the wall, offering a tired smile.

"What's up, guys?"

The lead cop eyed the barrel, then his glare turned toward Wolfgang. He sniffed in indignant disgust and lifted a lip. "You are under arrest!"

Wolfgang grinned. "Sounds great, buddy."

12

FRENCH JAIL SMELLED JUST about the same as any institutional building in America—a cocktail of sweat, stale coffee, and too little ventilation, but Wolfgang didn't care. He lay on his cot, facing the ceiling with his eyes closed, and just breathed.

He was alive. In the heat of the moments leading up to disabling the bomb, he'd never thought about himself. He'd thought about his team, he'd thought about innocent Parisians, and he'd thought about Megan. It wasn't until the bomb was about to detonate that he really considered his own stake in the game, and even then the imminence of his death didn't sink in until the jailer locked the door and Wolfgang had a moment to think.

He wasn't worried about being in jail. Sure, he'd stolen

a three-hundred-thousand-dollar car, scraped it up, broken several traffic laws, broken into a closed monument at night, and most auspiciously, been arrested next to a nuclear weapon. All those things would be cleared up by SPIRE, or they wouldn't. And if they weren't, if SPIRE disavowed him and left him in this cell . . . well, he was a man of many means. He'd get out eventually.

Right now he just wanted to lie on this bed, eyes closed, and enjoy being alive. The cot was stiff, and a stray spring jabbed into his back, but he didn't care. He could lie there for days, his eyes closed, a single image playing over and over in his mind—the image of him and Megan dancing at the gala, moving smoothly while the music played and the world around them faded out of existence.

He'd never met somebody so special that he thought about them this way or felt the things he was feeling now. He'd never met somebody that he thought he'd like to spend a lot of time with, and really get to know, and maybe even let her get to know him.

And yet, he knew it couldn't be. That was clear now. Sure, she'd only known him a few days, but she clearly didn't reciprocate the attraction he felt, and he thought he knew why.

Footsteps clicked against the concrete of the jail floor, and Wolfgang made a show of yawning without opening his eyes.

"Yo, Louis!" Wolfgang shouted. "When's breakfast? I feel like I'm entitled to some French toast."

"How about breakfast in the USA?" Megan stood just on the other side of the bars, leaned against them, staring at him with just the hint of a smile playing at her lips.

Wolfgang swung his feet onto the floor, breaking out into a grin as he walked toward her. "Finally! I thought you guys were gonna leave me here."

Megan shrugged. "That was certainly suggested, but you've got Lyle's watch. He wants it back."

Wolfgang laughed. "No way. They can bury me with that watch."

"Are you okay? Did they wash you off?"

Wolfgang nodded quickly, uneager to discuss the details of the French decontamination process. He appreciated being washed free of nuclear contaminants, but standing buck naked in somebody else's country while they sprayed you with a water hose . . . well. It wasn't a postcard moment.

More footsteps, and a cop appeared. It was the same cop who'd arrested him at the top of the tower.

The man's eyes were dark and full of disgust. He opened the door and held it back, sticking his nose in the air. "You are free to go."

Wolfgang grinned. "Don't mind if I do."

He and Megan walked back to the front desk, where he processed out. The paperwork he'd signed labeled him as

Paul Listener, and he remembered the passport he'd taken to the gala.

They think I'm Canadian.

The desk clerk handed him the passport, along with the watch and euro notes. "You have twelve hours to leave France, Monsieur Listener."

Wolfgang flashed her his standby grin. "No worries. I'll be home by then."

He followed Megan outside and ducked into the waiting Mercedes. It was Kevin's car from earlier that night, but there was no sign of Kevin or the others. Sunlight streamed over Paris from the east, bathing the car in golden light and reminding Wolfgang how good it was to see another day.

"They're waiting on the plane," Megan said as she slipped into the driver's seat. "We'll take off as soon as we arrive."

"How did you get me out? I mean, they have to think I was at fault for the bomb."

Megan shrugged. "Edric made some calls. SPIRE pulled some strings. I imagine that if we stuck around another few hours, you'd be arrested again, but all we needed was an opening."

"Thanks," Wolfgang said.

He watched as Megan piloted the car onto the highway. Her hair was held back in a simple ponytail, and she wore a leather jacket and jeans. Somehow, she looked even better than she had in the dress.

He looked away, his stomach tightening. "How mad is Edric?"

"Edric is more flexible than he lets on. A lot happened last night. Were it not for you, a lot more would have happened."

"What about Spider? I found his body—"

"In the alley, yes. Edric already spoke to the CIA. Apparently Raven pushed too hard and blew his own cover. Spider wasn't talking, and Raven eliminated him, rather than letting him go."

"Sloppy work. I can't imagine the CIA is pleased."

"They're not," Megan said. "I get the feeling Raven will be out of a job pretty soon. How did you figure it out, anyway? Your comm went dead."

Wolfgang tapped the watch. "The Geiger counter went off in my watch when I searched Spider's body. It shouldn't have done that unless he'd been recently exposed to radiation. That's when I realized there must already be a bomb. A dirty bomb made the most sense. Constructing an actual nuclear device would require resources and know-how that even a nuclear scientist like Spider couldn't have obtained on his own. But a dirty bomb is just nuclear waste packed around an explosive. I figured Spider could've obtained the waste. So, then it was just a matter of where he put it."

"How the hell did you guess the Eiffel Tower?"

"There was paint on his shoes. I'd read that the tower was being painted, and anyway, it made sense. Setting it off that high over the city would dramatically increase its effectiveness."

"Damn . . ." Megan shook her head, and Wolfgang thought he saw genuine respect in her eyes. "That was quick thinking," she said. "And quick driving."

Wolfgang laughed. "Yeah, too bad we can't take the Ferrari home. Hey, what about the Russians?"

"What about them?"

"Are they . . . alive?"

She nodded. "We ended up tasing the one outside. Your guy is gonna have one hell of a concussion, but he'll survive."

"I'm glad."

"You're glad?"

"He was never the enemy," Wolfgang said. "He was just doing his job."

Megan laughed. "Even so, I'd recommend you avoid dark alleys next time you're in Moscow."

"Hey, if it's up to me, I'll never *be* in Moscow."

The car grew quiet as they approached the airport. Megan rubbed her lip with one finger, glancing at him out of the corner of her eye. He didn't say anything, but he knew what she was thinking, and he was dreading the conversation.

"I know Kevin left his post," she said.

Wolfgang nodded. "Yep."

Megan put both hands on the wheel and let out a breath. "There's . . . there's something you need to know about him. And me."

Wolfgang faced the window. "You're exes. I know."

"Exes?" Megan's voice turned shrill. "Gross! He's my brother."

"Your brother? What do you mean?"

"How many definitions does *brother* have?"

"You have different last names."

"Well, okay. Half brother. We share a mother."

"Wait, so . . ."

Megan held up a hand. "Just listen, okay?"

Wolfgang sat back and waited for Megan to clear her head. She stroked hair out of her face, and he thought he saw a tear forming in the corner of her eye.

"Edric told you we lost a man on our last mission."

Wolfgang nodded.

"His name was James. We worked together for a long time." Her voice wavered a little, but she regained control. "Kevin and James were best friends. They used to hang out a lot outside of work. Hunting trips and football games . . . James was more like a brother. They were very close."

Again, she paused, then swallowed, as if the next thing she had to say was going to be the hardest. "James and I were also . . . a thing. I mean, we were together. Dating, or whatever. Edric didn't know, or at least he pretended not to know, because of course it was a bad idea. The thing is, we worked so well together, I guess he figured it didn't matter if we were involved."

Wolfgang knew where this was headed, and he felt like a miserable, disgusting jerk.

"Our last mission was in Damascus. Edric, Kevin, and James were in a two-story building collecting intel from a terrorist organization. Something went wrong. The terrorists found them there, in the building."

Megan looked out her window, and for a long moment, she said nothing.

Wolfgang felt an overwhelming longing to grab her hand—to have her stop the car so he could hold her. But he waited.

Megan wiped her eyes and nodded a couple times. "Kevin blames himself for what happened. He was closest to James and Edric when the gunfire started. A hand grenade went off and blew Edric out of a second-floor window. He broke his shoulder and humerus on impact, but Kevin was able to get to him before the fighters closed in. James never made it out."

Megan nodded a couple times, as if she were accepting the reality of what had happened all over again. "It's my fault. I should have been there. They left me behind because, you know, it's Damascus. Women can't just go places without being noticed. But maybe, if I'd been there . . ." She glanced at Wolfgang from the corner of her eye, as if remembering who she was talking to, then cleared her throat and sat up. "Anyway. I just thought you should know. I guess I was a little cold to you before. And Kevin came across a little ugly, I know. He's protective of me, and he feels like you're replacing James. He can't accept that."

Megan turned off the road and into the private airfield where the Gulfstream sat at the end of the runway, ready for takeoff. The others were already inside, and Wolfgang felt a strange comfort thinking about being around Edric and Lyle again. And Kevin.

"You won't have to worry about him now, anyway." Megan put the car in park. "Edric will fire him for leaving his post."

Wolfgang reached for the door handle, then felt Megan's hand on his. He flinched, lightning flooding his body, and when he turned, it surprised him to see her smiling.

She gave his hand a gentle squeeze. "I like you, Wolfgang. You're good at your job, and you're fun to have around. But you should know . . . I'll never become involved with somebody on my team again."

The exhilaration that flooded him only moments before crashed down like a house of cards. A weight descended into his stomach, and he nodded dumbly. Megan ducked out of the car, and he hurried to follow, feeling awkward and foolish as he ascended the steps into the plane.

The door shut automatically behind him, and he

followed Megan into the cabin where Edric and Kevin were. Lyle sat in the back, hidden behind a computer screen.

Edric jumped up and hurried across the aisle, smacking Wolfgang on the back with his good arm. "Wolfgang! Dammit, it's good to see you. Hell of a job last night. Hell of a job!"

The warmth in Edric's tone was more than Wolfgang had ever heard him express. As the captain called for them to fasten their seatbelts, he took a seat across the aisle from Kevin, feeling the bigger man's eyes on him the entire time. As the seatbelt clicked, he glanced at Kevin and saw him look away.

There was a shadow in his eyes—a little shame, or a little sadness.

The plane's engines whined, then the aircraft shot down the runway, lifting into the air like a bird.

As soon as the seatbelt light went off, Wolfgang turned to Edric. "Hell of a thing with those Russians."

"What do you mean?"

Wolfgang shrugged. "If Kevin hadn't seen them walking in and come to warn me, they probably would've got the jump on us."

Edric's eyes narrowed, and Kevin sat up. They both stared at Wolfgang. Lyle and Megan were watching him, also.

"He came to warn you?" Edric asked quietly.

Wolfgang nodded. "My earpiece was giving me trouble all night. Guess he couldn't get through. Right, Kev?"

Kevin's cheeks flushed, and he looked down. But he nodded. "Yeah . . . that's right."

Wolfgang could tell Edric wasn't fooled, but he said nothing. He stared at Wolfgang for a long moment, then grunted and slapped Kevin on the shoulder. "Good job, Kevin. Lyle, let's take a look at those earpieces."

Wolfgang walked to the tail of the plane, stopping at the minibar next to Lyle. He poured himself a water and sipped it, shooting Lyle a sideways glance.

The computer wiz smirked, then whispered, "There's nothing wrong with those earpieces if you charge them."

"Roll with me?" Wolfgang said.

"I guess I owe you one."

"Owe me one?"

Lyle's cheeks flushed red, and he turned back to the computer.

"Owe me for what?"

Lyle sniffed, and a grin tugged at his lips. "Oh, nothing. It's just that . . . the bomb was disabled after the second wire."

"What?"

Megan turned in her seat, and Wolfgang was suddenly aware that the entire plane was listening again.

He growled. "The *second* wire? What about the purple wire? You told me to pull the purple wire!"

"Sure," Lyle said. "That just disabled the clock."

Wolfgang slammed the glass down. "My god, man. I was about to have a heart attack!"

A ripple of laugher echoed through the plane, and Lyle broke into a grin. "Welcome to Charlie Team, Wolfgang."

THAT TIME IN CAIRO

BOOK 2 OF THE WOLFGANG PIERCE SERIES

———

"Egypt is full of dreams, mysteries, memories."
— *Janet Erskine Stuart*

———

[1]

September, 2011

EVEN IN LATE SUMMER, Buffalo was cool. Sharp wind drifted off Lake Erie and tore through the city like the revenging hand of God, searching for anybody who may be guilty of being comfortable. Only weeks from now, the snow would start, and a month after that, it would clog Buffalo, piled high against every building. For now, standing outside was still bearable, but the shortening days and sharpening wind were an omen of what lay ahead.

Wolfgang stood thirty yards from the building with his hands jammed into the pockets of a light windbreaker. From his vantage point on the sidewalk, he could see through the smeared windows and into the dingy interior of

Jordan Fletcher Home for Children. Harried workers ran back and forth, dressed in scrubs featuring safari animals, while children played in any number of small rooms with colorful walls.

These were the outcasts—the orphans and the lonely—children who were between foster homes or awaiting an impending adoption mired in red tape. Wolfgang knew their stories because he was one of them, and so was Collins.

Through the third story of the shabby building, Wolfgang could see her room. It was small, with a mechanical bed lifted into a seat. Collins's room was more akin to a hospital room than a child's bedroom. Sure, the same bright paints adorned the walls, and the same toys littered the floor, but Collins didn't run and play like the other children. She didn't laugh as loud or walk as fast.

And she never would.

Wolfgang found a park bench that faced the facility. The wooden slats of the bench creaked under his weight, but it felt good to sit. He watched the little room on the third floor. From this angle, he could just make out the top of the bed and the small, curly-haired head that rested against a pillow. Eyes shut. Cheeks pale.

Another blast of lake wind tore down the street, crashing around Wolfgang's windbreaker like water over rock, but he didn't move. He didn't even shudder. Wolfgang just watched the room, thinking of Collins, and for the dozenth time that year, he told himself to get up and go inside. Go to her room . . . sweep her up in a hug. Tell his baby sister that he loved her.

But he couldn't.

He closed his eyes and heard the crash of glass against hardwood. He heard the yell of a drunken man out for blood. The scream of a panicked woman shielding her children. The broken sob of a little girl, her breaths ragged and filled with pain.

"Throw that runt out!" the man had screamed. "No child of mine is defective!"

More glass shattered. More household items flew like artillery shells, exploding against marred drywall, already battered by a hundred such engagements.

And so it went, two, sometimes three nights a week—as often as the man found the bottle, and the bottle found the floor, and the little girl cried and sheltered behind her bruised mother while her older brother cowered in the shadows . . . and did nothing.

Wolfgang opened his eyes. They stung with cold tears as the wind intensified. He couldn't see Collins's head now, but he imagined he could. He imagined he could hear her breaths, each one filled with pain as the ravages of her disease clutched her body.

He stood up, leaning into the wind and hurrying across the street, then stopped in front of the smudged glass entrance and stared at the handle. Wolfgang turned to the right and approached the donation slot next to the door. He dug a thick envelope from beneath the windbreaker, packed with anonymous cash, and crammed it through the slot. Casting another furtive glance at the window, three floors up, he whispered to Collins as he always did. "I love you, and one day, I'll make it right."

Wolfgang's phone buzzed. He turned from the building and retrieved it, grateful for the distraction. There was a text message from a contact labeled simply as E.

HEADQUARTERS. 12 HOURS.

A flood of excitement filled him—enough to burn away the cold, but never quite enough to burn away the guilt. He shoved the phone back into his pocket and held out his hand for the nearest taxi.

———

BUFFALO MIGHT'VE BEEN in the throes of premature fall, but in St. Louis, summer was still alive and well. Wolfgang found Charlie Team waiting for him on the fourteenth floor of the Bank of America Plaza, and he scrubbed his shoes on the mat outside the door before ducking inside.

"Wolfgang! Better late than never," Edric called from the far side of the room.

Wolfgang blushed, glancing around the room to see Lyle sitting behind a computer at the table and Kevin standing

next to the minibar, mixing a cocktail. Megan sat by herself
next to the window, right where she had the first time he'd
met her four months prior. She leaned against the wall with
her legs crossed and stared out at the gleaming Gateway
Arch only a half mile away. She wore yoga pants and a
loose-fitting shirt that fell an inch short of her waistline. She
was beautiful in a simple, elegant way. He loved that.

"Like a drink, Wolf?" Kevin's commanding voice
boomed from the minibar, and the big man offered Wolfgang a reserved nod.

"A Sprite would be great," Wolfgang said.

Kevin reached for the soda as Wolfgang settled into a
chair. This was Charlie Team—an elite detachment of
SPIRE, a company specializing in professional espionage
services. They worked for whoever could pay their hefty
fees, conducting specialized undercover missions around
the globe. Their diverse capabilities were prominently
advertised in their name: Sabotage, Procurement, Infiltration, Retaliation, and Entrapment. SPIRE did it all.

Wolfgang joined Charlie Team earlier that summer
after working for SPIRE as an independent operator for
three years, conducting corporate espionage and entrapment rackets in mostly American cities. Now his missions
would carry him around the globe. In June, the team had
barely survived a delicate operation in Paris, which almost
cost a great deal more than their own lives. Wolfgang

thrived on that mission, winning the respect of the rest of the team, but failing to win everything he really wanted.

As Megan sat next to the window, he heard her words play back from moments before they left Paris. *"I like you, Wolfgang. But you should know . . . I'll never become involved with somebody on my team again."*

Wolfgang looked away, shoving his feelings deep inside a mental box and locking them there. Megan was right, after all. They were a team. They had a job to do. Getting involved with each other didn't play a part in that.

"Here you go." Kevin offered Wolfgang the Sprite with another reserved nod.

Kevin was Megan's half brother, and prior to the Paris mission, he was about as friendly with Wolfgang as a dog with a burglar. Wolfgang could still feel the awkward tension between them, fueled predominantly by Kevin's suspicions that Wolfgang was making a play for his sister, but at least Kevin was handing him drinks now instead of throwing punches. Wolfgang could appreciate the progress.

"Thanks, Kev."

Wolfgang sipped the soda as Edric approached his favored whiteboard and produced a red marker. Edric's right arm moved with a little stiffness—residual effects of a multi-point break from an accident in Damascus five months prior. The injury had hamstrung Edric in Paris, and Wolfgang wondered how much it would limit them on whatever mission lay ahead.

"I hope you guys had a nice break. We're back at it, and we're going someplace warm."

Edric started scratching on the board, and Wolfgang wondered why he bothered. It seemed needlessly time-consuming and repetitious.

"Cairo," Edric said, stepping back. "We're going to Cairo."

Edric grinned at the room as if he were awaiting a standing ovation, but Cairo wasn't exactly the warm, exotic locale Wolfgang had imagined. Nassau or Fiji would've hit the spot. Havana, even. Cairo?

Edric sighed, then turned to the board and drew a large triangle. "Cairo," he said. "Great Pyramids?"

Lyle started slow-clapping, and the others quickly joined in. Edric rolled his eyes and motioned to the table. "You're all jerks. Gather up."

Megan, Kevin, and Wolfgang joined Lyle at the table.

"Three weeks ago," Edric said, "a construction worker laboring on an apartment building in the Libyan village of Al Jawf uncovered a stone case that housed an ancient papyrus scroll inscribed with hieroglyphics. It seems he didn't really know what he'd found, but he thought it might be valuable, so he went into town and found an American W.H.O. worker and tried to sell it. The American had enough education to recognize the extreme age of the scroll and bought it from him, then called Libyan authorities."

Edric wrote on the board the entire time he spoke,

sketching words such as *scroll* and *W.H.O.* and connecting them with a mess of lines that, at first glance, made the entire story appear to be the structure of an elaborate bank heist.

"The Libyans deployed some researchers to take a look, and they determined the scroll to date back to around one thousand B.C., possibly a relic of the Library of Alexandria. Obviously a valuable find."

"Why do I detect the sordid stench of impending corruption?" Kevin asked.

Edric just smirked. "The Libyans confiscated the scroll from the W.H.O. worker and contacted Egyptian authorities. Apparently, Libya hasn't got much interest in ancient literature, but they thought they could make a quick buck. After some haggling, Egypt agreed to purchase the scroll. They sent scientists to authenticate it, then placed it in a protective, vacuum-sealed case . . ."

"And lost it," Megan finished.

Edric jabbed the marker at her. "Bingo. Someplace between Al Jawf and Cairo—amid a thousand kilometers of Sahara desert—the case went missing, along with its escorts."

"They drove straight through the desert?" Megan asked.

"Yep. The research team from Cairo hasn't been seen or heard from in six days, but one of the Land Rovers used in the convoy turned up in southern Egypt earlier this week, riddled with bullet holes."

"Shit," Kevin muttered.

"What's the value of the scroll?" Wolfgang asked.

Edric shrugged. "The Egyptians bought it for one hundred twelve thousand Libyan dinars. About twenty-five thousand dollars, US."

"Not a lot to kill for," Wolfgang said.

"No, not really," Edric said. "Except the Egyptians believe the scroll was worth more than ancient porn. Almost none of it was readable without restoration, but what snippets they gathered indicate the document to be some kind of burial record. The map to a tomb, if you will."

Silence filled the room as the morbid quality of the words sank in.

Edric nodded slowly, then sat down at the end of the table. "At least a dozen tombs of the pharaohs have yet to be found," he said. "When King Tut's tomb was discovered in 1922, they valued the contents at tens of millions."

Wolfgang let out a low whistle. "Plenty to kill for."

Edric nodded. "Grave robberies have accounted for the destruction of numerous ancient artifacts and national treasures in Egypt. The Egyptian government wants to be sure that whatever tomb is documented on the scroll isn't the next victim."

"So, they hired us to catch a book thief?" Kevin laughed.

"You could say that," Edric said. "Only, this book thief is well armed, probably not alone, and lost in the biggest desert on the planet."

Wolfgang fingered the dripping condensation on the outside of the Sprite can, evaluating the story and searching for inconsistencies or missing information. Then he grinned. "Well, *procurement* is in our name, right? Let's go procure a grave map."

[2]

SPIRE's GULFSTREAM G550 waited on the tarmac at a small private airport north of St. Louis. Wolfgang held the door of the Uber for Megan and offered her a warm smile. She nodded her thanks but said nothing as she hurried up the steps into the plane, her petite frame looking little larger than that of a child next to the big aircraft.

Wolfgang felt something sink inside of him as she disappeared inside.

"Hey, Wolf. Give me a hand?" Lyle said from the back of a utility van parked nearby. His nose was wrinkled up to hold the glasses on his face, and he beckoned.

Wolfgang hurried to the back of the van and looked in to see a box half the size of a coffin resting inside. "What the hell is this?"

Lyle grinned. "New toys." He jumped inside and pushed the box out.

Wolfgang caught the edge, and they lifted it up.

"Watch out. It's heavy," Lyle said.

The air whistled between Wolfgang's teeth as he stumbled backward. "You don't say . . . It feels like a case of bricks!"

The box must have weighed close to two hundred pounds and was packed so tight that even as Wolfgang struggled to regain his balance, nothing shifted inside. They wrestled it out of the van and up the steps into the waiting airplane. Lyle motioned toward the rear of the aircraft, and they stumbled past the plush leather seats, dragging the crate over headrests and slamming into Kevin along the way.

"Look out there, wiz," Kevin snapped, a drink in one hand.

Lyle shot Kevin a salty glare, then they set the case down just outside the plane's aft cabin.

A door clicked shut, then Edric emerged from the cockpit and motioned to the seats. "Lift off," he said.

Wolfgang slid into a seat, catching his breath and buckling his seatbelt. The aircraft's engines whined and spun to life, and a few minutes later, they shot skyward.

Lyle sat on top of his box, his short legs hovering an inch off the floor as he sipped water from a bottle. Wolfgang cast the box another curious look, then dismissed the mystery as his eyes landed on Megan again. She sat at the lone table, bent over a map of Cairo with a red pen in one hand. He recalled her studying maps of Paris prior to their last operation and remembered how helpful it would've been if he'd done the same.

I should join her.

"All right. Huddle up." Edric took a seat close to the group and accepted a gin and tonic from Kevin.

Wolfgang leaned forward and flexed his fingers. Memories from his last operation with Charlie Team flooded his mind and primed his body to spring into action again. Paris had been a stress-filled nightmare at the time, but now all Wolfgang could think about was feeling that rush of adrenaline again.

"The Egyptians have determined that the scroll went missing someplace in their Western Desert region," Edric said. "That area constitutes about 263,000 square miles, and two-thirds of the country."

"Well, that's helpful." Kevin snorted.

Edric sipped his drink. "It's a desolate place. Entire battalions of World War Two soldiers lost themselves in that desert, and it would be easy for us to do the same. So, the question is, how do we find our needle in that haystack?"

Wolfgang rubbed his chin and watched Edric. Charlie Team's leader rested his injured arm on one knee and leaned back, swirling his drink and watching his team with the faintest hint of a smirk.

He already knows how. He just wants us to figure it out.

Wolfgang scanned the team. Kevin was making a show of puckering his lips and glaring at the premium carpet in between gulps of whiskey. Megan shuffled through maps until she uncovered one of Greater Egypt, then tapped the Western Desert region with her pen. Lyle sat back and tried to hide a grin.

He knows, too. Figures. He probably hacked Edric's brain.

Kevin snapped his fingers. "Satellite! Lyle can hack a satellite again, and we'll just scan the desert."

Lyle shook his head. "After Paris, I'm having difficulty gaining access to any useful satellites. Most of them don't have the sort of high-powered, live cameras we need. Also, security has been . . . upgraded."

Edric grunted. "And besides, what exactly would you be looking for? Two guys with guns holding up a scroll in the middle of the desert?"

Kevin blushed and turned to the minibar to refresh his drink.

Wolfgang rubbed his chin, picturing the vast wasteland in his mind. Two hundred sixty-three thousand square miles . . . It was just too big. Impossibly big. It would be difficult to find an aircraft carrier in that expanse, let alone a book thief who didn't want to be found.

"Roadblocks?" Megan asked.

She looked up, still rolling the pen between her fingers. *She's guessing.*

"What are we, warlords?" Edric said. "Come on, guys. It's not that hard."

"We don't find them," Wolfgang said.

Everybody looked his way, and he sat forward.

"It's not possible. The desert is too big. For all we know, they aren't there anyway. They could be anywhere in the country by now."

"Go on," Edric said.

"We have to put ourselves in their shoes. If we stole the scroll, what would we need? We already know the scroll isn't fully readable, and anyway, it's written in a dead language. So, the thieves need to restore it before it can be useful, and then they need somebody who can translate it." Wolfgang snapped his fingers as the plan cemented in his mind. "In other words, we don't need to find them. We need to find the person they need. There can't be more than a few specialists in the country with the right kind of skills. We find that person, and the thieves will come to us."

Edric smiled and looked at Megan. "Kid's good."

Megan shrugged indifferently, probably perturbed that she hadn't solved the riddle first.

Edric reached into a briefcase next to his chair and retrieved a file. He opened it and shuffled full-page photographs across the table.

"Dr. Amelia Pollins. She's a British national currently employed by the Egyptian Museum in Cairo. She holds a PhD in Egyptology, with specialties including hiero-glyphics and the restoration of ancient artifacts."

"Well, her résumé checks out," Kevin said.

Wolfgang lifted the photograph from the table. Pollins looked to be in her late thirties, with ice-blue eyes and dirty-blonde hair. She had a somewhat stiff appearance, as though she were more comfortable in a laboratory than at a dinner party.

"Where's the museum?" Wolfgang asked.

"Downtown Cairo," Megan said, apparently eager to contribute after striking out. "It's massive, with thousands of artifacts. The scroll was probably headed there before being stolen."

Edric nodded. "It was, because Dr. Pollins was the specialist assigned to head the restoration and evaluation project. She knows more about hieroglyphics than almost anybody in the country, which is funny since she's not even Egyptian."

"Does she speak them?" Lyle asked.

"Speak what?" Edric said.

"Hieroglyphics."

The plane went silent for a moment as everybody waited for Lyle to laugh. He didn't.

"It's a dead language, wiz! Nobody speaks it." Kevin snorted, smacking Lyle on the shoulder.

"Actually, it's not a language," Megan said. "It's not even an alphabet, really. It's a different form of written communication—pictographic characters strung together to convey concepts, ideas, events, etcetera."

Edric waved a hand. "None of that matters. The focus is recovering the document, then the Egyptians can worry about what it says. We know Pollins is the likely target of the thief and agree that starting with her makes the most sense. Now, we need a plan of action."

Megan's back stiffened. "Wait, we're gonna use this woman as bait?"

"Not bait, no," Edric said. "We're going to provide her with close proximity, invisible protection, and nab her potential kidnapper before she knows a thing about it."

Megan folded her arms. "We're going to use her as bait."

Edric lifted both eyebrows. "Do you have a better idea? Better than roadblocks, I mean."

Silence filled the plane, then Megan nodded her defeat.

Edric walked to the minibar and poured himself a bourbon, then took a long sip. "After we land, we'll proceed to Pollins's office to locate her. Intel suggests she arrives early and leaves late, and we'll land about four hours before sundown, so we should have plenty of time to establish a perimeter and monitor her as she leaves."

"What if Wolfgang is wrong?" Kevin asked. "What if they aren't targeting this woman at all?"

Edric shrugged. "If they don't make a move on her

tonight, we'll reevaluate in the morning. Let's not compli-
cate things ahead of time. Lyle, are we good on communications? I don't want any more unexplained failures."

Lyle shot Wolfgang a sideways look, and Wolfgang
avoided his gaze. On their last mission in Paris, Wolfgang
had thrown Lyle under the bus, blaming a communications
failure while covering for Kevin, who had broken protocol
and left his post. Kevin had kept his job, and Edric probably
knew the comms had never failed, but Lyle still got harassed
about it.

"Won't be a problem," Lyle said. "I've devised a way to
reduce proximities between each of you and the core
antenna that routes all signals back to my computers.
Comms should be strong and reliable."

Edric nodded. "Terrific. Let's keep them that way."

He drained the glass, then waved over his shoulder as
he stepped over Lyle's crate and disappeared into the aft
cabin.

Lyle shot Wolfgang a sideways look. "You owe me one,"
he said.

Wolfgang motioned to the crate, eager to change the
subject. "What's in the box?"

Lyle's face lit up, and he scooted out of his seat. "Help
me open it. I'll show you."

They pried the lid off, exposing a mound of foam
packing peanuts inside.

Lyle scooped them aside, then lifted out smaller cardboard boxes. "You may remember that in Paris I had a lot of trouble staying connected to our satellite."

"You mean the satellite you hacked."

Lyle wrinkled his nose. "Hacked, borrowed, whatever. The point is, it occurred to me that we could maintain visual and radio connection a lot better if we weren't using a satellite at all, but something much closer to the ground. Something we controlled."

Lyle opened a long cardboard box and pulled out a black and sleek propeller blade, about fifteen inches long and made of carbon fiber.

"You bought a drone?" Wolfgang asked.

Lyle beamed. "Not just any drone, my friend. This baby is custom-built, with an aircraft aluminum frame, four high-torque electric motors, and eight carbon-fiber propellers. It can attain altitudes of over fifteen hundred feet—which isn't strictly legal, but whatever—and carries all the right electronic goodies to keep us connected and informed. Really, it's a remarkable aircraft."

Wolfgang knelt next to the box and helped Lyle unpack, fascinated by the precise detail of each part. The drone was fully disassembled, in maybe fifty different pieces, but Wolfgang held faith in Lyle's ability to assemble it correctly and on time.

"What about flight time?" Wolfgang asked. "You mentioned that it's electric. Your electric toys have a tendency to run out of battery."

Lyle feigned irritation, but Wolfgang knew he loved questions about his gadgets.

"Flight time is usually a problem for small drones, it's true. That's why I had this one custom-built, using a battery design very similar to the batteries used in modern electric cars. On a full charge, it can fly as long as two hours, using most of its power for takeoff and aggressive maneuvers, and running on only four propellers when cruising."

"That's a big battery," Wolfgang said. "How much does it weigh?"

"A lot. About eighty pounds, actually, which is why the motors had to be so big. It's kind of a catch twenty-two. You make a bigger battery for longer flight time, and that requires stronger motors to lift it, which weigh more, and therefore drain the battery faster. But with the carbon fiber and stuff, we cut weight wherever we could. The drone actually has a net payload capacity of forty pounds, after the weight of the battery."

Wolfgang watched as Lyle attached parts and tightened screws. The tech moved with the speed and efficiency of a child assembling a new Lego set.

"Just out of curiosity," Wolfgang said, "how much did this thing cost?"

Lyle grinned. "About twice what I told Edric, and he hasn't gotten the invoice yet. So, let's not worry about that."

[3]

It wasn't warm in Egypt; it was hot. As Wolfgang stepped off the plane and into the bright sun of mid-afternoon, he ran a hand through his hair and thought back to Buffalo, only a day prior. Cairo couldn't be more different from New York—with not a cloud in the sky, and open expanses of desert all around them. The sun beat down like the tail end of a rocket engine, pumping waves of heat over the desert and leaving everything feeling dry and desolate.

The private airfield lay about ten kilometers southwest of Giza, which was built on the western banks of the Nile River. Cairo itself was built along the eastern banks, and if Wolfgang squinted, he could make out the hazy glimmer of glass towers amid sandblasted stone ones in the distance, rising out of the desert. He held his hand above his eyes and swept his gaze along the horizon, hoping to make out the Great Pyramid, or perhaps the Sphinx.

"The pyramids are west of the city," Kevin said, stepping up beside him. "You can't see them from here, but we'll pass them on the way in."

Kevin offered Wolfgang a pair of Ray-Bans, and Wolfgang nodded his thanks.

"You've been here before?"

Kevin didn't answer, staring at the desert behind the shade of his glasses. Something about his posture was stiffer than normal, almost edgy, and Wolfgang suddenly wondered if Charlie Team had visited Cairo before. Maybe they found their way into Damascus—the site of their last mission before Wolfgang joined them—by way of Cairo. That mission had resulted in Edric's arm injury and the vacancy Wolfgang had filled.

"Huddle up!" Edric said.

Wolfgang and Kevin returned to the plane, where Edric stood with a map held in his good hand. Megan and Lyle appeared, both dressed in long-sleeve shirts and sunglasses. Megan's hair was suspended in her customary ponytail, and she was busy smearing sunscreen around her nose. Wolfgang realized he was staring and looked away before she caught him.

"There's a 4Runner and a van in the hangar." Edric jammed his thumb at a nearby hangar, then pointed to the map. "The Egyptian Museum is here, right in the heart of the city. You guys will take the 4Runner and find a place to park, then establish a perimeter. Lyle, what about comms?"

"I've got battery pack transmitters for everybody to wear on their hips. They aren't as covert as the smaller units, but the batteries will last longer. After nightfall, we can use the drone for additional surveillance and support."

"Perfect. Dr. Pollins should work until nightfall anyway." Edric squinted at the map, then pointed at the parking garage five blocks from the museum. "Lyle and I will park the van here and assume operational control. Megan, you've got ground control."

Edric rolled up the map, then led the way inside the hangar. A pure white, late-model Ford Transit van waited in the shadows. Next to it was a desert tan Toyota 4Runner, with dusty windows and muddy tires.

Edric threw open the back doors of the Ford, revealing Lyle's usual setup inside—a desk and rolling chair with a couple boxes full of odds and ends.

Edric opened one of the boxes and handed out pistols from inside. "Engagement rules are set to Code Yellow."

Wolfgang reviewed Edric's handbook of regulations in his mind. *Code Yellow: Armed, but do not fire unless fired upon.*

Wolfgang accepted the Beretta 92x Compact handgun and the shoulder holster that accompanied it. A silencer rode in a pouch next to the gun, and two extra magazines of ammunition were tucked into a pouch on the offside of the holster. He put it on, then fit a loose, long-sleeve shirt over it.

"Let me be clear," Edric said as he slid on his own holster. "This isn't Baghdad. Cairo is a civilized city. But it's not a safe place, either. Avoid contact, and avoid conflict. Use your best judgment when interacting with locals, and for God's sake, let's not get arrested this time."

Everybody looked at Wolfgang, and he blushed.

"I'm driving," Megan said, taking the keys to the 4Runner.

"Shotgun," Kevin shouted, shoving Wolfgang in the shoulder.

Wolfgang gritted his teeth as he gathered up his communications equipment and turned to follow.

Some things never change.

———

MEGAN POWERED the 4Runner out of the hangar and onto the road, her eyes sheltered by dark sunglasses that accentuated her round face. Wolfgang took the back seat, piling in next to a cooler full of sandwiches and water bottles. He absentmindedly wondered who prepared all of their equipment and had it waiting when they landed, then he shrugged the curiosity off. SPIRE was a massive company with a deep pocket. He just hoped the sandwiches weren't soggy.

Dust rose from the pavement as they plowed toward the city. The small buildings and narrow streets around them grew taller and wider as the sun continued to pound down. Megan turned the air conditioning up, providing a merciful stream of cool air, but Wolfgang still cracked a window and sucked in the dusty taste of the desert.

Everybody they passed smiled, and many of them waved. Wolfgang waved back, noticing civilians of every race and creed growing in numbers as they closed in on the city. Small children laughed and kicked soccer balls between houses, while dogs and other small animals chased each other in and out of the streets. Everything was sunburnt and dust-blasted, just the way he imagined it would be. Even so, there was an order and pride reflected in the carefully swept porches and clean houses. People here gave a damn, it was obvious, and that was more than could be said of many places he'd visited.

Wolfgang leaned back in the seat as Megan piloted onto the highway, then turned north. She chewed gum quietly, relaxed into the seat as if she were out for a Sunday drive, and Wolfgang marveled at her flawless composure. Megan never seemed to be fazed by anything—never seemed to be caught off guard. The only time he'd ever seen her become emotional was after the Paris job when she broke down while telling him about James, her boyfriend and the member of Charlie Team who died on the Damascus operation. Wolfgang had taken James's slot on the team and had ignorantly pursued Megan from day one.

Maybe if he'd known about James, he would've given her more space. Maybe he would have been kinder, and more subtle, and not so, well . . . himself.

Or maybe not. Because even now, sitting in the back of the 4Runner with the memories of Megan's pain so fresh in his mind, he still found it impossible to ignore her. He found it impossible not to remember dancing together at the gala in Paris, and the way her grey eyes shone like stars when she laughed, which wasn't often, but it was addictive. It was impossible not to think that maybe, if he kept trying, she'd give him the time of day.

Megan's lips twitched, and Wolfgang suddenly had the idea that she was staring—or glaring— at him through the mirror. He looked away quickly, turning to the window again, and then he saw them. Rising out of the desert, maybe five kilometers away, the glorious triangle shape of the pyramids dominated the horizon. He could see three of them from this distance—two smaller pyramids, with the Great Pyramid itself looming over them and punching almost five hundred feet into the sky. As Megan continued to plow toward the city, smaller pyramids came into view, clustered together south of the others.

"Pyramids for the queens," Megan said, answering his unspoken question. "The Sphinx is on the other side."

"You've been there?" Wolfgang asked, his gaze lost on the pyramids.

Megan grunted but didn't answer, and both Kevin and Megan stared directly ahead, their shoulders stiff.

So, I was right. They've been here before.

He opened a bottle of water and watched the pyramids grow slowly closer, then pass by a kilometer south of the highway. Moments later, they were enveloped by the city of Giza, and everything changed. Trees and greenery of all kinds appeared, jammed into flower beds and rising between buildings. People crowded around the sidewalks, bustling and shouting as the dust faded from the air.

Giza was packed to the brim with thousands of people clogging the streets. Horns blared, busses surged by, and music pounded from open-air restaurants. It was like any other big city, with a sun-blazed intensity that was both overwhelming and thrilling at the same time.

"How many—"

"Three million," Megan said. "Three million people live here. And you should know that."

Wolfgang looked back out the window, too distracted by the thrilling sights and sounds to be bothered by Megan's rebuke. She was right, anyway. He needed to study better and be more aware of the places he worked.

Buildings grew taller, and the people less packed as the 4Runner ground another few dozen blocks into the city. The residential and shopping districts faded into the business and government districts, and the children and dogs were replaced with men in business suits climbing in and out of black cars caked in dust. But the greenery was still there, fueled by the richer dirt near the Nile River.

Megan turned the 4Runner into a parking garage and found a spot on the second level. She shoved it into park and turned to Wolfgang. "I gather you've never been to this part of the world before."

Wolfgang shook his head.

"Figures. Well, here's your crash course on survival. Cairo isn't the kind of place where Jihadists are going to jump out of random buildings, guns blazing. We're not walking into the Wild West, here. Having said that, many of these people make their livings off of tourists. Ignorant, gullible, cash-rich tourists. Get my drift?"

"Be street smart," Wolfgang said.

"Be *very* street smart. Don't make eye contact when you don't have to. Don't speak unless you need to. And absolutely don't pull your weapon. Got it?"

The three of them unpacked the transmitters Lyle had given them and snapped them onto their belts before fitting wired earpieces in place.

"Charlie Lead, this is Charlie One," Megan said. "Comm check."

"I've got you loud and clear, Charlie One," Edric radioed back. "We're almost in position. Deploy your team."

Megan led them across the garage and down the stairs

to the first level. Wolfgang breathed in the deep scent of a foreign city, savoring the dirt and the strange food and the unfamiliar body odor. It was at once fragrant and foreign— the smelly cocktail of a new place full of new people.

I like this. I like being someplace new.

Megan stopped at the base of the garage and brushed her crimson hair behind one ear, then she motioned to the northeast. "The museum is three blocks that way. We'll split up and approach from different angles. Check in frequently, and try to blend in. Any questions?"

Wolfgang and Kevin shook their heads, and Megan nodded. "All right. Let's catch a book thief."

[4]

WOLFGANG BROKE TO THE RIGHT, shoving his hands into
his pants pockets and relaxing under the setting sun. The
suited business people, bustling city officials, and robed
Muslims that passed on all sides didn't even glance his way
as he covered the blocks and closed in on the museum.

Giza was a truly diverse place, and while Wolfgang was
certainly in the minority, he was far from the only white
male walking the streets with no apparent destination in
mind. Tourists blended with the locals and the business
travelers, wielding cameras and pointing at the most ordinary things. Europe, Asia, and America were all repre-
sented by throngs of families and individuals, all eagerly
seeking the most ideal places to snap photographs for social
media.

This would be an easier place to blend into than Paris had been, Wolfgang decided. He would stick to the sidewalks, keep his sunglasses on, and remain casual, while hoping that the book thief wouldn't be as subtle.

"Hey, Charlie Three, don't eat the meat," Kevin spoke suddenly, his voice booming through Wolfgang's earpiece.

"I'm sorry?" Wolfgang said.

"The street meat. Don't eat it."

Wolfgang hadn't even thought about food, but as if on cue, the rich scent of roasting lamb wafted toward him, and his stomach growled.

"Why not?"

"Because I said so."

Wolfgang squinted, then a slow smile spread across his face. "Did it disagree with you, Kev?"

Unidentified laughter rippled through the comms.

"It always disagrees with him," Lyle said. "Hey, Kev, tell Wolfgang about that time in Manila."

A grumble of curses filled the comm. "Forget I said anything. Just trying to help out the new guy."

"Don't be so salty, bro," Megan said. "We've all been in shitty situations."

Edric cleared his throat. "Okay, we've had our fun. Sharpen up, now."

Wolfgang bypassed the slow-roasting lamb vendor and turned eastward. The Museum of Egyptian Antiquities lay on the east bank of the Nile River, in the shadow of down-town Cairo. According to the brief Google search Wolfgang had performed on the plane, the museum housed over 120,000 artifacts and was originally built in the early twen-tieth century by an Italian construction company.

Wolfgang merged with a crowd of tourists and pressed his way across another bustling intersection as he tasted a slight dampness in the air. A hundred yards later, a bridge appeared, stretching across the Nile River with a pedestrian sidewalk on one side. A large sign in the middle of the bridge announced the end of Giza city limits and the begin-ning of Cairo. Wolfgang tilted his head back and looked to either side, admiring the tall buildings constructed on both banks of the water. For all intents and purposes, Giza and Cairo were the same metropolis, both with their cores situ-ated near the river.

He shoved his hands deeper into his pockets, then stepped onto the bridge. The setting sun gleamed against the slow-moving waters of the ancient river, and Wolfgang paused a moment to admire the beautiful landscape. It was at once ancient and modern, simple and mysterious. He imagined boats built of bound reeds drifting through the waters, and he recalled the ancient Bible tale of the Hebrew leader Moses turning the entire river to blood with a strike of his staff.

Staring at the river now, the gravity of the story hit him like it never had before, and he thought about the millions of ordinary people like him who had stood next to this river and thought about their lives. In the context of something so ancient and unchanging, how meaningless everything else felt. How temporary.

"Hey, hotshot!" Megan said. "Let's move. You're not a tourist."

Wolfgang looked for Megan but couldn't see her in the crowd. He hurried forward, crossing the bridge a few minutes later and stepping onto the east bank. The mass of the Egyptian Museum rose out of the buildings to his left, and he quickly found his post in its shadow. Wide streets full of rushing cars surrounded the museum on four sides, but there was a park in front of the main entrance, complete with sidewalks cutting through heavily irrigated grass.

Wolfgang found a bench with an unobstructed view of the entrance and surrounding streets and took a seat. "This is Charlie Three. I've assumed a position to the southeast of the main entrance."

"Roger that, Charlie One," Edric said. "Charlie One, Two, what are your positions?"

"Charlie One, east of the building, side entrance," Megan said.

"Charlie Two, north of the building, back entrance," Kevin said.

"Very good," Edric said. "Settle in. The target won't leave until after sunset."

———

THE LAST TWO hours of the day dragged by in slow motion. Wolfgang watched pedestrians pass by, some talking on cell phones, others listening to music on tiny earbuds. Better than half the people wore Muslim garb, and most of the women were accompanied closely by male escorts.

Tourists clogged the entrance of the museum, surging in and out, and snapping photos with obnoxious enthusiasm while their children shouted and cried, running up and down the steps and touching everything. It was funny, Wolfgang thought. The Western world viewed the Middle East as an unruly, uncivilized place. Yet, by far, the most unruly and uncivilized things he'd seen so far were Western tourists.

He leaned back and soaked in the warmth of the fading sun. It had already sunk behind the tall downtown towers of Giza, and he wondered what it would feel like once the sun was gone altogether. He'd heard that the desert was cold and windy at night, and this time of year, it could only be more so. Maybe he should have brought his peacoat.

His stomach growled, not for the first time, and he looked around for a street vendor. There were none close by, and he redirected his gaze at the museum, then took out his phone and glanced at a high-resolution image of Dr. Pollins, studying every detail of her features. It was going to be a one in a million chance to identify a single woman leaving the museum, but hopefully the crowds would thin as the light dimmed.

The museum closed, and the sun faded. As darkness fell over the city and streetlights flickered to life, the crowds did thin, with most pedestrians disappearing into cars or walking back across the river to their hotels and condominiums. An hour after dark, almost nobody surrounded the museum, save a few hippies sitting next to the river, talking in indistinct murmurs and smoking weed. Wolfgang wondered if it was legal here or if you could even grow weed in the desert.

He stood and stretched, walking casually down the sidewalk. He'd maintained sharp surveillance of his position all afternoon and was confident nobody had given him a second glance. But after dark, with fewer pedestrians around, it would be a lot harder to go unnoticed. Pollins had better hurry.

"Charlie Lead, sitrep all stations," Edric said.

"Charlie One, on-site," Megan said. "No sign of target."

"Charlie Two, on-site," Kevin said. "All clear."

Wolfgang rubbed his hands together, a shiver running down his spine as wind whipped off the surface of the Nile and tore through his thin shirt.

"Charlie Three, on-site," he said. "No sign of target."

"Copy that," Edric said. "We're deploying the drone now."

Wolfgang impulsively glanced skyward, but he knew

he'd never see Lyle's toy. The drone would hover hundreds of feet up, high enough that its whirring blades would go unheard by people on the ground, and dark enough that it could never be seen. Its giant eye of a camera would stare down, providing crystal-clear imagery of the museum and those around it. For two hours, anyway. Then the battery would need to be changed. He assumed Lyle had a spare.

"Stop picking your nose, Charlie Three," Lyle said.

Wolfgang grinned and casually flashed the peace sign at the sky. He returned to the bench and waited another forty-five minutes. The museum grew darker and more still, with lights fading from its windows as the staff departed one at a time. Wolfgang checked his watch, but it read 12:42 p.m. It was still set on St. Louis time, and he had no idea how many hours ahead Cairo was. He cursed himself again for his lack of preparation and swore it wouldn't happen again. He'd been distracted leading into this operation. The team deserved better.

"All channels, I have a possible contact," Kevin said suddenly. "Exiting the north side of the building and moving toward Charlie One."

Wolfgang stiffened and looked instinctively toward the north-facing side of the museum, where Kevin covered the back entrance. The employee entrance, probably.

I should have taken that side.

Moments ticked by in slow motion.

"Charlie Lead, I have a probable target," Megan said. "White female, about five foot six, exiting via the side entrance. I can't see her face. Charlie Eye, do you have a visual?"

There was a pause, and Wolfgang imagined he could hear the soft whirring of the drone high above, though it was probably just the wind.

"Copy that, Charlie One," Lyle said. "I have a visual, but not a face. Target is moving northbound on the east side of the museum."

"Close in and identify, Charlie One," Edric said. "Do not break cover."

Wolfgang tapped his foot on the ground, suppressing an overwhelming urge to stand and walk toward the museum. If that was Pollins, they'd need to move quickly. The thief could be anywhere, waiting in the shadows, ready to lunge out and kidnap her. Maybe he was in a car, planning to rush out and throw her in the trunk before she could resist. At five feet tall and under a hundred pounds, she'd fit just fine. Pollins would never have a chance.

"Target is turning toward me . . . hold one . . ." Megan said.

Wolfgang licked his lips. The dry desert wind, dampened by the Nile or not, was sucking the moisture from his skin.

"Target confirmed!" Megan hissed. "It's Pollins."

Wolfgang stood and began walking toward the east side of the museum even before Edric spoke.

"Close on the target, Charlie One," Edric said, "but remain in the shadows. Charlie Three, move in to assist. Charlie Two, return to the 4Runner and stand by."

"Come again, Charlie Lead?" Kevin said, an obvious challenge in his tone.

"You heard me, Charlie Two. Recover the vehicle and stand by."

Wolfgang could feel the tension on the line, but he understood Edric's rationale. Kevin was a capable operator, but he possessed the stealth ability of a charging rhinoceros. Better for Kevin to get the 4Runner.

"Copy that, Charlie Lead," Kevin said.

Wolfgang quickened his step, then took out his phone. It was lit up with a map of his current location, with blips on the screen where both he and Megan stood. A moment later, a new blip lit up the screen, moving slowly northward, then turning east at a much faster pace than he or Megan. That would be the drone.

"I have eyes on the target," Lyle said. "She's moving deeper into downtown."

Wolfgang quickened his stride. He caught sight of Megan moving through the shadows on his right, and then he saw Pollins about fifty yards ahead, stooped over and hugging herself. He guessed she must be cold and wondered why she hadn't brought a jacket to work. If this woman knew everything about Egypt, she should have expected the chilly winds. The temperature had to be below sixty now and still dropping.

"I see her," Wolfgang whispered.

"Fan to your left, Charlie Three," Megan said. "And don't crowd her."

Wolfgang moved to the north about twenty yards, keeping Pollins in sight as the blocks passed beneath his shoes. Half an hour dragged by, and they were still walking, now moving east of downtown and into a tightly congested neighborhood. Buildings were crammed together with no rhyme or reason to their geometry, with streets switch-backing and twisting around like the strands of a web woven by a drunk spider. These streets were narrower, too, providing Wolfgang with only glimpses of Pollins as she hugged the brick walls of the looming structures and plowed ahead in a straight line, only making alterations to her course when the winding streets left her no choice.

"Are we sure this is Pollins?" Wolfgang asked.

"Positive ID confirmed," Megan said. "She matches the picture."

"What's your concern, Charlie Three?" Edric asked.

Wolfgang sucked in a deep breath and broke into a soft jog, sliding one block over and struggling to keep Pollins in sight.

"She doesn't appear to be headed anywhere," Wolfgang

said. "She's just walking due east with her head down . . . and the buildings are getting shabbier."

Edric grunted but said nothing.

An uneasiness settled over Wolfgang, and he quickened his stride. He couldn't see Megan now. She should be a block to the south, struggling to keep sight of Pollins among the irregularly winding streets. The target was forty yards ahead, still marching forward with dogged determination, her head down as if she wasn't concerned with where she was headed. Something was wrong. Something didn't feel right. This wasn't the way a woman who knew the city and was headed someplace in particular would walk.

"Keep your eyes sharp," Lyle said. "You're moving into a rougher neighborhood."

Wolfgang didn't need to be told. The streets breathed a grungier air, with looming buildings that hung in shadows next to flickering streetlamps. What people were visible were all inside, moving behind dirty windows, while the streets and alleys in and around tall apartment buildings lay empty and dark.

Wolfgang reached up and unbuttoned his shirt down to his belly button, exposing the white undershirt he wore beneath and providing him easier access to the pistol—just in case. He could still see Pollins, marching relentlessly eastward, head down, arms hugging herself.

Then he saw the shadow moving out of an alley on her right, sheltered by two tall, dark buildings. The closest street was wide and empty, and before Pollins could cross it, the figure darted out of the alley and grabbed her, clamping a hand over her mouth and dragging her back into the darkness.

"Target is under attack," Wolfgang hissed. "I'm moving in!"

[5]

Wolfgang broke into a run, completing a forty-yard dash to the entrance as the pistol cleared his holster. He didn't want to use it. He didn't have time to affix the silencer to the barrel, and firing an unsuppressed handgun in a quiet place like this would almost certainly result in all the wrong kinds of attention, but he couldn't let Pollins get hurt, either. Charlie Team had already let this go too far—already let her life come into jeopardy.

"I can't get through!" Megan said. "I've got to go around the block. I'm coming!"

Wolfgang spun into the alley and raised the gun. Two men stood in the shadows, both clothed in black, both wielding glistening knives. One of them held Pollins against a wall, his thick forearm jammed beneath her throat, while the other was busy unbuckling his pants.

"Hey, you!" Wolfgang shouted.

The men looked up, their dark eyes growing wide at the sight of the gun. But instead of running away, the first man slammed Pollins's head against the wall, stunning her before dropping her to the ground. Then they bolted toward Wolfgang, knives gleaming.

Not good.

Wolfgang froze in indecision. Code Yellow only allowed him to fire if fired upon, but it said nothing about knives. And anyway, if he did fire, what then? They didn't need these people dead; they needed them alive so they could find the scroll.

But knives.

Wolfgang stooped, narrowly missing the first swing of the lead man's knife, then shot his fist up into that man's groin. As he stood, Wolfgang retrieved a fistful of dry dirt from the edge of the street and slung it into the eyes of the second man. The entire maneuver happened in mere seconds, all strung together like a perfectly choreographed dance move.

The first man stumbled and dropped the knife. The second man held his weapon but clawed at his eyes with his free hand. Wolfgang went on the offensive, kicking the downed knife away and driving his elbow into the neck of the first man. That guy went down, still writhing from the pain in his crotch as Wolfgang moved to the second guy.

The second guy wasn't so easy. He'd cleared most of the

dirt from his eyes, and he still held the knife. The man took a step back, brandishing the knife with a wolfish grin. Wolfgang lowered his head and charged, smashing into the guy's sternum and hurling him backward. It was a calculated move designed to shield his face and neck, but the man still swung, and the knife clipped Wolfgang's shoulder blade. His attacker made a frantic attempt to fend off the headbutt, but as Wolfgang's skull collided with the man's sternum, the air rushed from his lungs, and he stumbled back with a grunt.

They hit the ground, both tripping over scattered trash in the alley as the knife clattered to the dirt. That was a win, at least, but Wolfgang was thirty pounds lighter than his opponent, and this guy felt like the kind of man who didn't mind killing somebody tonight.

Dirt and rocks flew as the two of them flailed. Wolfgang kicked, attempting to prevent his attacker from rolling on top of him, but it was too late. A meaty fist struck him in the shoulder, deadening his arm and causing him to lose his grip on his opponent's shirt. Then the man struck again, this time smacking Wolfgang across the jaw. His head snapped against the packed dirt of the alley floor, and the world spun. In the distance, he heard the scrabbling of another fight from the mouth of the alley, then Megan cried out in muted pain. He could only hope she wasn't being slashed to shreds by the knife.

Wolfgang spat blood and twisted his head just in time

to dodge a second blow from his attacker. His mind swam, but he imagined he could see the bloodthirst in his assailant's eyes—the animalistic hunger of a violent man ready to kill.

Wolfgang twisted and shot up with his right hand, grabbing the man by the cheek and shoving his right thumb into the man's eye. He pressed with full force, and the man reared back in pain, struggling to break free. Wolfgang pushed harder, then shot his hips upward. The dislodged thug rolled backward, jerking his head and frantically trying to protect his eye. Wolfgang followed, rolling on top of him and lifting his hand to deliver a throat punch. His opponent, in spite of the blood streaming from his left eye, was faster. He shoved out with both hands and hit Wolfgang in the chest, slamming him against the wall of a nearby building. Wolfgang's head cracked against the bricks. Waves of dizziness and disorientation washed over him, and he suddenly wasn't sure which way was up. He couldn't move.

The guy got up and reached into the folds of his black robe. A moment later, steel flashed in the moonlight— another knife. Wolfgang coughed and tried to move, but the dizziness weighed him down as though he were underwater and steadily sinking.

Tires ground against the pavement, and headlights shone into the alley. The guy with the knife looked up, and fear flooded his face, then he turned and bolted away from the car. Wolfgang coughed and twisted toward the light.

The 4Runner sat at the end of the alley, headlights blazing. Wolfgang blinked in the glare and then saw Megan lying on her back. The first attacker straddled her with his forearm pressed against her windpipe, bearing down on her. She thrashed and tried to break free, but to no avail.

Wolfgang choked and stumbled to his feet, lurching toward her. Before he'd moved two yards, Kevin appeared from the 4Runner. He bolted across the alley and grabbed the attacker by the scruff of the neck. With one powerful heave, Kevin hauled him up and threw him against the wall, pinning him there with his feet dangling and his nose crushed into the brick.

Kevin's eyes blazed, the muscles rippling beneath the stretched skin of his arms. Then he cocked his right arm back and delivered a lightning blow to the back of the man's head. Bone crunched against brick as the man's face caved in, and then his lifeless body crumpled to the dirt.

Wolfgang swallowed, catching himself against the wall. He felt the urge to puke as he stared at the flattened and mangled features. Kevin shot him a glare, then turned quickly and bent over Megan.

Megan lay on the ground, gasping for breath and gently massaging her throat. Kevin bent over her and started to scoop her up like a child.

Megan brushed him off. "What did you do?" she said. "You killed him, you moron!"

Kevin frowned, confusion and anger crossing his face. "Killed him? Killed who?"

"The book thief, you fool!" Megan picked herself up, still rubbing her throat.

Pollins.

Wolfgang remembered the doctor and turned back down the alley. Pollins lay slumped against one wall, the bottom half of her shirt torn open and her head rolled to one side. Blood oozed through blonde hair, and Wolfgang broke into a run.

"I had to kill him!" Kevin spluttered. "He was gonna kill you!"

"Not once you threw him off me. Dammit, Kevin!"

Wolfgang ignored them and felt for Pollins's pulse. It was pounding. He tilted her head back and checked her face against the image on his phone. It matched perfectly, even with her eyes closed and her cheeks pale.

He rubbed her wrists, then gently massaged her temples. "Wake up, Doctor. You're safe now."

Pollins groaned, then blinked slowly. Her eyes were the same crystal blue as in the photograph, but now bloodshot and strained by panic.

"Where . . . where am I?"

"You're okay, Doctor. You're safe now."

Wolfgang offered her a warm smile.

Pollins's brow wrinkled. "Doctor?"

He nodded. "Yes. You're a historian, remember? You study Egypt."

Pollins stared at Wolfgang, still blinking, then she twisted, and Wolfgang saw something on the ground next to her. It was a small leather passport cover, stamped with a British flag on the face. He picked it up as Kevin and Megan continued to argue.

"We'll never find them, now," Megan growled. "You better hope that scroll is around here someplace."

"It's not," Wolfgang said.

The arguing ceased, and both of them looked his way.

"What do you mean?" Kevin snapped.

Wolfgang closed the passport. "I mean, these guys weren't our book thieves, and this isn't Amelia Pollins. It's her twin sister, Ashley."

———

THE HOTEL ROOM was warmer than the streets outside, with comfortable furniture and two king-size beds. They set Ashley Pollins on the end of one bed, and Kevin went to find her an ice pack and water while they waited for Edric and Lyle to arrive. Ten minutes later, Charlie Team gathered around Ashley, watching as she huddled at the end of the bed with an ice pack held to her temple.

"Are you okay, ma'am?" Edric asked.

Ashley's eyes were wide with fear, but the disorientation had faded. She looked away and said nothing. Edric pulled up a chair, motioning for the others to give her some space. They retreated to the corner of the room, and Edric spoke quietly.

"Ma'am, I need you to talk to me. We're looking for your sister."

Ashley surveyed the small crowd, her focus coming to rest on Wolfgang, her apparent rescuer.

She chewed her lip a moment, then looked back at Edric. "Who are you?" She had a gentle British accent.

"We're the good guys," he said. "We're here to help your sister."

"What makes you think she needs help?"

"Doesn't she?" Edric asked.

Ashley didn't answer.

Edric patted her on the hand. "I'm very sorry about your mishap, ma'am. I saw the stamp in your passport. Looks like you've only been in Egypt for a couple weeks. Did you come to visit your sister?"

Ashley glanced around the room again, then nodded.

"You live in England, right?"

"Yes."

"Are you and your sister close? I imagine you must be, being twins."

A solitary tear slipped down her cheek.

"It's okay, ma'am. You're safe now. We won't let anybody hurt you."

"It's not me," she mumbled. "It's Amelia."

"So, she's in danger?" Edric pressed. "They took her, didn't they? Somebody took your sister."

Ashley said nothing, but she met Edric's gaze. Even from across the room, Wolfgang could see the truth in her eyes.

Edric nodded. "They took her, and they told you not to tell anybody. If you did, she'd be hurt."

The truth was evident.

Edric sat back and folded his arms. For a while, he let the room fall into silence, then he nodded toward the others.

"This is Megan, Wolfgang, Lyle, and Kevin. I'm Edric. We work together."

"You're treasure hunters?" Ashley asked.

Edric cocked his head. "Why would you think that?"

Ashley's cheeks flushed, and she looked away, but the cat was out of the bag.

"Ms. Pollins, we need you to tell us what you know. We're not here about any treasure. We're here to protect your sister."

"You're too late," Ashley mumbled.

Edric placed a hand on Ashley's arm, then gave it a gentle squeeze and waited until she faced him. When he spoke, his voice was soft but as solid as granite. "Ashley, I know they took your sister. And I know they said they'd hurt her if you got help. But these people are no match for us. We're going to get your sister back, alive and unharmed. Okay? That's my promise to you. I just need your help."

Ashley chewed her thumbnail and surveyed the team again. "What do you need to know?"

6

ASHLEY POLLINS SPOKE SLOWLY at first, and then she seemed to cross a point of no return and gushed like a fire hydrant.

She lived in Manchester, and although she and Amelia were very close, they seldom saw each other since Amelia took the job at the Egyptian Museum. This year, Ashley had decided to take what she called a "long holiday" to visit her sister in Cairo for a couple months, but shortly after she arrived, Amelia had become engrossed in some special project that involved the Egyptian government. Ashley wasn't sure of the specifics, but she knew it was secret, and she knew it involved something discovered in Libya. Amelia had also mentioned the discovery of a new tomb—perhaps of a pharaoh—but she wouldn't say anything else.

"She spent a lot of time at the museum, and when she

was home, she worked in her apartment," Ashley explained. "She had photos of a document. She showed them to me, but of course I had no idea what I was looking at. It was some kind of scroll, with hieroglyphics on it. Amelia was trying to translate them. I knew it was important because whenever Amelia left the room, she locked the photos in a safe, even if she was just going to the bathroom. She was really paranoid about them being lost, I guess."

According to Ashley, Dr. Pollins had labored on like that, obsessing over the project until yesterday, when guilt for her abandoned sister finally caught up with her and she took Ashley out for a night in the city. They went to dinner, saw a few sights, and were walking back to Amelia's apartment when the attack came. Multiple men struck out of the shadows, pulling both Amelia and Ashley into the darkness. There was a struggle, but both women were heavily outmatched, and the next thing Ashley remembered was waking up in her sister's office at the museum to the sound of the phone ringing. She answered it and heard a computerized voice on the other end.

"They told me not to get help or Amelia would be hurt," Ashley sobbed. "They told me to stay in the office all day, then leave after dark and walk due east. No other direction. Just keep walking."

Megan stepped across the room and patted Ashley on the back. She offered her some sleeping pills, repeated Edric's promise to find Amelia, and advised her to get some sleep. Ashley took the pills and lay down, but didn't close her eyes. They were wide with fear and heartbreak as she stared at the empty ceiling.

Charlie Team retired to the adjoining room and closed the door behind them. Edric poured himself a drink from the minibar and took a long sip, then Kevin was the first to break the silence.

"How the hell did we not know Pollins had a twin sister?" Kevin shot Lyle a stormy glare.

Lyle scrunched his nose. "How is that my fault?"

"Because you're the wiz," Kevin snapped. "Because you're supposed to know things. Didn't you hack her Face-book or something?"

Lyle's back stiffened, but before he could object, Edric held up a hand.

"Enough. It doesn't matter whose fault it was. Bottom line is that we should've known, and we didn't. Now we move forward." He took a swig of his drink, then cleared his throat. "What happened in the alley?" Everybody was quiet, and Edric turned to Kevin. "You killed a man?"

Kevin nodded, and Edric muttered a curse.

"That's not great, Kevin. That's not great at all."

"It wasn't our book thief," Wolfgang said. "I think they were just thugs eager to rape a lost tourist."

Megan nodded. "I agree. We searched the body and found nothing. The guy was underfed and covered with needle scars. My bet is, whoever kidnapped Amelia told

Ashley to walk due east after nightfall because they knew she'd eventually be raped and killed. It's a much cleaner way to get rid of a witness than killing her themselves."

"I surmised as much," Edric said. "Which means these guys are smart, as well as violent."

Wolfgang rubbed his chin. "What about the photographs? Ashley said Amelia was studying pictures of the scroll. But we were told there were no pictures."

Edric swirled his drink and frowned. "I know. And that worries me. The Egyptians had to know there were pictures, but they refused to supply them to us. They must be worried that we'd make a play at the treasure ourselves. Maybe that's why Amelia kept them under lock and key."

"That doesn't make sense, either," Megan said. "If they have images, why wouldn't they simply deploy us to the site of the tomb to wait for the thieves? For that matter, they could simply secure the tomb. Sure, the scroll is historic, but I'm guessing they're paying us much more to find it than it's worth. And if they already know where the tomb is . . ."

Edric rubbed his lip but said nothing.

Wolfgang grunted. "There's more to the story. Something the Egyptians aren't telling us. Maybe there's something on the scroll that isn't visible in the pictures—the location of another tomb or other hidden artifacts. Regardless, our next step is obvious."

Everybody looked his way, eyebrows raised.

Wolfgang held out his hands. "We have to go to Dr.

Pollins's apartment and retrieve the images. If they abducted her in public, we can assume the kidnappers didn't know the location of her apartment, so the images are still there. If we can find them and have somebody translate them, we'll know where to find the kidnappers. The scroll will lead us right to them."

Edric swirled his drink again, then nodded. "I like it. Megan, go get the address."

Megan slipped into the adjoining room and obtained the address before Ashley fell asleep. She returned a moment later, and Lyle punched it into a computer.

He grimaced. "Well, it's not Fort Knox, but it's damn close." Lyle spun the computer around, and they all leaned in.

Amelia Pollins lived in a twenty-floor, high-security condominium tower on the eastern bank of the Nile. Her apartment was on the eighteenth floor, with a balcony facing the pyramids.

The complex was owned by a private company named IronGate that specialized in providing secure living in dangerous cities around the world. According to their website, they prided themselves in twenty-four-hour security featuring armed guards, a complex check-in system for guests, and a full array of lobby, hallway, and elevator surveillance.

"I didn't realize Cairo was that sketchy," Lyle muttered.

"It's not," Edric said. "Cairo is actually a pretty safe

place, Ashley Pollins's attack notwithstanding. But many places in the Middle East aren't safe at all, and I'd imagine Cairo is a great place for IronGate to showcase their product to potential customers who deal in this part of the world."

Lyle scratched his chin. "Well . . . Whatever the reason, it's gonna be a hell of a place to infiltrate. There's no chance we just walk in like the pizza guy."

"What about the elevator shaft?" Kevin asked, breathing whiskey breath over them.

Lyle shook his head. "I'll have to find some blueprints to be sure, but now that I think of it, IronGate owned that tower in Johannesburg. Remember, from last year? There were motion sensors in the elevator shaft. These guys really aren't joking."

"Stairs?" Wolfgang asked.

Again, Lyle shook his head. "Cameras. And secure access doors."

"So, we climb it from the outside," Kevin said.

Lyle pulled up an image of the tower from the company's website and zoomed in on the sleek surface of the exterior. The tower was round and encased in glass. Windows faced out on all sides, broken only by balconies that jutted out in an offset pattern, with the balconies of one floor slightly overlapping those of the floor directly beneath it.

"You'd have to climb the dead spaces in between the windows," Lyle said. "The face is sheer glass, so it'd be slick. Also, you can't climb straight up because of the way the balconies overlap. You'd have to shift back and forth, avoiding open windows where somebody might see you. It'd take a while . . . a couple hours. And no offense, but are any of you in that kind of shape?"

Silence. Wolfgang rubbed his temple with one finger and stared at the tower. Then he glanced at Megan and sized her up from head to toe. When he looked back at Lyle, he saw a smirk playing at the corners of the tech wizard's lips.

"You thinking what I'm thinking?" Wolfgang asked.

Lyle grinned. "I believe so. And it just might work."

———

"Aw, SCREW THIS," Megan snapped. "I'm not doing it."

She folded her arms, staring at the drone where it lay behind the van. The eight-bladed flying monster was a full ten feet across when fully constructed, and it vibrated as desert wind tore through downtown Cairo. They were parked on a quiet street two blocks from Amelia Pollins's condominium tower, and Lyle held out a rappelling harness to Megan.

"It'll work. I promise," Lyle said. "If we drop the battery out of the drone and power it with a cable, it'll lift up to one hundred twenty pounds. And you weigh . . . ?"

Megan's eyes blazed, but nobody spoke up to defend her.

"One twelve," she growled.

"Great. So we've got eight pounds of wiggle room." Lyle tossed her the harness, then knelt beside the drone and disconnected the power wires from the battery tray.

"Edric, I don't trust his toys," Megan said. "Remember what happened with the comm units?"

Edric patted the air with one hand. Wolfgang and Lyle's scheme had already won him over, and Wolfgang could see the impatience growing in his body language.

"He knows what he's doing, Meg. Nobody else is light enough to do it."

Megan jabbed a finger at Lyle. "He is!"

Lyle shrugged and spoke around the flashlight in his mouth. "Technically, I'm one twenty-one. But that's not the problem."

"What's the problem?" she said.

Lyle grinned. "Can you fly the drone?"

Wolfgang rubbed his chin, trying not to laugh. Megan glowered at each of them individually, then stomped around the van and put on the harness. It was designed for rappelling, not being hoisted beneath a giant drone like a teddy bear, but Lyle assured them it would suffice.

Wolfgang knelt beside Lyle and whispered low enough that nobody else could hear. "You're sure about this, right? She won't fall?"

Lyle took the flashlight out of his mouth. "Pollins's apartment is on the eighteenth floor. So, assuming fourteen feet per floor, that's about two hundred fifty-two feet up. The extension cord we'll be using weighs about eight pounds per hundred feet, so we have to calculate about twenty pounds for the cord."

"That puts you twelve pounds overweight," Wolfgang said.

"Yes, but I'm increasing the voltage to the motors. The battery runs them at about eighty percent output to save energy. Pushing them up to full power gives us an additional seventeen pounds of payload capacity—more or less."

"More or less? Hey, buddy. This is her *life* we're talking about."

Lyle looked up from the drone and met Wolfgang with unblinking eyes. "I'm very aware of what we're talking about."

Wolfgang stood up. "I'm sorry. You're right."

He shoved his hands into his pockets and circled the van. Kevin and Edric were helping Megan to adjust the harness to fit her slender body. It was too big for her, but with adjustment, it would suffice.

Kevin cinched a strap around Megan's shoulders, and then Lyle appeared with an iPad in one hand. "The elevators and stairwells run up the core of the building, with hallways connecting the apartments." He zoomed in on a blueprint image of the IronGate tower, and everybody leaned in. "Every apartment features a private balcony, along with floor-to-ceiling windows," Lyle continued. "However, there's dead space between each unit where there are no windows facing outward. That space is about fifteen feet wide and is found where the balcony of one floor is overlapped by the balcony of the floor above it. If we fly the drone directly up the path where the balconies overlap, it will never become directly exposed to a window."

"Just a couple dozen balconies," Megan muttered.

"Right," Lyle said. "Which is why Wolfgang will make sure they're empty before you lift off."

The group grew quiet as Lyle continued to stare at his iPad, nodding to himself. Wolfgang wasn't sure if he was as confident in the plan as he pretended.

"Any other questions?" Edric asked.

"What about the noise?" Kevin said. "How loud is it?"

"We've actually got a break on that," Lyle said. "The drone isn't quiet, but I was able to find exact specs on the glass the tower is encased in. It's pretty thick, designed to isolate city noises and to protect the building against sandstorms. The occupants won't hear a thing, so long as their balcony doors are shut."

Wolfgang ran the numbers through his head again. The total lifting power of the drone, minus so much weight for the cable, minus Megan's bodyweight, minus the weight of the harness . . .

"Maybe your shoes," he said hesitantly.

"What about my shoes?" Megan snapped.

"I was just thinking . . . You don't really need them. Could save a couple pounds."

"Seriously?"

Nobody said anything, and Megan cursed as she bent to untie her sneakers. "You morons would be lost without me. You really would." She kicked the shoes off, then waddled across the rough pavement to the back of the van. "Come on, wiz. Let's do this shit."

7

"T-minus one minute," Edric said. "Charlie Two, have you got the goods?"

Wolfgang held one hand over his ear, waiting for Kevin's reply to Edric. He stood across the street from Amelia Pollins's building and traced the outline of each floor, all the way to number eighteen. Dr. Pollins's balcony jutted out over downtown Cairo, pointed toward the Nile and the Great Pyramids beyond. It sported a four-foot metal railing and sliding glass doors. Those doors would certainly be locked, but under Megan's practiced hands, they would pose much less a challenge than the security downstairs.

"Just completed the pickup, Charlie Lead," Kevin said.

"Copy that," Edric said. "Deploying now."

Wolfgang turned back to the street that lay between himself and Pollins's apartment tower. Charlie Team's van was parked half a mile down the street to his left, its headlights set to dim as exhaust clouded beneath the rear bumper. With a little rumble, the van pulled away from the curb and turned toward the IronGate tower, driving past the main entrance before turning down the service alley on the far side. The alley sat conveniently eighteen floors beneath Pollins's apartment, with a clear vertical shot all the way to her balcony, along the windowless dead space Lyle had described.

The van ground to a halt.

"Charlie Three, what's your visual?" Edric said.

Wolfgang scanned the street in both directions, then looked upward at the balconies for any sign of smoking occupants standing near the railing and observing the streets below. It was after midnight, and the balconies, like the streets, were empty.

"Charlie Lead, you're all clear," Wolfgang said.

The back doors of the van popped open, and Lyle jumped out. A moment later, Megan appeared, and they pulled the drone out and set it on the concrete behind the van. Megan wore the rappelling harness cinched tight around her petite torso, with a thick strap running from between her shoulder blades to the bottom of the drone. A neat coil of cable lay on the ground, with one end running into the bottom of the drone and the other end connected to a Honda generator in the back of the van. Lyle leaned into the van and hit the start button on the generator, and Wolfgang heard a soft humming sound, like that of a distant lawn mower.

All eight blades of the drone spun to life as the generator pumped power into the motors, and a more present buzz joined the distant humming, exactly like that of a horde of bees.

It's loud. Is it too loud?

Megan stood back, staring fixedly at the vibrating, multi-bladed beast in front of her with something between dread and disgust on her face. Then Lyle shot her two thumbs-up, and she nodded reluctantly.

"Charlie Three, what's your visual?" Edric said again.

Once more, Wolfgang scanned the balconies and streets. They still lay empty, lit only by intermittent streetlamps spaced evenly along both sidewalks.

"Charlie Lead, all clear," Wolfgang said.

"Copy that. Charlie Eye, execute."

Lyle crouched in the back of the van and lifted a giant remote control, complete with thumb-sticks and enough switches to run a submarine. He nodded once to Megan, and she took another step back from the drone. All eight blades accelerated, spinning so fast that they appeared as solid discs. The buzz of the drone doubled, then tripled before it lifted off the ground with the grace and stability of Marine One. The drone hovered six feet off the pavement, the strap dangling down loosely to Megan's back, and the cable trailing the ground, then Lyle nodded again and the drone rose another six feet.

Wolfgang checked the balconies again, searching for anybody who may have heard the noise and stepped outside to investigate. So far, there was no one, and his gaze returned to the spectacle at the back of the van.

The strap tightened, and Megan hopped two feet off the ground, then came to rest again. She clutched the harness with both hands and clamped her eyes closed. Lyle shot a glance upward at the drone, and Wolfgang held his breath.

Lyle depressed a lever, and Megan rocketed off the ground like they had launched her out of a cannon. The drone surged into the sky, shooting a hundred feet up before Lyle could decrease the power. Megan swung like a para-trooper, her red hair tousled by the wind. She spun twice in a full circle, and Wolfgang met her gaze both times. Her eyes were wide, but she kept her mouth shut as she dangled only yards away from the condominium tower full of sleeping residents.

"Charlie Eye, what the hell!" Megan hissed.

"Sorry," Lyle said, his voice cracking a little. "Some-thing's up with the generator. It's pumping too much voltage into the motors."

"What does that mean?" Wolfgang asked.

Lyle shot him a glare from across the street, then waved

his hand dismissively and tilted his head upward. "Charlie Three, am I clear?"

Wolfgang checked the balconies, quickly counting the number of floors the drone had already passed. "You're good to go, Charlie Eye. Proceed upward. You've got about eleven floors to go."

Lyle applied gentle pressure to the throttle lever on the remote, and the drone rose again, slower this time. Megan still spun, and the drone wobbled a little as she passed the twelfth floor, then the thirteenth. Wolfgang couldn't make out her facial expressions anymore, but she still spun, her bare feet almost two hundred feet off the ground.

"Easy . . ." Wolfgang whispered to himself.

The drone continued to rise, but it dipped to one side now and shuddered under a blast of wind. Megan swung toward the building, extending her right leg just in time to ward off a balcony railing before she slammed into it.

"Sorry!" Lyle hissed. He fidgeted with the remote, and the drone dipped to one side, dropping ten feet and sailing twenty more away from the tower.

"*What* are you doing?" Megan said. Her voice carried an undertone of panic now.

"Hold still," Lyle said. "The wind is giving me fits!"

"I don't *care* about the wind!"

Wolfgang stepped into the street and shielded his eyes with one hand, quickly counting balconies again. "You've got three floors to go!"

"Hurry it up," Edric said. "I need that thing out of the air!"

Lyle pressed the power lever again, and Megan rose. The cable dangling from the bottom of the drone swung in the wind, blown around by consecutive blasts as the drone turned back toward the tower.

The seventeenth floor passed beneath Megan's toes, and Lyle eased up on the power. Her head crossed the bottom edge of Pollins's eighteenth-floor balcony, then Wolfgang saw a spark flash from the bottom of the drone.

"Charlie Eye!" he snapped. "You've got—"

Before he could finish the sentence, a shower of sparks burst from the edge of the drone near one of the four motors that powered the fifteen-inch blades. Wolfgang thought he saw smoke framed against the light of the moon, and one side of the drone dipped rapidly. Megan swung, her shoulder clipping the edge of the balcony, then she shot away from the tower as the drone stopped in midair, unable to rise any farther.

"It's smoking!" Wolfgang said. "I see sparks!"

"I know!" Lyle said. He fought with the controls as the drone continued to shudder under the next blast of wind, then the sparks turned to a flash of orange flame.

"It's coming down!" Wolfgang said.

The drone dipped as Megan swung toward the tower, then began to fall. She twisted in midair and leaned toward the balcony of the eighteenth floor, catching it with one hand as she flashed past. Wolfgang heard a muted grunt as she slammed against the railing, suspended by her left arm. The drone, now unimpeded by her weight, buzzed only a few feet from her head, powered now by three motors.

Wolfgang held his breath as Megan thrashed at the bottom edge of the balcony, a full two hundred fifty feet off the ground. With her free hand, she reached back and disconnected the tether from her harness, then lunged upward and caught the railing. A moment later, she hoisted herself up, jammed one foot beneath the railing, and then flipped over it and onto the balcony, falling out of sight.

Wolfgang breathed a pent-up sigh and ran a hand over his face. Despite the stiff wind, sweat coated his face and palms.

"What's going on?" Kevin appeared out of the shadows behind Wolfgang, breathing hard, a large paper bag in one hand. "You said sparks? Is she okay?"

Wolfgang waved him off. "She's fine."

He glared across the street at Lyle, who was sheepishly landing his wounded toy. The drone still smoked from one motor, and Wolfgang could smell the acrid stench of toasting electrical components. He wiped his nose and looked back up the tower.

"Charlie One, what's your position?" Edric said, his voice as calm and controlled as ever.

"I made it," Megan panted. "I'm on the balcony."

"Copy that. Proceed with the breach."

Lyle dragged the drone into the van, then quickly retrieved the two hundred feet of cable, the top end of which was blackened from the electrical fire. The rear doors of the van clacked shut, and Edric powered out of the alley.

Wolfgang checked his watch, then looked upward again. He couldn't see Megan, but he knew she was there, working her magic on the balcony door's latch. In only moments, she'd be inside the apartment, and that could trigger an alarm at the main desk.

"Door is breached. Moving in now," Megan said. Her voice shook a little, but her tone was even.

"Copy that, Charlie One," Edric replied. "Charlie Three, deploy."

Wolfgang accepted the paper bag from Kevin, then hurried across the street. Now that his mind had calmed a little from the panic, he could smell the rich aroma of Chinese food from the bag—takeout from a local place a couple blocks away. It was a favorite of Pollins's, according to her sister, a place she ordered from often while working late, although he doubted she'd ever ordered takeout that weighed over twenty pounds.

He mounted the steps to the glass door at the bottom of the tower and paused to catch his breath. He smoothed wrinkles out of his shirt and ran a hand through his hair, then depressed the call button. It buzzed.

The answering voice spoke in Arabic. "Marhabaan?"

"Food delivery for unit eighteen oh nine," Wolfgang

said, figuring that somebody on the other side had to speak English.

Silence from the other end.

Wolfgang heard Megan speaking through the comms, her voice soft and sleepy, with a hint of a fake British accent. It wasn't half bad.

"Hello? Yeah . . . no, I triggered it by mistake. Yeah, I ordered some food. Let him up."

Another pause, then the lock clicked and Wolfgang pushed inside. The desk guard motioned him over and gestured to the bag. Wolfgang set it on the counter, careful to avoid any slamming or clinking sounds, and untied the top. The guard clicked a light on and scanned the top of the bag, sniffing and poking at the paper cartons.

"ID?" he asked.

Wolfgang passed him a Canadian passport for Timothy Jenkins, a student from Toronto.

The guard checked the image, then flipped to the back and inspected the Egyptian visa. At last, he nodded and handed the passport back. "The elevator is to your left, Mr. Jenkins."

[8]

POLLINS'S APARTMENT was dark and smelled clean. Wolfgang slipped inside and flipped the lights on. Megan rattled
around in the next room, and books thumped against a
table.

"You find it?" Wolfgang whispered.

He crossed into the main living room and looked
around. The interior of the apartment was sparsely
furnished, with only a few decorations, all of which seemed
to have something to do with Ancient Egypt. There was a
desk along one wall, and Megan was bent over it, clicking
on a computer, her bare feet planted in the soft carpet.

"The pictures aren't here, and I can't find any notes,"
she said without looking up. "The computer is locked, also."

"What about the safe?" Wolfgang asked.

Megan motioned to the far wall of the living room,

opposite the balcony door where she entered. A canvas painting leaned against the sheetrock, exposing the metal face of a small safe in the middle of the wall, complete with a digital keypad and a metal lever.

Wolfgang walked to the safe and set the Chinese food down. The safe-cracking tools hidden in the bottom of the bag clinked, and he ran his hand across the face of the safe. It was a premium unit, built of thick steel with almost no gap between the door and the frame. He grabbed the bolt lever and pulled, curious if the safe would wiggle in the wall. It didn't budge.

"Charlie One, sitrep," Edric said.

"Charlie Three is here," Megan said. "Apartment is clean. Moving to wall safe."

"Copy that. Get a move on. You've already been in there ten minutes."

Megan motioned Wolfgang aside, then clicked her flashlight on and scanned the safe. She gestured to the bag. "Get that crap out of here. It stinks."

Wolfgang scooped the food cartons out of the bag and slid them across the tile floor, then he began to unpack the safe-cracking tools.

"You don't like Chinese food?" he asked.

"Not when it's made of goat."

"Goat? What makes you think it's made of goat?"

Megan snorted. "You think it's pork? This is Egypt. Hand me the stethoscope."

Wolfgang handed her the stethoscope, and she fit the earpieces in before pressing the cup over the face of the safe and twisting the bolt lever. She closed her eyes and bit the tip of her tongue. Wolfgang caught himself holding his own breath as he watched her slide the cup of the stethoscope over the face of the safe while manipulating the bolt lever.

Megan sighed. "It's fitted with a relocking system," she said, peeling the stethoscope off and tossing it to the floor.

"What does that mean?" Wolfgang asked.

"It means that if we defeat the primary bolt by force, secondary bolts will click into place and prevent us from opening it. We need the combination. Hand me the computer."

Wolfgang dug back into the bottom of the bag, bypassing the complex levers, screws, and the drill that would've been used to force the safe open. He found a handheld computer at the bottom of the pile, a little larger than a cell phone, with a black wire dangling from the bottom. Megan accepted it and peered under the edge of the keypad. There was a port, which the cable connected to with a soft click. Megan powered the unit on and tapped on it.

"Does the computer guess the combination?" Wolfgang asked.

Megan shook her head with a semi-irritated grunt. "The computer is for unlocking the safe in the event the battery in the primary keypad dies. That's the legal application, anyway. You can also use it to read diagnostics on weak or worn parts, which can give you an idea which keys are pressed most often. Charlie Eye, you with me?"

"Right here, Charlie One," Lyle said.

Megan read off the safe's model number, printed on the bottom right-hand corner of the door. Wolfgang heard the rattle of Lyle's keyboard on the other end of the comms, then a grunt.

"It's a good unit. The combination will be between eight and ten digits long, followed by pound. It's also got a lockout feature. If you input the wrong combination six times within a twenty-four-hour rolling period, the safe will lock down for twelve hours."

"Fantastic," Megan said. She poked at the handheld computer for a moment, then waited while a loading icon spun on the screen.

"Top inputs are one, nine, six, four, three, and two," she said. "In that order."

"Copy that," Lyle said. "Hold one . . ."

Megan unplugged the computer and brushed hair off her sweaty forehead. She stared at the lock and gently chewed a wad of gum.

Wolfgang scooped the useless safe-cracking tools to one side with his shoe, then stepped a little closer to watch the computer. "What's Lyle doing?" he whispered.

Lyle said over the earpiece, "Calculating possible combinations using known favored digits and personal information about Pollins. And don't use my name on comms."

Wolfgang felt his face flush. "Right. Sorry."

The minutes dragged on, and Wolfgang wondered how long it would be before the over-zealous security guard downstairs remembered the Canadian with the Chinese food and wondered why he hadn't checked out yet. Not long, probably, and then there would be trouble.

"Okay," Lyle said. "It could be her home phone number. All the frequent numbers match."

Lyle read off a ten-digit number, and Megan punched it in, followed by the pound sign. A red light flashed on the keypad, and the bolt handle wouldn't turn. Megan brushed hair out of her face again.

"No good," she said.

"Okay, try her birthday. Eight digits." Lyle read out the number, and Megan tried it. The red light flashed again, and this time something electronic buzzed inside the safe.

"No good."

Wolfgang stepped back and watched as Megan attempted a third combination. Again, the red light. Now she chewed harder on the gum, leaning forward and scanning the keypad with her flashlight for any sign of fingerprints or clues to deduct the combination from.

Wolfgang turned away, stepping to the large computer desk at the end of the room and clicking his flashlight on. Papers were scattered across the desktop, mixed with open books and empty coffee cups. Wolfgang shuffled through them, uncovering stacks of research papers and photographs of ancient artifacts. Most of the documents smelled musty and old, as if they'd lain on that desk since the time of the pharaohs. He flipped through a couple of the books, searching for hidden notes or significant highlights. The top book was written in tight lines of academic text, with photos of dead bodies being mummified. The next book was titled *The Black Death of Ancient Egypt*.

None of the books or papers were inscribed with an eight- to ten-digit number, with "safe code" scrawled beside it.

Wolfgang glanced around the room. The apartment was large, but aside from the stacks of empty takeout containers on the kitchen counter and the piles of research materials on the desk, the living space was almost empty. There were only a couple pictures on the walls—both canvas paintings of Ancient Egypt—and no TV set in front of the couch. No signs of a pet, or a favorite blanket, or even a well-worn novel. Everything about the apartment screamed of a person madly obsessed with her work, and nothing but.

Except there were little rectangular objects mounted next to the front door, and again next to the bedroom door. Wolfgang thought they were security devices at first—motion detectors, or cameras, even. But as he flashed his light across them, he saw blue and white paint, with a hint of gold script. Wolfgang stepped closer to the bedroom door, then peered down at the object. It was about three inches tall and rounded on the face, with a flat back mounted against the wall. The hollow object was made of wood and painted blue with a gold script carved into the face. A rolled piece of parchment stuck out of the top. Wolfgang bent closer as he heard Megan snapping at Lyle behind him.

"No good. That's five, Charlie Eye."

The script carved into the tube wasn't English or even written in the Latin alphabet. It was some other language altogether, and when he slid the tiny scroll out of the top of the tube and unrolled it, the same script was printed on the inside, consisting primarily of tiny black marks with little dots printed beneath them. It wasn't Chinese, and it wasn't Cyrillic or Arabic, but it shared characteristics with all three. It was a defined, organized alphabet, long-lost from the current of mainstream society.

Hebrew.

"Six four nine, one one one, three two one," Wolfgang said, turning to Megan.

Megan stood with her finger held over the keypad, only a millimeter away from punching in her sixth and final attempt. She frowned.

"What?"

"Pollins is Jewish," Wolfgang said, holding up the scroll. "This is called a *mezuzah*—the Hebrew word for *doorpost*. It's a tiny scroll inscribed with words from the Torah that some Jewish people put next to the doors in their homes. The specific inscriptions are from Deuteronomy, Chapter Six, verses four through nine, and Chapter Eleven, verses thirteen through twenty-one. That's nine digits."

Megan stood with her flashlight between her teeth and an "Are you serious?" look on her face. Wolfgang joined her at the safe.

"When I was a kid, my best friend's grandfather was Jewish. He kept mezuzahs on every doorpost in his home. I remember the references."

Megan took the flashlight from her mouth and accepted the tiny scroll, then scanned it. "I can't read this."

"Neither can I. It's written in Hebrew. But trust me, that's the combination."

"He's right about the references," Lyle said. "I just googled it."

Megan fingered the scroll, then glanced at the mezuzah mounted to the wall next to the bedroom door.

She shook her head. "That's too obscure. We've only got one combination left. We should trust the computer."

"No," Wolfgang said. "The computer is programmed to input known factors from her life—things like her birthdate and childhood street address. But people don't choose passwords based on their demographics, they choose them based on their identities. Look around you. There's *nothing* in this apartment that reflects personality. Nothing but sour food cartons and stacks of books from the museum. The only personal, individual thing is the mezuzah, because her religion is important to her."

Megan stared at the scroll again, then glanced around the apartment. At last, she cleared her throat. "Charlie Lead?"

"Your call," Edric said. "Whatever you do, hurry it up. You're going on twenty minutes."

Wolfgang placed a hand on her arm. "Trust me. This is it."

Megan handed him the scroll, then twisted to the keypad. Her finger danced over the keys as Wolfgang recited the numbers, then she hesitated over the pound sign. Wolfgang nodded again, and she pressed it. There was a pause, and they held their breath, waiting for the red light.

The keypad flashed green. Wolfgang felt a flood of relief washing through him, and he realized he hadn't been as confident as he thought. Megan grinned and twisted the handle. The bolts slid back with soft thunks, and Megan pulled the door open and shone her flashlight inside. The safe was empty except for a lone manila folder on the top shelf. Megan slid it out and tore the top open, then shone the light inside. Photographs. Four or five of them, taken with the aid of powerful lighting, illuminating the tattered and aged remains of a scroll.

"Charlie Lead, we've got it," Megan said, still grinning. She turned to Wolfgang and smacked him on the arm. "Nice job," she whispered.

Wolfgang felt a flood of elation, but he only nodded, unsure what to say. Her smile radiated brighter than the sun, and he suddenly realized that it was the first time he'd ever seen her genuinely smile.

Damn, it's a good look.

Megan swung the safe shut and turned toward the door. They made it only halfway before Lyle's voice burst over the comms.

"Charlie One, you're busted! Security is headed your way."

MEGAN TUCKED the folder beneath her arm and motioned for the door. "Let's move!"

Wolfgang dipped for the safe-cracking tools scattered across the floor, but Megan shook her head.

"Leave them. It won't matter after we recover Pollins."

She paused next to the door to slip her bare feet into a pair of Pollins's sandals. They weren't a perfect fit, but they'd have to work. Then they slipped out the front door, and Megan turned to shut it. As she did, the elevator doors rolled back, and footsteps thumped against the carpet. Wolfgang looked up as two men in black suits hurried into the hallway. Their jackets were unbuttoned, exposing Glock handguns fixed to their hips, and their death stares killed any hope he had that this wasn't going to be a confrontation.

"Stay cool," Megan whispered. She brushed the hair behind her ears, and they started down the hallway, walking casually straight toward the two men without giving them so much as a glance.

"Stop right there!"

The first man was tall—an American, with the kind of haircut and cookie-cutter glower that screamed Marine Corps. He put one hand on his gun and held out the other. The second man stood two paces back, his hand next to his gun, his feet arranged in a perfect weaver-shooting stance. His skin was darker, and his jacket hung over beefy shoulders that jutted up and out awkwardly, like a bulldog.

Megan made a show of looking from one guard to the next, then popped her gum like a high school delinquent. "What's up your ass, boys?"

Wolfgang heard a hint of a Toronto accent creep into her voice, and he took his cue.

"Ma'am, I need to see some identification," Marine said, his hand still resting on the Glock.

Megan glanced at Wolfgang with a "What the hell?" expression, then produced a Canadian passport.

Marine took it and scrutinized it a moment, then glared at Wolfgang. "You're both from Canada?"

Wolfgang nodded.

"Who are you visiting tonight?"

Megan took that one. "Dr. Amelia Pollins. She's a friend."

"I thought you were delivering food," Marine said, turning back to Wolfgang.

"I was. I work at the Chinese place. They let me take home the leftovers."

This time, Bulldog spoke, directing his question at Megan. "Did you check in downstairs?"

She shrugged. "Maybe. Can't remember. It was yesterday."

Megan popped the gum again, and the guards continued to glare them down.

Bulldog moved toward Pollins's front door. "I'm just gonna check with the resident before we let you go."

"She's asleep," Megan said. "Hell of a hangover. Been drinking all day."

"Is that right?" The guard paused mid-step, then turned back. A little smile played at the corners of his mouth. "Drinking all day?"

Oh, crap.

Megan shrugged, but Wolfgang saw her legs tense.

"Tequila, man," she said.

The guard smirked. "You know, that's funny, because every year, the big dogs at the corporate office send out a little gift for the residents. You know, something to show our appreciation."

He took a step forward, the smile growing at the corner of his lips.

Not good.

"Anyway, this year they sent a nice bottle of wine. But when the concierge delivered it to Dr. Pollins, you know what she said? She says, 'You keep it. I don't drink.'"

Yep. That's a wrap.

The guards exchanged a "busted" look. It only took a split second—just one bro congratulating another on his supreme Sherlock skills—but it was a split second too long. Wolfgang and Megan sprang into action at the same moment, Megan taking Bulldog and Wolfgang taking Marine. The guard had three inches and probably forty pounds on Wolfgang, all of it muscle, but the groin is immune to the protections of big biceps and handguns, and Wolfgang had learned long ago that a shin to the groin was about as effective as a hand grenade in a fuel refinery. Marine's eyes popped outward as the blow smashed home, then he fell forward with a guttural moan so sincere Wolfgang almost felt sorry for him.

Behind him, Wolfgang heard a commotion of arms and legs flailing, followed by a thump on the carpet. He turned to see Bulldog writhing on the floor, his right arm bent behind him at an unnatural reverse angle. His handgun lay scattered around him, fully disassembled.

"Let's go!" Megan shouted. She swept past Wolfgang, grabbing his arm and hurtling toward the stairwell.

"Charlie Lead, requesting immediate evac!" Megan snapped as she flung open the door to the stairwell, and they rushed downward two and three steps at a time.

"Copy that, Charlie One. Arranging evac now." Edric spoke with the practiced calm of a man whose back had been driven against the wall a thousand times, and Wolfgang felt reassured, like a kid hearing the calming voice of a parent.

Megan flipped from landing to landing with the elegance of a jungle cat as Wolfgang stumbled to follow. They made it to the fourteenth floor before doors burst open somewhere beneath them, and screaming voices shouted upward. An alarm went off, and red lights flashed from the walls.

"Charlie One, be advised, the building is on full alert," Lyle said. His voice was as steady as Edric's. "All exits are going into auto lock. Reserve security is moving in from the lobby."

"Shit!" Megan said. She slid to a stop halfway down the stairs between the thirteenth and fourteenth floors, then leaned over the railing and stared down the space between the steps. Boots thundered beneath them, and she shook her head. "No good! We've got to get out of here."

Wolfgang rushed back up the steps to the fourteenth-floor landing, then slammed his body against the door. It wouldn't open. He tried again, but the door was bolted.

"Charlie Eye!" Wolfgang said. "The doors to the stairwell are locked. What do we do?"

From the far side of the comm unit, Wolfgang imagined he could hear Lyle breathing through tensed lips as he pounded on a keyboard, searching for a way out of the stair-well. That was how it worked in the movies, right?

Megan shoved past Wolfgang and rushed to the wall, where a mounted red box housed an ax and a fire extin-guisher. Next to it was a trigger for the fire alarm. Megan pulled the trigger, and a new shriek joined the existing alarm, followed a moment later by a shower from the over-head sprinklers.

The door locks clicked open.

"Think on your feet, Wonderboy," Megan said, pushing the door open. "Fire protocol trumps security protocol."

They spilled onto the fourteenth floor and found it to be a carbon copy of the eighteenth. Plush carpet covered the hallway, which was lined on either side by luxurious wooden doors with identical little lamps next to each one. Only this time, the carpet was wet, and sleepy-eyed resi-dents poked their heads into the hallway as the fire alarm continued to blare.

Megan slid to a stop and looked toward the elevator. The LED display above the door showed the car at the tenth floor, and it was headed up.

"Is there another stairwell?" Wolfgang said.

"It's at the end of the hall," Lyle said. "But you won't get far. Security protocols probably call for them to lock down all stairwells."

Megan and Wolfgang exchanged a glance as the elevator hit the thirteenth floor. Wolfgang imagined half a dozen beefy copies of the guards upstairs, all armed to the teeth and ready to avenge their humiliated comrades.

"Charlie One, get out of there," Edric snapped. "Our mission does not allow for you to be caught!"

Wolfgang's mind spun as he saw Megan continue to hesitate. He realized that she was as lost as he was, and the thought galvanized his mind into action. He turned to the nearest apartment door and saw a Latina woman wearing a cosmetic face mask poke her head out and glare at them. He visualized the apartment on the other side and assumed it looked a lot like Dr. Pollins's apartment, at least in layout. There would be a short hallway, then a kitchen on the right, a living room on the left, and the balcony straight ahead, hovering almost two hundred feet off the pavement.

The balcony.

"I've got it!" Wolfgang said. He grabbed Megan by the elbow and rushed toward the woman, motioning her aside and dragging Megan behind him.

"Excuse me!" Wolfgang said. "Lovely night, isn't it?"

The woman shrieked as Wolfgang and Megan plowed through. The apartment on the other side was nothing like Pollins's—this one was a wreck, with piles of laundry and household knickknacks everywhere. It smelled heavily of sour food, and a cat scurried by as Wolfgang rushed into the living room. Despite the mess and the smell, however, the balcony door was right where it should've been, and Wolfgang made a beeline for it.

"What are you doing?" Megan demanded.

"Thinking on my feet!" Wolfgang said. He threw the sliding glass door open and hurried onto the balcony, turning to the left and peering down.

The side of the tower gleamed with polished glass and metal, reflecting the city lights of Cairo. From where Wolfgang stood, he could see the next four balconies jutting out of the round tower in a spiral pattern, overlapping each other by about half their width as they wound toward the ground. The next in line stuck out like a stair step, fourteen feet below.

Close enough.

"Wait . . . What are you thinking?" Megan shook her head and stepped back a pace as Wolfgang hauled himself up onto the railing, tucking his toes onto the edge of the balcony outside the railing before twisting around to face Megan. "I'm not thinking, Meg. I'm getting the hell out of here!"

Wolfgang squatted on the outside of the balcony, transitioning his hands to the bottom of the railing before kicking his feet out and allowing his body to fall. His legs swung freely as his hands tightened around the bottom of the metal spindles, then he looked down. The floor of the balcony below him now rested about eight feet beneath his shoes—a jarring fall, but not a fatal one.

He let go of the railing. His body dropped like a bomb, clearing the eight feet in a split second before his feet slammed into the concrete beneath him. The impact sent pain shooting up his legs and through his knees, but he minimized some of the shock by allowing himself to crumple into a roll, hitting the balcony floor on his hips and shoulder before returning to his feet. Wolfgang panted and dusted himself off. Then he looked up to find Megan. "Come on!"

Megan hesitated, looking down the face of the tower to the cold pavement two hundred feet below. She swallowed, then turned to the door as shouting voices and thumping boots erupted from the Latina woman's apartment.

That was all the motivation she required. Megan threw her legs over the rail and repeated Wolfgang's move. By the time she landed, Wolfgang was already moving to the next railing, climbing to the outside before lowering himself into a monkey-bar-style hanging position, then dropping the final eight feet. The next fall hurt worse than the first, but adrenaline blinded the pain as the two of them proceeded from balcony to balcony, dropping fourteen feet every time and moving slowly around the circumference of the tower.

"Charlie Lead! We're on our way," Wolfgang said.

"We see you, Charlie Three," Edric replied. "There are no balconies below the fourth floor. Jump to the awning over the main entrance. We'll pick you up there."

Wolfgang threw his legs off the railing of the sixth-floor balcony, knocking over potted plants and a bird feeder. A moment before he released the railing, the sliding glass door of the fifth-floor balcony hurtled open, and Marine appeared, his eyes bloodshot and his Glock clamped in one hand.

It was too late to stop. Wolfgang let go of the railing and dropped straight toward him. The guard's eyes bulged, and he had no time to move. Wolfgang's left foot hit him in the sternum, knocking him onto his back, and then Wolfgang crashed down with his butt smashing the guy's face like a boxer's glove. The guard shouted in muffled pain, and the pistol skidded across the floor of the balcony.

Megan landed next to Wolfgang and grabbed his hand, then shot a quick foot into Marine's groin as the big man twisted to grab her by the leg. Projectile vomit exploded across the balcony as Megan and Wolfgang flipped over the rail and dropped to the final balcony. They could see Charlie Team's van now, hurtling down the street toward the main entrance of the tower. The roof of the main entrance portico lay only ten feet below them, but there was an eight-foot gap between the edge of the balcony and the edge of the roof. Megan hesitated, gauging the distance as she panted for breath. Blood oozed from cuts on her palms, and her pants were torn, but her eyes were alight with the thrill of the run.

Wolfgang gave her a reckless wink that was far from sincere, then threw himself over the railing and into midair before he could think twice. The roof of the awning was fifteen feet off the ground, increasing his total fall to twenty-five feet if he missed it and hit the asphalt instead—a certain bone-breaker, but he didn't have time to second-guess himself.

Cool Egyptian air blew through his hair and tore at his jacket as he fell like a cannonball, arcing through the air toward the edge of the roof. Only a split second after he jumped, he knew he wouldn't make it. The edge of the roof was a foot too far, and Wolfgang leaned forward and caught it with one hand as he hurtled down. His fingers scraped against metal as his full weight descended on his right arm. He grunted in pain, then heard the squeal of tires on pavement. The van slid to a stop directly beneath him, and Wolfgang let go of the roof. He fell the last couple feet and landed on the roof of the van like a dead body hitting a baking sheet, his head spinning.

The back door of the van popped open, and Kevin jumped out, already hurling grenades at the main entrance of the tower. A moment later, the air flooded with thick, grey smoke, clouding the cameras and shielding the view of the guards rushing in from the lobby.

Wolfgang coughed and blinked. His head swam, and the tower above him swayed in the dim light of the moon. He was vaguely aware of something falling toward him, sliding through the air toward the van's roof like a cruise missile.

It was Megan.

Wolfgang rolled to the left just in time to avoid being

crash-landed on by his fellow agent. A bullet struck the van near Wolfgang's elbow, and then powerful hands dragged both him and Megan off the roof and onto the ground. He landed on the concrete in a heap, every joint erupting in pain. Kevin pulled them both into the van as Lyle stomped on the gas and Charlie Team rocketed to freedom.

[10]

BACK IN THE HOTEL, Lyle stood next to the minibar, sucking on a Yoo-hoo. "I've got scans of the images routed to headquarters."

Wolfgang didn't know Yoo-hoos were available in Egypt, but somehow, he wasn't the least bit surprised Lyle drank them.

The tech wiz burped, then wiped his mouth. "We should have a translation back within a couple hours."

Wolfgang nodded and adjusted the icepack on his right knee. His entire body ached—his back, his knees, his ankles, and the soles of his feet. If he closed his eyes, he could imagine himself crashing from one balcony to the next, wincing with each impact.

Smooth idea. Really. Grade-A work.

"You all right?" Megan spoke from his left. She wore sweat-pants and a sweatshirt, with her hair dripping down her back. Megan had opted to soothe her swollen joints with hot water as opposed to ice and now looked ready to run a marathon.

Wolfgang grunted as if their recent exploit were no more significant than a trip to the grocery store. "Never better. Just a little stiff."

She smirked and settled down on the couch next to him. He caught a whiff of her shampoo and couldn't resist stealing a sideways glance.

She brushed hair out of her eyes and wiggled into the couch. Her skin glistened, and even though she was without makeup, he found himself lost in the smoothness of her complexion.

Megan twisted toward him, and Wolfgang looked away, switching the ice to his left knee.

"You did a good job," she said. "You thought quickly and took action. It got us out alive."

Wolfgang shrugged, feeling his cheeks flush. Had any other member of Charlie Team extended the compliment, he would have basked in the praise. But with Megan, he felt bashful. Awkward.

"You pulled the fire alarm," he said. "That got us out. I just started jumping."

Megan chuckled.

"What?" Wolfgang asked.

"I was just thinking . . . I'm still gonna kick your ass for that damn drone."

Wolfgang grinned. "You think you've got it in you?"

She punched him in the shoulder, and he winced as pain rocketed down his spine. "Okay! I tap out."

She laughed again, but the door opened, and Edric stomped in from the adjoining suite, followed closely by Kevin.

"You two made a hell of a mess," Edric said, his voice a mixture of amusement and genuine irritation. "Turns out my theory about IronGate placing a building in Cairo for demonstration purposes was right on the money. We just waltzed up to their prize show car and pissed all over it."

Megan grinned again.

Wolfgang realized he'd never seen her this relaxed before and wondered if she were secretly an adrenaline junkie, still riding the high of her fix.

"We got what you wanted," Megan said. "A simple thank-you would suffice."

Edric shot Wolfgang a challenging glare, and Wolfgang elected to take Megan's side. It wasn't a tough choice.

"The lady has a point," he said.

Edric muttered something about hotheads as he navigated to the minibar and poured himself a tumbler of scotch. Wolfgang was suddenly aware of Kevin standing in the background, eyeing him with a renewed coldness.

"What?" Wolfgang mouthed.

Kevin said nothing, and Edric returned from the bar.

"Regardless of the outcome, the point remains. We won't be welcome in Cairo much longer. As soon as Lyle hears back about the translation, I want everybody ready to go. Standing plan of action is to locate the tomb and recover Pollins and the scroll"—Edric paused and gestured toward Megan and Wolfgang with his glass—"*without* fireworks." He tipped the glass back and finished the drink in one gulp. "Ice those knees, Wolfgang. We aren't home free yet."

———

"IT's RIGHT THERE." Lyle pointed to a spot on one of Megan's maps. The five of them gathered around a hotel bed, now spread with notes and more maps. The point Lyle gestured to was east of Cairo, maybe twenty kilometers from the city in an expanse of open desert occupied only by occasional industrial complexes.

Megan leaned close, inspecting the spot and tracing her finger back toward the city. She shook her head. "That can't be right. That's open desert."

Lyle shrugged. "The linguist who translated Dr. Pollins's images of the scroll indicated that the tomb was close to Cairo. Ancient landmarks are difficult to use because not all of them still exist. But they're pretty sure the area we're looking for is someplace over here, east of the airport."

"But that's in *Cairo*," Megan said. "Cairo wasn't founded until A.D. 969. During the time of the ancient Egyptians—the time of the pharaohs—most Egyptian civilization was concentrated far inland, near the ancient city of Thebes, or modern-day Luxor." Megan shuffled to a bigger map of Egypt, then pointed to a spot about four hundred miles south of Cairo. "Here. This is where the Valley of the Kings is. King Tut's tomb was discovered there, along with many others."

Wolfgang frowned. "But the pyramids are near Cairo."

"The pyramids are west of Cairo, in Giza, because Giza sits on a rock plateau that is uniquely suited to building a very heavy pyramid but is *not* suitable for digging an underground tomb. By the time the Egyptians switched to digging underground tombs like King Tut's, they'd migrated south. An underground tomb in Cairo doesn't make sense for the era."

"How do you know all this?" Kevin asked.

Megan sighed. "I *read*. You should try it."

Edric held up a hand. "It doesn't matter. All of you are missing the point. We're not looking for an undiscovered tomb—we're looking for a kidnapped woman and some stolen Egyptian property. Finding the tomb isn't our prerogative."

The group glanced impulsively at the door into the adjoining suite. Ashley Pollins still lay in bed, as she had all day. They'd given her sleeping pills, food, and encouraged her to take a shower, but all she would do was sit on the end of the bed and stare at the television, waiting for news of her kidnapped sister to appear. The thought of her bloodshot eyes brought a hush over Charlie Team, and Wolfgang stared at his shoes.

"Lyle," Edric said, "how sure is the translator?"

Lyle pushed his smudged glasses up the bridge of his nose. "Impossible to be sure. The best they can give us is a general location in the desert. There are so many industrial complexes around that it's difficult to believe a tomb could lay undiscovered so long."

"It doesn't matter if there's a tomb or not," Edric replied. "It only matters if our kidnappers think there is."

"What if Dr. Pollins lied to them?" Megan asked. "They kidnapped her to translate the scroll, but she could've made something up. Sent them on a wild goose chase anywhere in Egypt."

Kevin shook his head. "She knows they had her sister, and she doesn't know they sent her sister to die. They'll use that to motivate her."

Wolfgang nodded. "Plus, she's obsessed with Egyptology. She's not going to waste time in the desert when there's a chance to find this thing—a chance for her to write her name in the history books."

Edric grunted agreement. "I agree. We work with what we have, then. My arm is still giving me hell, so Lyle and I will take the van and maintain operational control. The rest of you will take the 4Runner and head on-site. Lyle, how's the drone?"

Lyle's face turned dark, and he indulged in an involuntary pout. "Pretty messed up. I managed to replace most of the burned wires and reinstall the battery. It'll run."

"Good. We'll put the drone in the air for communications and a live video feed."

Edric rolled up the map, then glanced around the bed. "Whatever happens, don't forget why we came here. Our primary objective is to secure the scroll. Our immediate secondary is to rescue Dr. Pollins. Then we extract. Are we clear?"

Everybody nodded.

"Excellent. Let's hit the sand."

[11]

The desert outside of Cairo was as desolate as the Saudi Arabian wasteland only a hundred kilometers farther east. As Wolfgang stepped out of the 4Runner, a blast of sandy wind tore at his clothes and ripped the door from his hand. He blinked back the dust, then quickly pressed sunglasses onto his face. Megan appeared a moment later, dressed in canvas pants and a loose canvas jacket that barely concealed the pistol she wore in a shoulder holster.

Wolfgang glanced back into the 4Runner and saw Kevin at the wheel, eyeing him with that frosty glare again.

What's with this guy?

"Charlie One, sitrep," Edric called.

Wolfgang looked involuntarily to the sky, but he couldn't see Lyle's drone. It was either too high to make out or lost in the glare of the desert sun.

"We're half a klick offsite," Megan said. "Moving in now."

"Copy that. Charlie Two, remain on standby."

Wolfgang looked to Kevin again and wondered if he was angry because Edric had become comfortable with pairing himself and Megan while leaving Kevin for backup support. Kevin's operational specialty was combat, which most of their missions required little of. That left Kevin doing the grunt work—driving, setting off fire alarms, picking up Chinese food. It had to suck, but Wolfgang didn't have time to worry about it. He liked being on the leading edge of the action. He liked the thrill, the danger, and the pressure.

Most of all, he liked being close to Megan.

The two stepped away from the road and started into the sand. Cairo International Airport lay only a few kilometers to the northwest, and Wolfgang could hear the roar of a jet preparing for takeoff. He saw the glittering towers of Cairo rising from the desert. The city was a stark contrast to the desolation directly ahead and to his right. As they topped a slight rise in the sand, they paused, and Wolfgang held a hand over his eyes, sure that he was being blinded by the sun, in spite of his sunglasses.

But the yellow blob in front of him wasn't blindness—it was desert. Stretching out to the north and to the east for miles on end, the desolation was almost complete. Fields of packed sand, windblown and empty, were broken only by crisscrossing dirt roads and small compounds of industrial buildings. A few personal vehicles and an occasional semi-truck crawled toward Cairo in the distance, and black exhaust rose from a tower in the middle of one of the complexes. Otherwise, the desert was as vacant as an ocean.

And so damn large.

Wolfgang let out a low whistle. "That's a lot of ground to cover."

Megan dug a pair of binoculars out of her pack and scanned the desert. She adjusted the focus on the binoculars from time to time as she panned to different points in the sand. Then Wolfgang saw her back stiffen just a little.

She leaned forward, adjusting the focus again. "Charlie Eye," she said. "Did Pollins own a car?"

There was a pause over the comms as Lyle checked his notes. "Let's see . . . Um, yeah. A 2004 Chevy Cobalt. Grey. Usually parked at the museum. Why?"

Megan lowered the binoculars and broke into a fast walk back toward the 4Runner. "Because I see it."

———

"Drive!" Megan said, slamming the door of the 4Runner. Kevin had already started the engine and was shoving the SUV into gear before Wolfgang even shut his door. They bumped off the road and into the desert, cresting the small rise Megan and Wolfgang had just stood on, before dipping into the valley beyond. Dust exploded around the 4Runner's tires, clouding the side windows in mere seconds as Wolfgang clutched the back of Megan's seat and tried to keep his head from slamming into the ceiling.

"What did you see?" Wolfgang asked.

Megan ignored the question, guiding Kevin across the surface of the desert with a pointed finger. Wolfgang leaned between the two front seats and watched as the landscape unfolded in front of them. From a distance, everything looked flat, but closer in the desert was an uneven expanse of dips and rises, with small ravines and random pits sprinkled among them. Kevin had to turn rapidly on a number of occasions to avoid ramming one wheel of the 4Runner into a hole, but they gradually approached the spot Megan identified, and then Wolfgang saw the car.

It sat behind a sharp rise, sheltered from view except for the right rear quarter panel and wheel. The car was a dark grey four-door, small enough that the rise completely covered the front two-thirds of it. Kevin stomped on the brakes, and the 4Runner ground to a halt fifty yards away. Megan reached for the door handles, but Kevin held up a hand.

"Wait." He dug beneath the driver's seat and produced an AR-15 rifle with a shortened barrel and a collapsible stock. With a quick flip of his hand, Kevin deployed the stock, then chambered a round. "Charlie Lead," Kevin said, his voice calm but commanding. "We've located a grey Chevy Cobalt matching the description of Pollins's car."

"Copy that, Charlie Two. Charlie Eye has a view from the drone. The vehicle appears to be abandoned, but we can't tell for sure."

"Understood," Kevin said. "We'll check it out on foot."

"Copy that. Take it slow."

The group piled out of the SUV, and Wolfgang unbuttoned his shirt to make sure his Beretta was accessible. It rode beneath his arm, a friendly and reassuring lump next to his side. His heart pounded as the three of them fanned out, taking the car from different angles. Kevin led, his shoulders low and the rifle riding just beneath his line of sight. Every move he made was elegant and balanced, and Wolfgang wondered what Kevin had done prior to joining Charlie Team.

This isn't his first time in a desert, holding a gun.

Kevin held his hand up, signaling for Megan and Wolfgang to wait while he circled quickly around the rise and cleared the vehicle. A few seconds passed as Kevin faded from view, and Wolfgang braced himself for gunfire.

Kevin's voice boomed over the comms. "All clear."

Wolfgang let out a pent-up sigh and followed Megan around the rise. As the car came into view, Wolfgang panned the face of his smartwatch across the rear bumper of the Chevy. A camera was built into the watch and fed directly back to one of Lyle's computers.

"Do you have the license plate?" Wolfgang asked.

"Copy that, Charlie Three," Lyle replied. "The plate number matches her registration. That's Pollins's car."

Wolfgang knelt behind the car and felt cautiously near the tailpipe, then tapped the pipe directly with his index finger. It was cold. He stood up and checked the back passenger side door. It was unlocked, and a quick sweep of the interior revealed nothing of value—some cigarettes, fast food wrappers, and chewing gum. But there was mud in the footwells of the passenger seat and one of the back seats. The kidnappers took her car from the museum and used it to drive her out here. But why?

Wolfgang stepped away from the car, peering at the dirt. The steady wind that blew across the desert brought with it an endless wave of dust, quickly filling shallow footprints. Wolfgang didn't see any tracks or trails leading away from the car, but there was no reason to drive out here, in the middle of nowhere, unless . . .

Wolfgang swept the landscape immediately around the car, shielding his eyes with one hand, his gaze skipping from rock to shallow dip to scruffy desert bushes. He almost missed it on the first pass, sliding right by to the next dip, then snatching his attention back to the spot in the dirt fifty yards away.

Wolfgang broke into a jog. "Over here!"

His feet pounded against the packed dirt as he focused on the spot. With each passing yard, the disturbance on the desert floor became more distinct—a flapping, sand-colored piece of cloth pinned down by a rock and ravaged at the edges by wind. Wolfgang thought he saw another piece of cloth a few feet away and parallel to the first, also pinned down by a rock and covering the space in between.

"I've got it!" he shouted again.

"Wolfgang!" Kevin snapped. "Hold up!"

Wolfgang kept running. He cleared the final twenty yards to the spot and ground to a halt, scanning the dirt. He could clearly see the cloth now, pinned down in two corners by rocks—stretched tight and covered in sand.

It's hiding something.

Wolfgang broke into a grin, the excitement over-whelming the trepidation he'd felt only minutes before.

"This is it!" he shouted, waving the others forward.

"Wolfgang, wait!" Megan said.

Wolfgang took another step closer to the nearest rock and felt the ground vanish beneath him. His foot landed on what looked like sand but turned out to be part of the cloth, and he fell forward face-first.

His face and shoulders slammed into more sand-covered cloth that gave way into a gaping hole beneath. Before he could shout or grab for the edge, Wolfgang was somersaulting downward with darkness surrounding him on every side. He coughed and thrashed his way free of the cloth, still falling. Then his butt slammed into hard, smooth stone, and he continued to free-fall downward. He clawed out on all sides, desperately searching for anything to break or even slow his descent, but all his fingers touched was empty air as cold stone slid beneath his back.

Suddenly, Wolfgang's feet hit more stone, but it wasn't a floor; it was a slight turn in whatever kind of tunnel he was rocketing through. He flung both arms out to grab hold of a free edge as he shot through the turn. He was falling too fast.

The surface beneath his back was flatter now, but all light from the desert surface far above had long faded. Wolfgang slid another five or eight seconds, then he felt the surface beneath him turn from stone to sand, and his free fall converted into a flipping hurtle down a gentle slope.

Everything was pitch black, and the air was thick and rank with unknown smells. Wolfgang thrashed for something to break his fall as he continued to flip and roll downward. Sand clogged his face and filled his clothes, and then he slammed into another stone wall.

Wolfgang lay still, his mind spinning. He was vaguely aware of dirt and rocks beneath his back, and as he blinked into the blackness overhead, a sixth sense told him he was in some kind of cave. Maybe it was the sounds he'd detected as he fell or just the reality that there was only dirt beneath him, not over him.

It didn't really matter. His heart pounded, and his entire left side throbbed in pain from the collision with the wall. He forced himself up on his elbows, wincing as pain shot through his bruised hips and ribs.

"Charlie Lead?" he coughed. "Can you hear me?"

Nobody answered over the comm. Wolfgang reached a dirty finger up to his ear and felt for the earpiece, suddenly realizing he didn't feel the familiar pressure of it riding in his ear canal. Wolfgang sat bolt upright and blinked rapidly, feeling for the earpiece again. Sand ground in his ear as he fished around with his finger, but he felt nothing.

Wolfgang's heart rate spiked, and he gasped for air. He spat sand from his mouth and turned around, feeling with his hands for the side of the slope. Panic overtook his mind, and he shook all over.

Light. I need light.

Wolfgang felt through his pockets, digging past a pocket knife and a small roll of local currency. The Canadian passport fell out, and then he felt the familiar touch of cold steel from the LED penlight he kept in his pocket. He pulled it out and fumbled with the switch, still panting for air. The light came on and flooded the space in front of him, illuminating the face of a dead man lying only inches away.

[12]

WOLFGANG GULPED BACK a scream and thrashed backward, almost dropping the light. The olive-toned man that lay at his feet was tall and dressed in dark clothes. His neck was twisted to one side at an unnatural angle, his eyes wide and frozen into a death-stare.

"Hello?" The voice was distant and faint.

Wolfgang's heart beat so loud he wasn't sure if he heard the call, or just imagined it. He forced himself to calm down, clawing his way backward up the sandy slope until he was a few yards from the body, then he scanned the light upward.

He sat at the foot of a sand dune packed with rocks sloping downward from the roof of the cave about fifty feet up. Only it wasn't a cave. The light wasn't powerful enough to shine all the way to the ceiling, but Wolfgang could make out flat stone walls rising behind the dune, and at the top of the dune, he could make out the square outline of the hole he'd shot out of during his wild descent. It was square and black with no sign of light from the outside world streaming through.

It's some kind of chute . . . leading into what?

Wolfgang rubbed sand from his eyes, then placed his free hand into the dune to brace himself. His fingers sank into the sand and touched something hard and round. He frowned and twisted, panning the light over the spot and sweeping the sand away.

Wolfgang choked, thrashing backward again. The object in the sand was a human skull, decayed to the point where almost none of it remained, but the shape was unmistakable. He swallowed a panicked shout and clawed his way to his feet, struggling for balance at the bottom of the dune.

"Hello?" the voice said.

This time, Wolfgang was sure he heard it coming from the far side of the sandpile, off to his left, where the light was too weak to shine. The skull lay in between him and the voice, as did the body, but the prospect of another human in this dark cavern of death sounded like salvation itself. Wolfgang stumbled around the skull, struggling for balance and keeping away from the body as he panned the light forward.

"Hello?" the voice said for the third time. It was weak,

almost a whimper, and Wolfgang thought it was female. He could hear fear in the tone—the same fear that still pounded in his blood with every heartbeat.

"Hello?" Wolfgang called back. "Where are you?"

He struggled for balance as he circled the bottom of the dune. The voice didn't answer him, but he heard a soft cry, like a child sobbing. Wolfgang clung to the flashlight as if it were his sole hope for survival—which it might've been. Sand filled his clothes and ground against his feet from the insides of his shoes, but he kept thrashing forward, flashing the penlight from side to side as he saw another wall rise out of the darkness.

Then he saw her. From the first glance, he knew the little figure nestled in the crevice between the bottom of the dune and the nearest stone wall was Dr. Pollins. She looked just like her sister, identical in every detail. Amelia lay with most of her torso out of sight, buried in the sand. Only one arm, her neck, and her head poked out. As the light flashed across her face, Wolfgang saw pure panic in her eyes. Tears ran down her cheeks, and her hair was twisted into a tangle of sand and sweat.

"Dr. Pollins?" Wolfgang said.

Amelia lifted her free hand toward him as he hurried forward, kneeling in the sand beside her and placing the penlight in his mouth. He dug with both hands, pawing sand away from her torso.

"My leg . . . it's broken," Amelia said.

Wolfgang spoke around the light. "Stay still, Doctor. I'm going to get you out." He quickly unearthed her torso and other arm, then moved to scoop away sand from her leg. As he did, his fingers touched something hard, and he recoiled.

More bones.

He moved to her other side and scooped the sand away. Gradually, he shifted enough sand to expose everything from her knees up, then he reached down and pressed his arms beneath her back, gently lifting her up and out. Amelia groaned but allowed him to pull her free before setting her back down in a sitting position, her back resting against the stone wall.

"Water?" she asked.

"I'm sorry. I don't have any." Wolfgang looked back up at the ceiling and scanned the penlight over the mouth of the chute.

Megan and Kevin would be working for a way to free him. They would need rope—a lot of it—and he didn't remember having any in the 4Runner. Without communications, he had no way of telling them to send down water or more lights.

Wolfgang panned the light around again, taking in the full bulk of the sandpile, then glimpsing the dead man lying at the bottom.

What's going on here? Is this the tomb?

Wolfgang flinched when Amelia grabbed his arm, and he was impressed by the strength in her fingers.

"We have to get out," she said.

"We will, Doctor. My friends are coming, okay?"

Amelia shook her head. "We have to go now."

There was a fear in her eyes that transcended the natural panic of being stuck underground. It was deeper and more immediate. Was she descending into shock?

"Are there other men?" Wolfgang asked, motioning to the body at the foot of the sand dune.

"No," Amelia said. "Just him." She swallowed then motioned to her left.

Wolfgang turned the light in that direction, following her line of sight. For the first time, he saw a black doorway in the far corner of the room, barely visible even when he pointed the light directly at it. Wolfgang's heart skipped, and he felt a wash of excitement in spite of their predicament.

The tomb.

"A pharaoh?" Wolfgang asked.

She shook her head, but when she opened her mouth, he couldn't hear the words through her dry voice.

Wolfgang leaned closer, pressing his ear next to Amelia's lips so that she could whisper.

"Death," she said. "Plague."

"Plague? What are you talking about?"

Amelia beckoned him forward, and he leaned close again.

"This tomb . . . There was a plague, long ago. Black Death."

Wolfgang jerked away, rushing to his feet. He stepped away from the sandpile, recalling the bones buried beneath the dune. The reality of what he was looking at sank in, and he remembered Amelia's apartment and the books opened on her desk. He remembered the highlights and the pages opened to a passage about a plague in Ancient Egypt.

This wasn't the tomb of a pharaoh. It was the mass burial site of an ancient civilization ravaged by a disease that tore through society like an angel of death.

Wolfgang pressed himself against the wall, facing the sandpit. Everything made sense to him—why the Egyptians wanted the scroll back so desperately, even if they already had pictures of it. The scroll wasn't the map to a burial site packed with treasure; it was a map to a burial site packed with bodies and possibly disease.

Can bodies this old still harbor the plague? Surely the bacteria must be dead now.

Amelia coughed and waved Wolfgang toward her again. He hesitated, forcing himself to breathe.

Don't panic.

Wolfgang knelt next to Amelia and held his ear close to her mouth.

"Listen," she said. "The bones can't hurt you. It's been too long. But . . ." She swallowed, then coughed.

Wolfgang put a hand on her arm and waited for her to calm herself.

"In the next room," Amelia continued, "are the catacombs. You can't touch the mummies. Do you understand?"

Wolfgang nodded slowly. Mummies. That meant this plague was far older than the Black Death that ravaged Europe in the Middle Ages. This disease must date back to Ancient Egypt itself. Could it really be alive for that long? Surely not, but Wolfgang wasn't about to take the chance. He shone the light back up at the ceiling, searching for the mouth of the chute. He found it, but there was still no sign of a rope or a light or any communication from Megan and Kevin.

It's only a matter of time. Stay calm.

Wolfgang gave Amelia a gentle squeeze on the shoulder and smiled at her. "We're going to get you out, Doctor."

Amelia nodded. "My sister?"

"Ashley's safe. We already found her."

The relief that crowded over Amelia's face was evident. Wolfgang gave her shoulder another squeeze, and then he thought about the second man. There had to be a second man, after all. The first man had uncovered the chute, and he and Amelia had fallen into it. He fell face-first and broke his neck on impact, and Amelia fell to the left side of the dune and triggered enough of a landslide to bury her, breaking her leg somewhere along the way.

But there had to be a second man because somebody had covered the hole. Actually, there was probably a second and a third man, because there was dirt in all four floorboards of Amelia's car. After Amelia and the first man fell, the second and third men covered the hole because they had the same problem Kevin and Megan had—they needed rope. So, they covered the hole to keep it hidden and took a second vehicle to get rope.

And now they're coming back.

As if on cue, far away through the chute, Wolfgang heard the distant pop of gunfire, followed by the faint roar of an engine. The sounds were too weak for him to make out specifics, but he thought he heard more than one gun and more than one vehicle.

Wolfgang huddled in the darkness and lowered the light, listening to the noises far above. Gunfire meant that the kidnappers had returned to find Kevin and Megan at their hole, and they were prepared to defend it because they still thought the chute was the mouth of a royal tomb, not a mass burial site. Wolfgang thought about Megan as he heard another string of distant pops.

God, let her be okay.

He'd barely breathed the prayer when the explosion detonated, shaking the ceiling above and sending tremors into the floor. Wolfgang stumbled for balance and looked up

as bits of sand and rock rained down from the ceiling overhead. He pointed the light to the ceiling and saw cracks
spreading across the stone, fifty feet up. The cracks spread,
then several large stones broke free and hurtled toward the
sand. A split second later, a ripping, crumbling sound
echoed through the chamber, and the entire ceiling began to
cave in.

Wolfgang didn't have time to worry about a mummified plague awaiting him in the catacombs. He snatched
Amelia up by both arms and hurtled across the sandy floor,
dodging falling sections of ceiling. She grunted in pain, half-
dragging behind him, her broken leg scraping the floor and
bouncing on chunks of rock.

They hurtled through the open entrance to the catacombs and the consuming darkness beyond. There was a
deafening boom as his feet crossed through the doorway,
and then a wall of sand and sordid air pelted his back,
hurling him forward. Both he and Amelia crashed to the
ground, tumbling over one another as a deluge of rocks and
sand filled the doorway directly behind them. Wolfgang
came to rest on his butt, his back slamming against a rock
wall as the sand poured in. He thought the deluge would

drown them both, but the sand reached the top of the doorway and stopped, completely blocking their escape.

Wolfgang sat in the shadows, the penlight still clutched in one hand. It trembled as he lifted it and stared at the wall of sand and rock. The gunshots and engine noises ceased. In an instant, even the roar of the cave-in fell silent, and all he could hear was the total stillness of the tomb he was locked in, mixed with his and Amelia's ragged breathing.

Wolfgang forced himself not to panic as he panned the light to his right, farther down the hall. The stones that made up the tunnel on either side weren't like those of the cavernous room behind them. These walls were inscribed with hieroglyphics and covered in colorful drawings of an ancient world. Wolfgang stumbled to his feet and leaned against a wall, sweeping the light down its length. He knew nothing about what he was looking at, and of course he couldn't read the hieroglyphics, but the painted imagery was brutally clear.

Death by the thousands. The images displayed in perfect clarity the swollen, blackened faces of men and women in an ancient world. They lay on the ground, their mouths open, their eyes closed. A sweep of his light farther down the hallway revealed images of animals lying in piles, with fire rising from them and men and women standing back and covering their faces.

Then more bodies. Pictures of piles of bodies and of robed priests lifting their hands toward Heaven, and of fire raining down from the sky to consume cities. Every perfect detail of this ancient artwork was preserved in such vivid clarity that it looked to be only hundreds of years old, not thousands. In this tomb of silence, where wind and water never touched the stone, there was nothing to deteriorate the art—nothing to wash away the story of the death that visited.

Wolfgang looked down at Amelia. She stared at the paintings, her eyes alight with a fascination that eclipsed his own.

This is what she's dreamed of . . . a discovery to put her in the history books.

Wolfgang wiped his lip. Right then, he didn't care about history. He didn't care about artifacts and old plagues. He only cared about being trapped, and the fact that whatever oxygen they had left to breathe was a finite resource.

Then he heard the distant sound again—a soft grinding, and then a gentle tremor in the floor. He snapped the light toward the ceiling, where dust fell from the tight spaces between the stones. The vibrations in the floor grew louder and stronger, and he couldn't tell from which direction it was coming, but the cloud of dust overhead thickened.

It's all caving in.

Wolfgang stuck the flashlight in his teeth and bent to scoop up Amelia. She didn't resist as he lifted her onto his back and held both of her hands over his shoulders.

As he ran, the rumbling behind him grew steadily

louder, now accompanied by a shower of dirt so thick it was difficult to see. Wolfgang's mind clouded in panic as the hallway on either side of him flashed by, dimly lit by the penlight. He choked on dust and sprinted toward the darkness ahead as the floor shook beneath him.

A loud crash sounded, followed by a shockwave that ripped through the tunnel. Wolfgang hurled himself forward, his mind blinded by an overwhelming desire to get out. Whatever he had to do, wherever he had to go, he had to leave.

The end of the tunnel came abruptly, opening up into a wide chamber with a high ceiling. The crash and boom of the collapsing passage behind him grew louder, and dust rained down from overhead. Wolfgang looked around the chamber, choking on dust as the light cast eerie shadows around him.

There were bodies everywhere, lying on pyres and wrapped in white burial strips with their arms crossed over their chests. Mummies—dozens of them—were lined up in neat rows all across the room. Wolfgang would have been shocked, or maybe even terrified, but the threat of the impending cave-in was too present to ignore.

Wolfgang dashed across the room, weaving between the pyres as Amelia bounced on his back, one leg hooked around his waist and the other flopping next to his hip. She choked in a pain-filled scream, but he kept running, reaching the far wall of the tomb as bits of rock fell from overhead.

Then he saw the next door. It was framed in the middle of the far wall, filled with blackness, but he thought the floor of that passageway led upward, not downward. Wolfgang sprinted for the opening without pausing to think. Chunks of rock crashed down around him, one of them striking a pyre and obliterating it in a shower of dust. Wolfgang choked and slid through the door as more explosions of rock on rock burst from behind him.

The floor of the passageway did indeed lead upward—but only at a slight incline. Wolfgang ran like he'd never run before, and Amelia bounced along on his back. A sudden tremor in the floor sent him crashing against a wall, and the light flew out of his mouth. He stumbled and looked back, but there was no time to go back for the light. The floor beneath him shook like an earthquake as the chamber caved in and the flashlight disappeared into the dust cloud.

Wolfgang ran up the passage. He couldn't see anything now, and he could barely breathe. Everything was a choking, suffocating smog of dust and darkness, and the desperation that set in was unlike anything he'd ever felt.

I can't die here.

Wolfgang imagined Megan's face that night in Paris when they danced together at the art gala. He remembered the black dress she wore, the mocking smirk she gave him when he struggled to keep up with her smooth dance steps.

What a strange thing to think about, he thought, here at the
edge of eternity. Of all the memories in his life, he thought
about that night. He thought about Megan.

I'm going to see her again.

Wolfgang stumbled forward, still clinging to Amelia
with both hands. His shoulder struck a rock wall, and he
immediately turned and felt around in the darkness until he
found an opening again. The tunnel switched back on itself,
like a stairway in a building, and as he stumbled into the
next passage, he felt a slight incline beneath his feet.

That's all I need.

Wolfgang wheezed and almost fell as another tremor
rocketed through the floor. He heard the tunnel behind him
collapsing, and he leaned forward into the run as the floor
beneath him became steeper.

Then he saw light. It happened all at once as the tunnel
suddenly leveled out, and bright sunlight streamed through
a hole in the ceiling. The momentary hope that flooded his
mind was quickly extinguished, however, as cracks shot out
from the ceiling, and more chunks of rock fell to the floor,
followed by a deluge of sand.

Wolfgang could see clearly now. Beams of bright light
shot through the ceiling on all sides as the roof collapsed,
and he could see the surface of the desert fifteen feet overhead, but the gaps in the roof allowed a tidal wave of sand to
crash in. Within seconds, the surge covered his feet and
worked its way up his legs. Wolfgang thrashed free and

fought upward, dragging Amelia behind him as rocks and sand poured in on every side, but he already knew the effort was useless. There was no way he could fight his way out while dragging another person—however small—on his back.

It's me ... or her.

Wolfgang fought his leg free again, coughing and ducking his head to avoid the spray of sand. It was like a shower in a fancy hotel, blasting in from all sides. No sooner did he jerk one leg free than the desert tsunami buried it again, up to his knee now. It was becoming increasingly difficult to find stones to stand on, and even though massive chunks of the roof were now gone and there was little risk of being hit in the head by rocks, the gaps only left more room for sand to pour in.

"Climb on my shoulders!" Wolfgang shouted.

Amelia thrashed on his back, but to no avail. Her broken leg dangled next to him, quickly becoming buried by the sand.

"You have to climb on my shoulders!"

He couldn't move his legs now, and there was no longer a point in trying. His best bet now was to lift Amelia onto his shoulders and maybe get her far enough from the floor to somehow avoid being buried.

Amelia tried to climb, but her body was weak, and Wolfgang couldn't help much.

"Climb!" he said.

Amelia couldn't move. She clawed with both hands, but her broken leg kept her from obtaining any usable leverage.

She's going to die with me.

A whirring, buzzing noise came from someplace above them, and he looked up into the bright sun, blinking away the sand and searching the sky. The buzzing grew louder, coming in from his right . . . or maybe his left.

Lyle's monstrosity of a drone rocketed out of the sky like a helicopter descending on a war zone. The big black machine blasted down on them with all eight rotors spinning, sending up another cloud of dust that was almost too intense to see through. The drone's motors slowed a little, then it began to drop. Wolfgang noticed the strap that hung down from the middle of the drone. It was the same strap Megan had used to fly into Amelia's apartment, and at the end, the rappelling harness still swung like a life buoy.

Wolfgang reached up, his fingers scraping the bottom of the harness as the drone hovered ten feet overhead. He remembered Lyle talking about the weight of the battery and reserve lift and motor output—all things Wolfgang didn't understand or really care about.

It can't lift her . . . not with the battery. But it can help.

Wolfgang snagged the harness on his second attempt and pulled down, looping one side of it beneath Amelia's left arm, then helping her to get her second arm through the other side. The sand was up to his waist now, pouring in a little slower than before, but still rising inches per minute,

with no signs of stopping. Wolfgang was completely immo-
bile from the stomach down, but Amelia still had a fighting
chance.

He gave her hand a squeeze and shouted over the roar
of the drone. "Climb out, Doctor! You've got to climb!"

Amelia gave him a brief nod, then Wolfgang flashed a
thumbs-up at the drone's belly-mounted camera. The drone
surged to life and shot upward, its accession slowing almost
to a stop when the strap became tight. Amelia grunted in
pain but then began kicking her good leg and using her arms
to claw her way up the side of the deluge of rocks and sand.

The drone strained overhead. Wolfgang thought he saw
smoke rise from its motors, and he pushed upward on the
bottom of her shoe. She groped upward at the shifting pile
of sand and rocks, and then Dr. Amelia Pollins broke free
and disappeared over the side of the collapsing tunnel.
Wolfgang coughed and grabbed at the wall in a last
desperate attempt to free himself. The sand had almost
reached his armpits, and in another minute it would cover
his face. He'd be buried alive.

What a strange way to die. At least I saved Amelia.

Wolfgang pawed sand out of his eyes, then took a deep
breath.

I wish I'd gone upstairs to see Collins.

The sand rushed in on all sides, up to his shoulders, and
Wolfgang looked up at the sun, hoping to catch sight of the
blue sky far above. Then something rocketed through the

air and smacked him in the face. The object landed directly in front of him, coiled up like a snake and trailing back over the edge of the tunnel.

"Grab on!" somebody shouted.

Wolfgang flailed out with both hands and caught the rope. He wound it around his right arm and clamped his left hand around the tail end. Then he heard the familiar growl of Charlie Team's Toyota 4Runner.

The motor roared, and Wolfgang's body ached as the strain descended on him. He felt like he was being pulled apart, like an insect between the chunky fingers of a child. Then the suction of the sand around his legs gave way, and he rocketed upward, plowing headfirst through the sand and over the side of the tunnel. Dirt filled his mouth, and he skidded along the rough surface, rolling through rocks before coming to a stop twenty feet beyond the tunnel.

He came to rest on his back, his arms still outstretched, and he heard the beat of footsteps nearby. Dirt exploded next to his head as somebody's knees crashed down only inches away. A gush of water descended on his face, washing away the dirt and running over his dry lips in a glorious, unbelievable surge of pure goodness. He gulped at the stream and caught his breath, sucking in as many mouthfuls as he could before the water was suddenly taken away.

Then someone leaned over him, blocking out the sun.

Megan.

"Wolfgang! Are you hurt?"

Megan's eyes filled with a level of concern he'd not seen before. Despite the pain that still throbbed through his body, Wolfgang felt suddenly awkward, as if she'd walked in on him in the bathroom.

He ran his tongue over busted lips, then offered a sheepish grin. "Hey, Meg. Found that tomb we were looking for."

[14]

WOLFGANG WAITED ON THE GULFSTREAM, a glass of Sprite in one hand and an ice pack in the other. He moved the pack every few minutes from his neck to his shoulders, then his thighs, then his back.

Absolutely everything hurt. Every joint, every muscle. It was like a giant had grabbed him by the feet and slung him into a block wall multiple times, then stomped on him for good measure. All his major joints were swollen, and aggressive rope burns ran down the length of his right arm. No matter how he adjusted himself in the plush seat of the private jet, Wolfgang couldn't get comfortable, but all things considered, he wasn't too worried about it.

I'm alive.

The single thought raced through his mind over and over, like a CD with a scratch on it, repeating the same lyric from the same song for all of eternity. When he closed his eyes, he saw the sand again, closing in all around him, and all he could think was . . .

I'm alive. I shouldn't be, but I am.

He adjusted the ice pack to his neck and glanced to the tail of the plane, where Lyle was busy disassembling what remained of his drone. The motors were cooked, apparently —something about overstressing them with too much payload. After dropping Amelia on the dirt outside the tunnel, the drone had crashed into the ground and wrecked half of its propellers, along with some of its superstructure. Lyle was pissed, but Wolfgang figured he'd get over it.

As of yet, nobody else was on the plane. Wolfgang and Lyle had sat there for the better part of the morning, alone except for Charlie Team's pilots, who never left the cockpit while Edric worked to clean things up with the Egyptians. There was apparently a lot of confusion and no short amount of angst about what had happened near the airport, and even though Charlie Team used a private airfield outside the city, the Egyptians would not let them take off until certain questions were resolved. Questions like: "Why was there a gunfight in the middle of the desert?" "Are you responsible for the invasion of the IronGate tower?" And Wolfgang's personal favorite: "Who's going to pay for the mess?"

Wolfgang had a pretty good idea that SPIRE would not be paying for any mess. Sure, there was a network of gaping holes in the desert near the airport where various tombs and tunnels had caved in, but if what Amelia said about those tombs was true, it was probably just as well if they remained buried. After Wolfgang slid down the chute into the first room and found Amelia, everything that transpired above ground was pretty much as he had guessed. There was, in fact, a second and a third man, and after covering the hole to keep it out of sight, they had gone back to the city to get some rope. Apparently, Amelia's car wouldn't start, so they walked back to the road and caught rides, then returned in a large stolen truck.

The gunfight that resulted when they attacked Kevin and Megan ended when Kevin accidentally shot out the gas tank of the truck, which eventually set off an explosion and triggered the cave-in. During the course of the gunfight, both men had been shot—probably by Kevin, although he wouldn't admit to it—but neither man was killed. They were now in Egyptian custody.

Wolfgang turned to the nearest window at the sound of a car grinding to a halt outside and watched as Edric, Megan, and Kevin piled out. They were accompanied by an Egyptian police officer, who shook Edric's hand and said a few words before the three of them climbed the stairs and entered the plane. Edric proceeded immediately to the cockpit and said a word to the waiting pilots, then walked to the minibar and poured himself a drink.

Wolfgang eased the ice from his neck to his right thigh,

watching Megan out of the corner of one eye. He remembered the look on her face when he'd first seen her, only moments after being saved from the mouth of the desert. The concern in her eyes . . . the sincerity in her voice.

She'd have looked that way for anybody on the team. Don't read into it.

Wolfgang told himself that multiple times, but he still wanted to read into it. He still wanted to think that maybe . . .

"That was one hell of a mess," Edric said. He took a seat across from the others as the plane's door hummed shut. Only moments later, the aircraft began to roll, and Wolfgang fastened his seatbelt.

Edric took a sip of the drink and shook his head. "Dr. Pollins is in the hospital being treated for a broken leg, a couple fractured ribs, and no small amount of shock. Her sister is with her."

"So, is it true?" Lyle asked.

Edric swirled the drink and cocked his head. "About the plague?"

Lyle nodded.

"It's true that we didn't find the tomb of a pharaoh," Edric said. "Dr. Pollins believes that the catacombs Wolfgang so graciously uncovered were used sometime during the waning years of Ancient Egypt, primarily to bury plague victims. At first, they would've used the catacombs, but when the plague got out of hand, they started dropping bodies straight down the ventilation shoot that Wolfgang fell through and then dumping sand on top of them. Hence the giant pile of buried bones you landed in."

Wolfgang grimaced, recalling the sand dune and the skulls he'd touched. It wasn't a memory he was eager to relive.

"Of course," Edric continued, "Dr. Pollins's real concern wasn't the bones, but the mummies in the next room. Mummification is a very precise art that preserves a body to an incredible degree. The concern is that the disease may have been preserved, also."

"That's absurd." Kevin snorted.

Edric shrugged. "The Egyptians disagree, apparently. That's why they called us in, after all, and it's why they denied that there were photographs of the scroll."

"Was the scroll ever found?" Wolfgang asked.

Edric shook his head. "Not yet. They might find it, but it may have been incinerated when the truck blew up. In context of the discovered tombs, it's a small loss."

"They should've told us the truth from the start," Kevin said.

The plane's engines wound up, and then the nose began to rise.

Wolfgang tried to ignore the throb in his head. He cast a quick look at Megan, hoping she wouldn't notice, but their gazes met. Wolfgang flashed a quick smile. Megan smiled back, just a little, then rolled her eyes and looked away.

"Let the record state," Lyle said, "that once again, it was my gadgetry that saved the day."

Megan snorted. "Your gadgetry can go to hell. I better never see that damn drone again."

Kevin laughed. "Nobody would've had to save the day if Wolfgang hadn't gone jumping into tombs for no reason at all."

Wolfgang smiled but didn't bother to defend himself. The plane climbed, and Egypt faded, and he looked out the window and thought about Amelia and her sister, reunited in the hospital. Two innocent lives saved, a little money made, and a few bad guys banged up and locked up. Sure, his entire body hurt and he would never again set foot in a basement, let alone a cave, but all things considered, it was mission accomplished in his mind.

He leaned back in the seat and thought about Megan again, allowing himself to imagine that the look in her eyes when she leaned over him in the desert wasn't generic—that it was just for him. The thought may have been a fantasy, but it was enough to block away the rest of the pain and pave the way into exhausted sleep.

THAT TIME IN MOSCOW

BOOK 3 OF THE WOLFGANG PIERCE SERIES

"I would wake up in Moscow . . . my heart beating fast,
feeling bitter and helpless."
— _Alfred Schnittke_

[1]

November, 2011

THE INSIDE of the dealership smelled like the interior of a country club—or, at least what Wolfgang imagined a country club smelled like. Truth be told, he'd never set foot inside a club of any sort, or even a restaurant fancier than a Longhorn Steakhouse.

But Elite Motorcars of Kansas City had that ambiance —that sort of low-light, vaguely smoky, even-if-nobody-was-smoking vibe that brought to mind images of men in suits sitting around a poker table and swapping jokes about compound interest while deciding the fate of the world. It was the kind of place where Wolfgang expected to be offered a snifter of bourbon, not a bottle of water. The kind of place that he never in his wildest childhood memories imagined he would set foot, let alone set foot with a wad of cash in his pocket the thickness of a Bible.

"Good afternoon, sir."

Shoes snapped against the polished tile floor to his left as Wolfgang glanced around the glistening showroom at an array of expensive cars—Maseratis, Mercedes, Jaguars, Land Rovers, and Porsches. He indulged in a boyish grin and turned to the approaching salesman.

"Hey, there. I'd like to buy a car."

The salesman—maybe he called himself an *automotive concierge*—wore a suit that cost ten times the value of Wolfgang's entire wardrobe. Pinstriped, with an understated tie, and shoes with leather soles. The man was tall, bald, and carried himself with the attitude of somebody who was accustomed to addressing people by their last names and was comfortable doing so. He wore narrow glasses with metal frames and squinted at Wolfgang with a gaze that was both pitying and condescending all at once.

"You'd like to buy a car . . ." the man said, then stared at Wolfgang's feet.

Wolfgang nodded, then glanced down to see if there was gum on his shoe. He looked past his washed-out jeans from Walmart to his scuffed sneakers from the sneaker warehouse in Chicago—buy two pairs, get a third pair free.

Wolfgang looked up and nodded. "Yeah, a car. I was thinking a two-door, maybe a convertible."

"A *convertible*." The man said the word as if it were an

ancient racial slur he was only semi-familiar with but still offended by. "You mean a *cabriolet*?"

Wolfgang shrugged, looking back at the cars. His eye was drawn to a sleek coupe in bright yellow. It was a Mercedes coupe, small and agile-looking, with a retractable hard-top. "Sure, whatever."

The salesman sighed, at once a patient and exhausted sound. "I'm not sure we have the sort of motorcar you're looking for, young man. I feel compelled to say that the vehicles we stock are in the moderate to significant price bracket."

Wolfgang frowned. "Huh?"

Again the salesman stared at his shoes. Again Wolfgang checked for gum.

"Our cars are expensive," the salesman said, lowering his voice as if he were divulging nuclear launch codes.

"Oh, yeah." Wolfgang dug the stack of hundreds from his pocket and ran his thumb over the end, then tossed it to the salesman. "I'm not sure if that's a moderate or a significant amount. What do you think?"

The salesman's eyes bulged as he caught the wad. He blinked, ran his own thumb over the end of the wad, then looked up with a smile bright enough to overload a solar panel. "I don't believe I caught your name."

Wolfgang offered his hand. "Wolfgang Pierce. Tell me about the yellow one."

Ten minutes later, Wolfgang sat in the plush leather

seat of the coupe and hit the start button as Stanley—his name was actually Stanley—slid in beside him, adjusting his glasses and talking faster than an auctioneer on crack.

"Brand new from Mercedes, this is the 2012 SLK55 AMG, featuring a special-order paint finish that the Germans call *Streetfighter Yellow*. I have to tell you, Mr. Pierce, it's an exquisite machine. Truly a work of art. Crafted leather interior, a deluxe entertainment system, and suspension designed to make every trip a path carved through the clouds."

Wolfgang was barely listening as the car rumbled to life and the dashboard lit up with enough lights to shame a Christmas tree. He grinned, feeling the rumble of the coupe shooting up his spine. Everything around him felt premium. His mind flashed back to the beat-up pickup trucks and rusted-out sedans of his childhood, many of which were lucky to run at all.

Look at me now.

Stanley held out a pair of gloves, shooting Wolfgang that solar-flare smile again. "You'll want these."

"For what?"

Stanley blushed, then lowered his voice again. "Driving gloves, Mr. Pierce. All true enthusiasts wear them."

Wolfgang waved his hand as he steered the car through the open showroom door and into the parking lot. "I'm new to cars, Stanley. Not life."

He hit the button to lower the top, and the Mercedes's

roof retracted into the trunk with a low whine, allowing bright sun and gentle wind to stream into the car. It felt amazing.

Stanley dropped the gloves into his lap with a dull sniff, then motioned toward the street.

"You'll want to take it onto the freeway, Mr. Pierce. The quality of the ride is truly—"

"Is it fast?"

Stanley frowned. "Mr. Pierce, this is a *Mercedes*. The nuance of the driving experience cannot be simplified to a word as limited as *fast*. To appreciate a car like this, you really—"

Wolfgang hit the gas. The nose of the car bucked upward as the engine roared and the back wheels spun. A moment later, they rocketed out of the parking lot in a wild slide, tires screaming and the engine throbbing. Wolfgang felt equal parts adrenaline and fear rush through his system as the tires grabbed and rocketed them onto the multi-lane street that faced the dealership. Horns blared, and cars swerved past. Stanley screamed. Wolfgang clutched the wheel with both hands and broke the turn as the car shifted, then he felt something in the base of his spine like the explosion of gunpowder detonating behind a cannonball. He was pinned to the seat as the nose lifted again and everything around him turned into a slow-motion light show of extrapolated colors.

Engine noise, tire smoke, and the incessant screaming of

the petrified salesman next to him all blended into a glorious crescendo of sensational overload. Wolfgang cut the wheel to the left, sliding through a light as it turned red. A moment later, they were on the freeway, and the speedometer zipped past one hundred. Wind ripped through his hair and Wolfgang threw his head back and shouted, cutting in between cars and trucks as the Mercedes clung to the pavement as though it were on rails. He'd never felt anything quite like it—power, flash, and thrill.

And Stanley screaming. Wolfgang took them two miles down the freeway, then abruptly swerved off the highway and slid to a stop at a fuel station. The engine wound down and throbbed with glassy-smooth perfection, unstrained by its sudden workout.

Stanley sat panting in the passenger seat, and Wolfgang ran a hand through his hair. His fingers still trembled with adrenaline overload, but the sensation felt good. It felt like *life*.

"I'll take it!" he said, looking for the first time at Stanley. The salesman sat quaking, his fingers wrapped around the edges of his seat so tight that his knuckles turned white. To his credit, he hadn't wet himself, but Wolfgang sniffed a couple times just to be sure.

Stanley brushed the wrinkles out of his suit with two sweaty hands. He adjusted his tie, wiped his glasses, then nodded. "That's most excellent, Mr. Pierce. I'm so glad you like it. If we can find our way back to the showroom, I'd be delighted to draw up the papers."

Wolfgang absentmindedly stroked the smooth leather of the steering wheel. In the back of his mind, he heard a soft, distant voice, and the words came back to him as clear as if they had been spoken the day before. *"You'll go far one day. The world will be yours."*

Wolfgang blinked, then looked out the window. Stanley rambled on next to him about service packages and premium warranties, but Wolfgang wasn't listening. He was in another place, at another time, standing barefoot in the kitchen as his mother leaned over the stove, cooking up a box of Hamburger Helper. Her left eye was swollen, almost shut, and her dirty hair hung over a bruised neck. *"You'll get out of here. If it's the last thing I do, I'll see you out of this hellhole."*

"Mr. Pierce?"

Wolfgang realized he'd zoned out as the memory took over. He turned the car back toward the highway, driving gently this time. There was no rush. The phone in his pocket buzzed, and he dug it out. He punched in the passcode as Stanley mumbled something about "complete cellular integration," and Wolfgang saw a single text message light up the screen from a contact labeled only as *E*.

"Gonna have to expedite that paperwork, Stan," Wolfgang said. "I've got to be in St. Louis by five."

AFTER PARKING the Mercedes in a garage across the street, Wolfgang ascended to the fourteenth floor of the Bank of America Plaza in downtown St. Louis. The entire fourteenth floor—like most of the building—was vacant, save for the unofficial operational headquarters of Charlie Team, the elite espionage unit that Wolfgang was a member of. Charlie Team was the third operational unit of SPIRE's field division, and SPIRE—a private corporation specializing in sabotage, procurement, infiltration, retaliation, and entrapment—was America's elite provider of for-hire espionage services.

At least, Wolfgang thought so. He joined Charlie Team five months earlier after spending three years as an individual operator running minor corporate sabotage gigs. Since then, Charlie Team had conducted high-stakes operations in Europe and Africa, both of which delivered levels of adrenaline Wolfgang had hitherto only dreamed of, not to mention paychecks that outstripped his lifestyle by an order of magnitude.

Hence the Mercedes.

Wolfgang stepped through the office door and was immediately greeted by the acrid odor of cigarette smoke. He wrinkled his nose, glancing around the darkened room, but saw none of his teammates gathered around the table or the marker board on the far wall.

Then he saw Megan leaning next to the floor-to-ceiling window at the far end of the room, a cigarette smoldering in one hand as she stared out over the Mississippi River. Wolfgang nudged the door shut and shuffled toward her, feeling his heart rate quicken as the sun glimmered off her tanned skin.

Megan was petite—barely five feet tall—but two missions with her taught Wolfgang that size was no measure of ability. Megan was distant and elusive—a personality shrouded in shadow that, no matter how many times he tried to get to know her, still remained aloof. He'd at first attributed her distance as some manner of arrogance or condescension with the new guy on the team, but there had been flashes now and then of a deeper warmth to her that gave him hope—hope that maybe she'd give him the time of day. Because besides being mysterious and interesting, Megan had the sort of confidence and subtle good looks that made a man stare. Wolfgang was staring now.

"Nice car," Megan said before taking a pull of the cigarette.

Wolfgang frowned. "You saw it?"

She laughed. "It's bright yellow, Wolf. Everybody saw it."

Wolfgang felt suddenly self-conscious, and he shifted, staring down at his tennis shoes. Still no gum, but the smudges bothered him now—as did the cheap jeans.

Why didn't I stop to change? She shouldn't see me like this . . . not while she looks this good.

"I don't know. I guess I liked the color," he mumbled.

Megan laughed again, softer this time. Smoke drifted from her mouth, and she waved for him to sit. "Chill, dude. It's a nice car. I just didn't take you to be a car guy."

Wolfgang sat down, pulling his legs toward his chest and watching as she sucked on the cigarette. He hated the smell of smoke and the stench of sour clothes forever permeated by it. But right then, it didn't bother him so much.

Megan caught him staring and gestured toward the pack of cigarettes sitting on the floor next to her.

Wolfgang shook his head. "No, thanks. I don't smoke."

She turned from the window and leaned back against the wall, taking another pull and staring at him with quiet grey eyes that left him wondering what was happening behind them. The kind of eyes that told you Megan only said about five percent of the things she thought, but that the other ninety-five percent was well worth his time.

"You don't smoke," Megan said. "You don't drink. You don't cuss. What's with you, anyway? Religion?"

Wolfgang looked away, weighing the questions one at a time. Ever since he'd first met Megan, the day before the Paris job, he'd longed for a time like this—a time when they were alone and could talk. Now that the moment had come, he felt thrown off guard. All his usual charisma and wit fled him quicker than the Mercedes powering onto the freeway, and he felt like a silly little kid.

"Not religion," he said, still not looking her way.

Megan said nothing for a long moment, then grunted. "I get it. I won't pry."

Idiot. You can't expect her to talk to you if you won't talk to her.

"My father was a drunk," Wolfgang said, looking up. "He beat my mother all the time. He smoked a lot, too. When he was really mad, he'd burn her stomach with the cigarettes." Wolfgang winced as he spoke, then turned away and stared out the window.

Fool. You said too much. What the heck is wrong with you?

Megan said nothing, but when Wolfgang looked back, she stared at him with the cigarette lowered next to her knee. Her eyes were softer now, and when he met her gaze, she didn't look away.

"I'm sorry," she said, her voice soft but strong.

Wolfgang's cheeks flushed.

What was I thinking? Now she sees me as a pansy.

He cleared his throat, feeling his old wit return as he shoveled the memories back into their graves and reburied them with willful denial. "It's a pretty sweet car," he said, flashing a grin. "You should take a ride with me. Maybe someplace downtown. Maybe someplace with good food."

A smile played at the corner of her mouth. "You never give up, do you?"

Wolfgang shrugged. "It's just a meal with a coworker. Can't object to that, can you?"

Megan rolled the cigarette between two fingers and cocked her head. "I told you, Wolfgang. I'm not getting involved with anybody on the team. But"—she hesitated, then shrugged—"you know, dinner with a coworker, maybe."

A rush of elation overwhelmed Wolfgang as the door swung open and the remaining three members of Charlie Team burst into the room, headed by Edric, the team lead.

"On your feet, guys!" Edric said, clapping his hands. "We've got work to do."

CHARLIE TEAM GATHERED around the plastic conference table as Edric assumed his position in front of the whiteboard. He wore a blazer over a T-shirt, and Wolfgang realized it was the first time since joining Charlie Team that his boss wasn't wearing a cast or a sling over his left arm. During a botched mission in Damascus, Edric had fallen two stories and wrecked his shoulder, elbow, and forearm. It was also that mission that claimed the life of James—Wolfgang's predecessor and Megan's former boyfriend. Hence her unwillingness to date a team member.

Wolfgang took a sip of water from a bottle and then glanced to the end of the table at the last two members of Charlie Team—Kevin, a fellow operator, and Lyle, the team technology wiz. Lyle was all the clichés—short, wiry, and awkward, complete with smudged glasses that didn't fit his face. But he was a warmhearted man once you got to know him, and Wolfgang was pretty sure Elon Musk knew less about gadgetry and computer technology than Lyle.

Kevin was another story. Big, muscular, and moody, he was Megan's half brother and aggressively protective of her. He and Wolfgang had a love-hate relationship born out of Wolfgang's repeated attempts to build a bridge and Kevin's repeated refusals to meet him halfway.

You can't win them all.

"All right." Edric spoke from the whiteboard, where he was busy jotting something down with a red marker. As he stepped aside, Wolfgang saw the word, and a rush of adrenaline as strong as that brought on by the Mercedes hit his system.

"Moscow," Edric said. "We're going to Mother Russia."

Edric paused theatrically, but nobody reacted. This was Charlie Team. They could've been told they were going to North Korea and they wouldn't have blinked, but behind his forced passiveness, Wolfgang's heart thumped.

Moscow. The heart of enemy country for espionage operatives. The hornets' nest.

He'd never been, of course, but he imagined Moscow the way he saw it in the movies—grey, cold, locked in ice and snow, and infested with enemy operators with wits and skill sets every bit as sharp as his own.

This is gonna be fun.

"You guys give me nothing," Edric said, rolling his eyes.

Megan waved a finger. "It's almost December, Edric, and you're sending us into an icebox. You want theatrics, call Bravo Team."

A ripple of laughter erupted, and Edric turned back to the marker board. "Okay, I see how it is. Let's get down to brass tacks, then."

He wrote, and the room fell silent. "The target is Pasha Koslov, code-named *Trident*. He's a Russian-born chemist with a specialty in airborne transmission of manufactured agents."

"Chemical weapons," Wolfgang said.

Edric nodded. "Essentially, yes. Koslov began his career working with air fresheners for the Russian equivalent of Proctor & Gamble, but his peculiar talents quickly caught the attention of the Ministry of Defense. They"— Edric made air quotes with two fingers—"'acquired him,' and he's been working in Moscow for the past four years, most recently on a project to design new types of chemical weapons that offer higher rates of transmission, penetration of protection equipment, and cost-effectiveness."

"I thought chemical weapons were illegal," Kevin said.

"The Geneva Convention outlawed their use in warfare, effective 1928," Edric said. "In 1997, the Chemical Weapons Convention, by power of the United Nations, outlawed the development, production, retention, stockpiling, or acquisition of chemical weapons. So, yes, they're illegal. Your point?"

Kevin blushed. "I just thought, if we know this guy is developing chemical weapons for Russia, wouldn't that be a problem for the state department?"

Fair question.

Edric jotted on the whiteboard again. Wolfgang wondered what the point of the whiteboard was. Why couldn't he just brief them on the details?

"As I mentioned earlier, Koslov is code-named Trident. That name was assigned to him by the CIA, where he has served as an undercover informant for three of the past four years."

Wolfgang's mind spun, quickly connecting the dots. "That's why they can't involve the state department. America would have to disclose how they got the information, which would self-sabotage their own intelligence efforts."

"Bingo." Edric circled a word on the whiteboard and stepped back. "MAD. Mutually assured destruction," he said. "It's kept us safe against the Ruskies since Kennedy was in power, and it's just as effective against chemical warfare as nuclear. If the Russians are willing to risk an international scandal by producing chemical weapons, what else are they willing to risk? The position of the Pentagon is that America is better able to protect herself than the UN is. So, for eighteen months, Trident has fed us data on the developments underway in Russia, which has given our scientists time and information with which to build anti-chemical weapons gear, inoculants, and . . . well . . ."

Wolfgang sat forward. "And matching weapons. That's where MAD comes in, right? They won't use it on us if we can use it on them."

"You didn't hear it from me," Edric said. "Who knows what the CIA is up to? The bottom line for us is that things in Mother Russia are starting to disintegrate. Koslov wants out. I'm not sure if the pressure has gotten to him or if the Russians are getting suspicious. Either way, he's demanding that the CIA extract him immediately, or he's going public with what he knows."

"And at this point, that burns America as much as Russia," Megan said.

"Pretty much. Which is why the CIA made a phone call to their trusty friends at the SPIRE Corporation. Our mission is to extract Koslov from Moscow and deposit him in Minsk, where the CIA will take over."

Lyle spoke for the first time, pushing his smudged glasses up his nose and leaning forward. "I know I always ask, but why can't the CIA do their own dirty work?"

Everybody laughed, and Edric motioned to Wolfgang. "You wanna say it this time?"

Wolfgang leaned back. The answer was obvious. It was always the same answer to the same question. "Plausible deniability. If we get caught, the CIA wants to distance themselves from the operation."

Edric recapped the marker and settled into his chair. "Actually, it's a little more severe than that. The CIA isn't just distancing themselves, they're transferring blame. If our mission goes sideways in Russia, they're not just going to disown us, they're going to burn us. The CIA will pin the entire Trident operation on SPIRE."

The stillness in the room was deathly.

"That's a risk SPIRE is willing to take?" Megan said.

Edric nodded. "I spoke to the director myself. The CIA is writing an extra-large check for this assignment. A seven-figure check. Charlie Team's cut has been tripled."

Kevin let out a low whistle, and Wolfgang sat back. He remembered his last checks from the Cairo and Paris jobs. Together, they were enough to buy the Mercedes and lease a condo outside of St. Louis for a year, with several grand left over. At triple his usual cut, the Moscow job was worth over a hundred grand—more money than Wolfgang really knew what to do with.

But is it worth it?

Wolfgang glanced around the room, watching the dollar signs spin behind Lyle's and Kevin's eyes, but not Megan's. Hers were deep, and distant, and strong. And so damn beautiful.

It's absolutely worth it.

"When do we go?" Wolfgang asked.

"The plane is being fueled as we speak," Edric said. "We fly directly into Moscow, and from there, we make contact with the CIA operator code-named Sparrow. Sparrow is a native Russian brought on by the CIA to be Koslov's handler. They'll brief us on Koslov's current whereabouts and schedule, and from there we'll formulate a plan to get him out of the city. Minsk is about seven hundred kilometers west of Moscow. We may use a train."

Edric sat forward. He interlaced his fingers and met each of their gazes, one at a time, before he spoke. "I can't overstate the gravity of this mission. SPIRE's entire reputation hangs in the balance. Not only that, but Moscow is one of the most dangerous places in the world to attempt this sort of operation. Spies, SVR informants, and national police are everywhere. One false move, and the success of the mission could be the least of our worries. You could die in Moscow, or worse, be responsible for a teammate dying. To add further complication, we'll be limited in what we can bring with us. Even landing at a private airport, Russian Customs are likely to search the plane. That means no weapons and only limited tech gear. I'm setting operational protocols at Code Yellow."

Code Yellow—the bottom tier of three tiers of operational parameters that Charlie Team worked within. Wolfgang couldn't remember the exact limitations of Code Yellow, but the essence of it had already been explained. They were going in unarmed.

Wolfgang's first two missions with SPIRE had been

intense and certainly life-threatening, but the severity he felt from Edric now put a damper on everybody.

"What's our cover?" Megan asked.

"The three of us are banking executives from New York, flying in to meet with a Moscow-based investment firm," Edric said, motioning to Megan and Lyle. "Wolfgang and Kevin are our private security team."

Wolfgang processed the information, still a little stunned at the prospect of being unarmed someplace so potentially hostile. He recalled his last encounter with a Russian operative—the big man he nicknamed Ivan during their Paris operation. He and Ivan had engaged in a no-holds-barred brawl in the bathroom of a fancy Parisian hotel, and Wolfgang had come within an inch of losing his life. As had Ivan.

"Well," Kevin grunted, "we better do it. Wolfgang's gonna need spinners for his car."

Everybody chuckled.

"Does *everybody* know about my car?"

"Bright yellow Mercedes in downtown St. Louis?" Lyle said. "Dude, the mayor is probably scrambling to find out which Chinese business mogul is visiting."

"What I don't get"—Kevin leaned forward—"is why yellow? Don't you think it's a little, I don't know . . . piss colored?"

"There might be something in that," Megan said. "A nickname, maybe. You haven't got a nickname yet, do you?"

"We can't call him *Piss*. That's just mean," Lyle said, but he was laughing.

Wolfgang waved his hands and sat back. "Have your laughs. You're all jealous, and you know it."

"Sunshine," Edric said. "It's kind of a sunshine color, wouldn't you say?"

"Sunshine Pierce!" Kevin slapped the table. "Let's go to Moscow."

[3]

SPIRE's GULFSTREAM G550 boasted a range of almost eight thousand miles, putting Moscow well within range from St. Louis, but they needed flight logs that showed Edric's team of "banking executives" leaving New York, so Edric had the pilot land at LaGuardia, where they refueled and checked in and out of airport security. Kevin picked up a couple pizzas from an airport pizzeria, and ninety minutes later, they were in the air again and headed east.

This was only Wolfgang's third trip inside the plane, headed out on a new mission, but it already felt a little like home. The plush leather seats and well-stocked snack bar made for a comfortable transition around the globe. Even so, he felt vaguely naked without the presence of his Beretta holstered beneath his jacket or any backup weaponry stowed in the cargo hold.

To his surprise, he also felt uneasy without the stacks of obscure crates that were usually packed around the tail of the plane, housing Lyle's complicated array of high-tech gadgetry that had been instrumental in Charlie Team's success in both Paris and Cairo.

Lyle looked just as nervous, sitting in the back and sifting through the three bags of electronics Edric had allowed him to bring.

Wolfgang stood up, sipping from a can of Sprite as he made his way to Lyle's table and sat down across from him. "You okay?"

Lyle looked up, then pushed his glasses up his nose. "Fine. Why wouldn't I be?"

Wolfgang chuckled. "You're beet red and sweating. What's up?"

Lyle surveyed his small pile of equipment. "I don't like being under-equipped. I've got two computers and some communications hardware. No surveillance gear. No tracking technology. I don't even have the drone."

Wolfgang recalled the giant drone Lyle had employed in Cairo and wasn't altogether sure he missed it.

"You're the wiz, Lyle. You'll make it work. Plus, don't forget the watch."

Wolfgang tapped the smartwatch on his wrist, and Lyle nodded impatiently. The watch was far more than a time-piece—it boasted an array of detection sensors and a camera that fed video footage back to Lyle's computers.

"Huddle up!" Edric called from the middle of the plane.

Wolfgang slid out from the table and took a seat in a captain's chair, facing the middle of the plane.

Edric tapped on an iPad as the others gathered in. "We'll land around midnight, local time. I've arranged for a limo to pick us up at the airport and transport us to the Hilton Moscow Leningradskaya, where we'll be staying."

"Isn't that a bit . . . loud?" Wolfgang asked. "A limo, a fancy hotel. I thought we were flying *under* the radar."

"We are, but the Russians are accustomed to international travelers behaving in a certain way—especially rich travelers like bankers. Calling a cab and staying at the DoubleTree would draw more suspicion than the limo and the Hilton. We'll hide in plain sight."

Kevin grinned. "Doesn't bother me. Do they have a spa with a hot Russian masseuse?"

"I should ask," Edric said. "I could use a massage while my security detail stands guard."

Kevin rolled his eyes. "Funny, really. So, when do we meet Sparrow?"

"First thing in the morning. We'll get the details of the meetup via secure email after we reach the hotel. Sparrow will supply us with Koslov's immediate location and schedule over the next two days. Koslov is expecting an imminent extraction but hasn't been briefed on our identities or timeline, for obvious reasons. Koslov works daily at the Russian equivalent of the Pentagon—their military headquarters. It's literally called the Main Building of the Ministry of Defense and is located on Arbatskaya Square. Ideally, we'll pull Koslov on his way to work when his absence is least likely to be noticed. Extracting him from the Ministry of Defense headquarters would be next to impossible."

"When will the Russians know he's missing?" Megan asked.

"Good question," Edric said. "We can assume they have him under some sort of surveillance—probably digital—while he's at home, and he probably has some kind of tracking device for when he runs his errands. Koslov probably knows about all of that, and he can help us disable it. Anything he doesn't know about will be trickier, which is why I want to pull him on his way to work. His home is likely wired with all kinds of bugs and detection devices, but it's highly unlikely that the Russians are tasking somebody to follow him to work, so that will be our point of opportunity. Once we nab him, we're looking at half an hour before the Russians know."

Kevin whistled again. "We can't get out of Moscow in half an hour. No way. And once we clear the city, there will be roadblocks. Checkpoints. It's a helluva long way to the Belarusian border."

"About two hundred eighty-five miles, to be exact," Edric said.

"Sheesh," Wolfgang muttered. "It would be easier to break him out of Gitmo. What's your play?"

Edric puckered his lips. "I've got some ideas. Let's meet with Sparrow first. In the meantime, you guys should sleep. We land in eight hours."

Edric disappeared into the aft cabin, leaving the group huddled around the table, exchanging dubious looks.

"Be easier with some gear," Lyle muttered.

"Be easier with some weapons," Kevin added.

Megan rolled her eyes. "Be *easier* with a battalion of tanks, but we don't have that, do we? You're all a bunch of pussies."

Kevin and Lyle waved her off, then found their way to the minibar, still muttering to themselves.

Wolfgang watched them go, then leaned across the little table between himself and Megan. "They're right, you know. Edric doesn't seem to have much of a plan on this one. And the stakes are higher than usual."

"He's got a plan," Megan said. "You really think he's sleeping back there?"

Megan dug into her carry-on and produced a small stack of books and folded maps. It was her custom to study up on their destination during their flight. Wolfgang had witnessed her doing it on the way to both Paris and Cairo, and both times, her trivia knowledge had proven useful.

She waved her hand dismissively as she spread a map

across the table. "Give me some room. I've got my own work to do."

Wolfgang looked down at the map, then slid closer to the table. "Mind if I join you?"

She glanced up, raising one eyebrow. "Is this another lame attempt at a pickup? Because it isn't gonna work."

"In Cairo you said I should know more about the cities we operate in. I think you're right. Surely, you can't object to a study partner." He gave her a wink, matched with his most innocent smile.

She stared him down a moment, then a smile tugged at the corners of her mouth. "Okay, boy wonder. Just stay on your side of the table. And find a pen. You're gonna need to take notes."

———

THE G550 TOUCHED down exactly eight hours later, around eleven p.m. local time, its thick tires squealing against cold Russian tarmac. Wolfgang sat next to the window, peering out at the city lights as the plane circled twice, then made its final approach. Moscow was nothing short of massive—nine hundred seventy square miles in size, with a population of over twelve million, according to Megan's study material, making it every bit as large as New York City.

Snow encased the city like a blanket, piled high next to

the airstrip as the plane rolled toward a hangar. Wolfgang couldn't see people, but the lights from downtown Moscow were so bright, they reflected off the low-hanging cloud cover and shone over the airstrip, almost like ballpark lights.

"Wolfgang, let's go!"

Edric appeared from his bunk room, dressed in a premium business suit, matched with leather shoes and gold cufflinks. Lyle was similarly dressed. But when Wolfgang stood, he saw Megan appear from the bunk room, and the breath caught in his throat. She wore a conservative women's pantsuit with a white blouse and no jewelry, yet somehow, the fitted garment made her look more glamorous than a ball gown would have. She'd pulled her hair up into a bun and applied only a little makeup, all to downplay her appearance, he figured.

It wasn't working. At least, not with him.

"Carry the bags," Edric said, motioning to the stack of suitcases near the door. They contained clothes for appearance but housed Lyle's laptops and the communications equipment they would need. If the Russians searched the bags and found anything, it could be dismissed as equipment for Wolfgang and Kevin—the bankers' security detail.

"How's it feel doing the grunt work?" Kevin asked as he and Wolfgang scooped up bags.

During their last two missions, Wolfgang had assumed primary roles alongside Megan, leaving Kevin to perform backup functions. Kevin wasn't pleased with the arrangement and wasn't shy about saying so.

"Oh, you know me, Kev. Happy to save the world in any capacity."

The airlock on the door hissed, then swung open, and the automatic staircase descended toward the tarmac.

Wolfgang stumbled back, the air frozen in his lungs as a gust of Russian wind tore into the plane. It wasn't just cold —it was hard and sharp, like a baseball bat being rammed down his throat and smacked against his lungs. He gasped for air and swallowed, then watched as Edric ducked through the door and stepped down the stairs as if he were disembarking onto a Caribbean island.

"Holy cow," Wolfgang muttered. He glanced at Kevin and knew his fellow operator wanted to make a snide comment but was too busy recovering from the cold himself.

They stumbled after the others, down the stairs, and toward the stretch limousine waiting twenty yards away. It was black, built out of an elongated Hummer, and its tires were caked with packed snow and ice. Exhaust fumes gathered beneath the rear bumper.

"Put the bags in the back," Edric said, motioning without meeting Wolfgang's eyes.

He followed Kevin to the rear, while the limo driver hurried to open the door for Edric, Megan, and Lyle.

Wolfgang fumbled with the bags as his fingers turned

numb. Even through his thick cotton pants and his favorite peacoat, the wind sliced through him as though he were naked. "I take it back," he said. "Grunt work sucks."

Wolfgang hurried to shut the rear door, but Kevin stuck his arm up and blocked it.

"Are you screwing my sister?" Kevin's eyes were as cold as the wind, and his tone cut just as much.

Wolfgang blinked. "What?"

"You heard me. Are you screwing my sister?"

"No." Wolfgang dusted snow off his shoulders and turned toward the limo door.

Kevin caught him by the arm and turned him back. "I'm watching you, Wolf. I see the way you look at her. You're a good operator, and you cut me a break back in Paris, but you leave my sister alone, you hear? Back off." Kevin slammed the rear door, still glaring Wolfgang down, then walked past him and slid into the limo without a word.

Wolfgang was stunned. For a moment, he forgot about the cold and thought about Megan. The depth of her grey eyes and the way her mouth twitched when she tried not to smile. Even though Kevin shared nothing in the way of resemblance or personality with his half sister, it was no secret he was protective of her.

He can back off.

"Wolfgang! Get in here." Edric shouted from the limo.

Wolfgang shrugged off Kevin's aggressive warning and ducked inside the car. The interior was warm, with plush leather and a minibar with thermoses of hot Russian tea. Edric, Megan, and Lyle sat in the rear, stiff-backed and indifferent to their security detail. Wolfgang shut the door behind him and found a seat across from Kevin. The bigger man avoided his gaze as the limo slid into gear and turned toward Moscow.

[4]

In his imagination, Wolfgang pictured Moscow as something of a winter wonderland. It wasn't. What should have been white was grey, and what should have been grey was black. Snow mixed with mud, oil, and debris piled up next to the buildings, and the sky was glum with not only clouds but the smog of automotive and industrial fumes.

The only splashes of color came from the occasional nightclub or bar that flashed past the limo on the way into the heart of the city. There were plenty of tall buildings, all rising out of the muck and reaching into the cheerless sky like fingers of a desperate humanity starved for sunshine.

The streets themselves were crowded, as Wolfgang would have expected in any city this size. Cabs, buses, and the occasional brave motorcyclist wound their way through the heart of the city, impervious to the time of day or temperature. Wolfgang wondered what it must be like to live in a place like this—so cold and crowded and stained by decades of controversial history.

Only, to the Russians, it wasn't controversial history, he realized. It was simply *their* history, and much like Americans, they probably didn't overthink it. This was home, cold or not, crowded or not.

Wolfgang leaned back in his seat and indulged in a brief smirk. He'd had similar thoughts about Cairo only a few weeks prior. It was the polar opposite of Moscow in almost every way, yet people there also called it home. He wondered if a Russian or an Egyptian had ever visited St. Louis and asked themselves, "Why would anyone live here?"

The limo swung and glided down the big streets like a yacht, slowly winding its way deeper into the city until at last it slid to a stop under the portico of the Hilton Moscow Leningradskaya, towering twenty-one floors above street level. Edric flashed Wolfgang a look that said "showtime," and Wolfgang nodded. As soon as the Hummer stopped, he pushed the door open and stepped out, flinching in the blast of bitter wind before stepping to the side and waiting for Edric, Megan, and Lyle to climb out. They each waited without so much as glancing his way, and Wolfgang helped Kevin unloaded the luggage while the others hurried inside.

As Wolfgang towed the baggage into the hotel, he tipped his head back to glimpse the towering spire that jutted from the top of the building. He'd read about this building in one of Megan's travel books. It was built in 1954, one of seven sister buildings constructed during that time in the Stalinist neoclassical style—a mixture of 1930s American architecture and Russian neoclassical architecture that was already a fading memory.

The hotel, now renovated and operated by Hilton, was an homage to another time—a dark time, when the iron fist of the Communist Party held Russia in a death grip both colder and more deadly than the wind that now whipped through his coat.

"Wolfgang! Let's go," Kevin called from the steps.

Wolfgang hurried to follow. Edric checked them in to their suite, and the five of them piled into the elevator. Wolfgang sucked in deep breaths of warmer air and glanced at Edric. Before he could speak, Edric shook his head once and tilted his head toward the ceiling of the elevator. Wolfgang shot a quick look up and saw a security camera poking out of the woodwork, staring down at them like an eagle eying its lunch.

Crap. Is the entire hotel wired?

The elevator dinged to a stop, and they piled out onto dense red carpet. Their suite was just as fancy, featuring two rooms with giant king beds and a small sitting area in between. None of them spoke as they shut the doors, then Lyle knelt beside one of his bags and unpacked. A moment later, he opened what appeared to be a shaving kit, but after removing a razor and a cloth, he exposed some manner of electronic device housed inside that featured a switch and a row of lights. Lyle flipped the switch, then worked his way around the room, holding the device close to lamps, furniture, and wall molding.

Edric held a finger to his lips, and the group waited while Lyle conducted a ten-minute sweep of the suite, then returned and offered a nod. "It's clean."

"Very good," Edric said, walking to the minibar and pouring himself a glass of brandy. "Go ahead and unpack."

Lyle was already setting up computers on the table in the middle of the room, arraying laptops around himself and connecting them with wires. Wolfgang recognized some of Lyle's gadgets from previous missions, but conspicuously missing were Lyle's big screens, heavy-duty listening and communicating equipment, and boxes of "special purpose" gadgetry.

Wolfgang settled beside Lyle and watched as he input passwords into the computers, instantly converting them from innocent bankers' laptops into custom-programmed espionage processors.

"Do you use the hotel Wi-Fi?" Wolfgang asked.

Lyle chewed the tip of his tongue. "Any network I link

into can be used to track our location, so I piggyback onto cellular networks, which is actually more difficult to pinpoint since the devices are made to be mobile. With a little IP scrambling, we can stay hidden to the casual observer."

"What about the intentional observer?"

Lyle shrugged. "Best way to hide from a bloodhound is not to wake him up."

Wolfgang wasn't exactly sure what that meant, but decided not to press. Lyle needed to focus. Instead, he got up and walked to the window, pushing aside the curtain and staring out at the streets of Moscow. They stretched away as far as he could see into the Russian horizon.

Megan stepped up beside him, a drink in one hand. She pointed directly ahead. "There's the Kremlin. You can't see it at night, but it's just on the other side of those buildings."

"It's crazy," Wolfgang said, "to be this close."

"Russia isn't the Soviet Union. A lot has changed. And a lot hasn't, I guess." She took a sip of her drink, then turned away, leaving Wolfgang standing alone.

"We'll sleep in shifts tonight," Edric said. "Just to be safe. Wolfgang, you'll take the first—"

"Guys!" Lyle called from the computer, his voice an uncharacteristic shout. "We've got a problem."

Wolfgang and the others rushed back to the table, where Lyle leaned close to his primary computer screen.

"I logged into the secure server, just to check, and

there's an email from the CIA. Sparrow wants to meet . . . right now."

Edric scanned the screen, and his brow furrowed into a frown.

"What do you mean, right now?" Kevin asked. "The meeting was supposed to be tomorrow morning."

"Something went wrong," Edric said. "Sparrow moved up the timeline. Lyle, are there any other messages?"

"That's the only one. We can reply, but there's no guarantee anybody will see it before Sparrow's deadline."

"Shit," Edric muttered. He stepped away from the computer and took a sip of his brandy.

The room fell silent as everybody watched the tension play across his face.

"We can't go," Kevin said. "If the five of us leave now, we're certain to attract attention."

"Not only that," Megan chimed in, "we don't have enough intelligence. If the CIA is going to move it up on us like this, they owe us more details. I say we email them back, then wait for a response."

Edric scratched his cheek, then checked his watch. "No. We can't afford to wait. If Sparrow is under pressure, that probably means Koslov is under pressure, also. The CIA may not have additional details. The only way to be certain is to talk to Sparrow."

"It could be a trap," Wolfgang said. "What if the Russians busted Sparrow and now they're setting us up?"

"That's doubtful," Edric said. "Sparrow would have some kind of coded passkey—a word or an expression used to let the CIA know everything was kosher. Something he wouldn't have used if he were under duress."

"What if the Russians flipped him?" Lyle asked.

"If they flipped him, there would be no reason for him to advance the meeting and spook us," Edric said. "He'd just wait until tomorrow."

Everyone exchanged looks, then Edric set down his glass. "Wolfgang, you're coming with me. The rest of you stay put. Lyle, we need some comms."

Edric moved to his suitcase and stripped out of his business suit, quickly changing into a warmer and more flexible outfit suitable for an evening surfing the Moscow bars.

Wolfgang and Megan moved toward him as Lyle shuffled through his bags to find the communications gear.

"I don't like this," Megan said, lowering her voice. "We're going in blind. We need to wait."

Edric shook his head. "We can't afford to wait. If Sparrow is in trouble and we miss him tonight, we may not make contact tomorrow. If that happens, we have zero chance of completing our objective."

"I realize that, but—"

Edric held up a hand. "I've made my call. You, Kevin, and Lyle remain here. Wolfgang will be my backup. Two of us leaving the hotel shouldn't raise much attention."

Edric pulled a heavy overcoat around his shoulders,

nodded to the onlooking Charlie Team, then turned to Wolfgang. "You ready, Sunshine?"

———————

WOLFGANG FOLLOWED Edric into the blustering Moscow night, walking two blocks before Edric hailed a cab and told the driver in broken Russian to take them to the Red October district. Wolfgang flashed him a curious glance, but Edric waved him off. The cab driver took off, bolting into traffic and yanking them through turns between sips from a water bottle. Wolfgang caught a whiff and guessed that whatever the driver was drinking, it wasn't water.

Fifteen minutes and two near-death experiences later, the cab slid to a stop, and the driver muttered something in Russian. Edric handed him three one-thousand-ruble banknotes and waved away the change. The driver rocketed off only a millisecond after the door shut behind them.

Wolfgang started to speak, but Edric held up a finger. "Don't talk. Just listen. I brought you because you think better on your feet than Kevin does, and because I need Megan at the hotel to get everybody out in case things go sideways. Sparrow's message stipulated that we meet him in the Red October district at one a.m."

Edric gestured ahead, and as they walked, Wolfgang saw through the darkness to the towering bulk of a red brick building sitting on a slight rise directly ahead. Another ten

yards, and Wolfgang realized that the slight rise was actually an island situated in the middle of the Moskva River
with bridges connecting it to the rest of the city. At the
southern tip of the island, lit by powerful spotlights, the
statue of Peter the Great shot out of the river and reached
for the sky.

Wolfgang remembered it from reading about Moscow
on the plane and realized they must now be in downtown,
with the Kremlin only a stone's throw to the other side of
the island. His stomach twisted into a knot, and Edric
nodded at him once as if to say he knew what Wolfgang was
thinking.

"Stay loose and alert. Sparrow is meeting us at a nightclub called Bar Gypsy. It's on the island."

Edric paused at the edge of a pedestrian bridge sheltered by the shadows of an apartment building and reached
into his pocket. He passed Wolfgang an earpiece, and they
slid the tiny units into place while making a show of
rubbing their hands and glancing around as if they were lost
tourists.

Edric whispered, "All channels, this is Charlie Lead.
Comm check."

"Charlie Eye, online," Lyle said.

"This is Charlie One," Megan said.

"Charlie Two, loud and clear," Kevin said.

Wolfgang hesitated, still rubbing his hands together for

warmth. His official call sign was Charlie Three, but he could hear the tension in his teammates' voices.

He grinned at Edric. "This is Sunshine, ready to rock."

Edric flashed a brief smile. "Copy that, Sunshine. Let's roll."

WOLFGANG FOLLOWED Edric across the bridge while looking down at the black depths of the Moskva River. Chunks of ice dotted the water, crashing into one another as they slowly churned downstream. He shivered and looked back up. The lights of the Red October district were bright now, shining from rows of brick buildings as the faint beat of nightclub music made its way through the walls. He thought about being inside, in the warmth, and walked a little quicker.

Edric led the way, stepping off the bridges and waiting for traffic to clear before leading Wolfgang onto the island. They turned left, moving toward the statue of Peter the Great, and the music grew steadily louder. Tourists and locals alike stood close to the buildings, leaning over and talking quietly while they smoked. He caught the scent of marijuana and wondered how the hell a person grew weed in a place like this. Was it trucked in? From where?

Edric nodded at a tourist who asked him for directions, then shrugged and said, "*Ya ne govoryu.*"

The tourist scowled and stumbled on, clearly drunk enough to pass out at any moment.

Ahead, Wolfgang caught sight of the backside of the statue, and just before it, bright disco lights blasted from the dirty windows of the last building on the island. The music was loud now, and more tourists gathered at the end of the island, walking in and out of the nightclub through a door guarded by a burly man in a thick coat—who was also drunk. Over the door in large, multi-colored neon lights were the letters: GYPSY.

"Once we're inside, we split up," Edric whispered. "Stay close enough you can see me, but not so close that Sparrow will put us together."

"How will you find him?" Wolfgang asked.

"Prearranged activity signals. Just follow my lead."

They approached the door, and Wolfgang fell back a couple paces, allowing a young couple to slide into line ahead of him. The guard glanced at Edric's fake ID only momentarily before waving him through. The couple did the same, then Wolfgang flashed a smile and withdrew his fake Canadian passport.

The guard peered down at him, his eyes bulging and watering. He swayed on his feet a moment, and Wolfgang choked on the blast of vodka fumes assaulting his face. The guard waved him through without so much as glancing at the passport.

Inside, the music was as jarring an assault as the cold had been. Pounding, pulsating club beats rocked the old brick walls as people jammed in next to each other on every side, fighting their way to and from the bar and trampling each other as they approached the DJ stand. In the middle of the room was a rectangular pool built out of bricks with fountain jets shooting streams of water out from the edges and toward the middle. Coins glistened from the bottom of the pool, and drinks were stacked along its edges. Colored lights flashed from overhead, and fake palm trees rose from the extremities of the room, bending towards the middle.

What the heck kind of place is this?

Wolfgang searched the collage of faces, suddenly aware that he had lost sight of Edric. He stood on his toes and swept his gaze around the room, but the flash of the lights made it difficult to discern faces.

"Charlie Three, tone it down," Edric said over the earpiece. "Nine o'clock, ten yards."

Wolfgang stopped and turned toward his nine o'clock, where Edric stood at the bar, casually talking to the bartender. After the bartender passed Edric a beer, Edric dropped a ruble note on the counter and then turned away without looking at Wolfgang.

Wolfgang breathed a sigh, irritated with himself for

having allowed Edric to escape him, and then for allowing his stress to become obvious.

Stay loose. Stay focused.

Wolfgang moved to the edge of the room, relaxing his shoulders and taking a moment to smile at a girl as she stumbled past. She smiled back, her drunken eyes watery and distant, and Wolfgang couldn't help but compare her to Megan. Certainly, the girl was pretty, and had she been in control of her own drool, she might have been beautiful. But there was a shallowness to her posture, a simplicity to her personality that was evident at first glance. It made him think of Megan and the way she laughed and how quickly her mind worked.

Wolfgang moved past the girl as she made a sloppy attempt of grinding on his leg, then glanced over his shoulder. Edric had moved to the pool and dropped three coins in it, then he removed his jacket and hooked it over his left arm before taking a seat at the far end of the club. He laid the jacket on the table, then set the beer down before unbuttoning the top two buttons of his shirt and leaning into the corner.

Those will be the activity signals. Now we see if Sparrow is for real.

Wolfgang settled into the shadows and winced as the first flash of a headache set in. The harsh cold, now replaced by the oppressive music, was too much for his tired, jet-lagged brain to handle. The first wave of pain passed but was then replaced by another more prominent pound.

The DJ jumped up onto his table, then planted his face near a mic and shouted a long stream of excited Russian. Everybody cheered, and the lights flashed, then the music grew even louder.

"Charlie Three, what have you got?" Megan said.

Wolfgang cupped a palm over his right ear, blocking out some of the noise as he tried not to shout his response. "Charlie Lead is in position. All clear."

"Any sign of target?"

"Negative."

Wolfgang glanced around the room, searching for somebody who stuck out from the rest—maybe a white male in a trench coat with "CIA Spy" written across his back. His eyes landed on the girl from a few moments earlier, and he watched as she danced with a man twice her age, laughing and grinding against him. She stumbled, caught herself on the edge of the pool, then puked into the water.

I'll bet that happens a dozen times a night.

He rubbed his lip and closed his eyes for just a moment, soothing the headache by blocking out the lights. It was a momentary reprieve, but it helped. When he opened his eyes again, somebody sat at the table across from Edric.

"Charlie One, I have the target with Charlie Lead," Wolfgang said. He moved a few feet to the right, keeping close to one of the fake palm trees as he gazed across the crowd to where Edric sat across the table from a woman.

Of course Sparrow could be a woman. Why not?

Wolfgang hadn't considered this possibility, and for a second he wondered if the woman was another drunk girl hitting on Edric. But no, the body language was all wrong for that. They both sat casually, neither looking the other in the eye as their lips moved.

The woman brushed her hair behind her ear and took a sip from a beer. She was tall and skinny to the point of looking malnourished, with raven hair and pale European skin. She set her hand on the table, palm down, and when she lifted it, Wolfgang caught sight of something small on the table—a flash drive, maybe. She covered the item with a cocktail napkin and passed it to Edric without a word. Edric accepted it and nodded once.

"They're wrapping up," Wolfgang whispered. He glanced around the room, his instincts kicking in as he remembered that Edric needed surveillance.

"Is Sparrow still there? Has he said anything?" Megan asked.

"Sparrow is a she. They're talking now. I think—" Wolfgang froze, the blood turning to ice in his veins as his gaze passed over then ratcheted back to a big, dark-haired man on the other side of the room. His black eyes were as penetrating as spotlights, and his enormous nose twisted to one side.

Twisted by being broken. Broken by being smashed with a toilet lid.

Wolfgang recognized him. In fact, Wolfgang was responsible for his broken nose—a parting gift he'd left the Russian during the Paris mission. He'd nicknamed the man Ivan, and the two of them had engaged in a knock-down, drag-out that almost killed them both.

Wolfgang's mind froze as he struggled for his next move. Run? Signal Edric? Hide?

It was too late. Ivan's sweeping gaze passed across the room, sliding past Wolfgang and then ratcheting back, just as Wolfgang's had. Their eyes met, and momentary confusion passed across Ivan's face—the confusion a person feels when they see somebody familiar but in the wrong context.

A wolfish grin spread across Ivan's face, and he lifted a finger. "*Yemu!*"

Almost immediately, everything went to hell. Three more Russians, all of them as big and butt-ugly as Ivan, surfaced from the crowd. Two of them turned toward Ivan, then followed his pointing finger, but the third pointed toward Sparrow and let out another shout. "Zhenshchina!"

At that call, the first two turned back toward Sparrow, and Wolfgang saw the panic cross through Edric's eyes.

"All channels, abort!" Edric snapped, then he flicked at his ear, and Wolfgang saw the earpiece drop out. Edric ground his shoe over it, obliterating it, then rushed for the nearest door.

"What's going on?" Megan shouted. "Charlie Three, what do you have?"

Wolfgang didn't have time to respond. Ivan was bolting through the crowd like a running back, plowing people out of his way as he crashed toward Wolfgang. "Hello, Amerikos!" His voice boomed like a loudspeaker as the gap between them melted away.

Wolfgang dove to the ground, just missing Ivan's clutching hands as he skidded to the floor, sliding toward the pool over puddles of spilled drinks. People screamed, and high heels stabbed at the floor on all sides while the music continued to pound. Wolfgang heard a gunshot, then rolled to his left just in time to miss a stampede of drunks surging toward the door. He grabbed the edge of the pool and hauled himself to his feet, his head swimming. A quick glance over his shoulder confirmed that Edric and Sparrow were gone, leaving nothing behind except the coat and the half-finished drinks. He glimpsed the three Russians surging through the back door, shouting as one of them waved a pistol, but he didn't have time to follow. Ivan was just behind him, his feet pounding like a herd of elephants.

"Welcome to Mother Russia, Amerikos. How good you are to visit!"

Wolfgang whirled to see Ivan only feet away, his eyes alight with enraged fire. Ivan's right hand disappeared into his coat, and Wolfgang winced, bracing himself for a handgun. But Ivan's fist reemerged clad in a pair of brass knuckles, the tips of the weapon glistening. "Now I give you bruises vodka will not treat!"

Ivan charged, and Wolfgang had no chance of outrunning him. He dropped his hand to the edge of the pool and wrapped his fingers around the first thing he touched—a martini glass. With a flick of his hand, he flung the alcohol into Ivan's face, then slid to the right. The big Russian stumbled, then slipped on a puddle as he fought to wipe the liquor out of his eyes. Wolfgang pressed his advantage, moving in and driving his foot into Ivan's shin.

The Russian went down with a grunt of pain, but Wolfgang didn't wait to see where he fell. The club was almost empty now, the music stuck on short repeat as people screamed and sirens rang in the distance. Wolfgang bolted for the door, just sliding through it as Ivan clambered to his feet and dashed after him. The big man bellowed so loud Wolfgang felt it in his bones, and the sound sent a chill up his spine.

Oh, crap.

Wolfgang slid outside and frantically searched for a place to hide. There was nothing. The sidewalks between the buildings and the river were desolate, save for a waist-high wall that rose from the edge of the island, protecting people from the icy currents below.

The river.

His mind spun into action, and he rushed toward the wall as Ivan barreled out of the club just behind him. The big man roared in delight at the sight of his quarry, and Wolfgang sprinted for the wall—ten yards, then five—then he was at the wall, throwing one leg and then the other over the top.

"You will not swim tonight, little fish!" Ivan yelled as he ran.

Wolfgang pushed himself off the edge of the wall, his feet coming to rest on the last few inches of pavement on the other side, only a breath away from the precipice. He crouched below the top edge of the wall as the river churned five yards farther down. He imagined he could feel waves of cold radiating up from the water, promising hypothermia and impending death if he slipped.

Ivan's feet pounded, and Wolfgang braced himself, clutching the top lip of the wall with his left hand and keeping his right hand free. Then Ivan's face appeared over the top of the wall, scowling down toward the river as he reached out with both hands to break his charge.

Wolfgang never gave him the chance. Reaching out with his right hand, Wolfgang grabbed a fistful of Ivan's shirt and yanked forward. The violence of the motion, combined with the momentum of Ivan's charge, was too much for the Russian to counteract. He rocketed over the top of the wall, both arms flailing for something to grab onto. There was nothing, and Wolfgang released him only a split second before being jerked downward himself.

Ivan crashed the final five yards through the air with a

frantic howl, then hit the water with a splash large enough to wash away an island nation. Wolfgang winced as icy water pelted his exposed skin, but there was no time to wait around. He hoisted himself back over the wall and dropped onto the sidewalk, searching for Edric. His boss was gone, as was Sparrow, but in the distance, Wolfgang heard shouting and the slamming of car doors.

His head spun in momentary panic as his fingers turned numb in the cold, his headache forgotten in the rush of the moment. Conflicted thoughts crowded his mind as he suddenly realized that during his fight with Ivan, he'd lost his earpiece, cutting him off from the rest of the team.

Wolfgang ignored the momentary panic he felt as something clicked in his mind—something Edric had purposefully left behind. Wolfgang rushed back into the nightclub, clearing the full length of the dance floor in a few quick strides before snatching up Edric's coat and rocketing back to the door. He could hear police cars rolling over the automotive bridge fifty yards away, sirens blaring.

Wolfgang pulled the coat on, wrapping the warm garment close around his shivering body before digging his hand into the pocket. His fingers closed around the flash drive as he dashed back across the pedestrian bridge.

[6]

THE HOTEL ROOM door hadn't yet closed before the remaining members of Charlie Team burst around the corner, already peppering Wolfgang with questions. He shut the door and held up a finger, gasping for breath and still shaking from the cold.

Without the earpiece, Wolfgang could not communicate the resolution of the nightclub fiasco to Megan and the team, leaving him with nothing to do except find his own way back to the hotel. He ran five blocks from the Red October district before he found a cab, and since he'd forgotten the Russian part of the Hilton's name, and since he couldn't speak any other Russian, all he could do was repeat "Hilton!" and point in the general direction of the hotel.

The cabby took him halfway before becoming frustrated and demanding payment, at which point Wolfgang remembered that Edric's rubles were in his pants pocket, not his coat pocket.

So Wolfgang ran again, the cabby halfheartedly chasing him for two blocks before giving up. Now, a full hour after hurling Ivan into the icy depths of the Moskva River, Wolfgang was back in the hotel room, freezing cold and exhausted.

"What happened?" Kevin bellowed, his face a shade of hellfire red.

Wolfgang wheezed and held up a finger again.

"Back off," Megan snapped. "Lyle, make some coffee. Kevin, find some blankets." She patted Wolfgang on the back, helping him to clear his throat, then guided him into the sitting room.

He sat down and rubbed his hands up and down his arms. A moment later, Kevin appeared with a blanket, tossing it at him with a semi-disgusted scowl. Wolfgang took it without shame, wrapping it around his shoulders as his heartbeat finally slowed.

How is it possible to run so hard and be so cold?

"Where's—" Kevin started, but Megan glared him into silence.

A couple minutes passed, then Lyle appeared from the minibar with a Styrofoam cup of coffee. Wolfgang slurped down a scalding sip and nodded his thanks. He didn't like coffee, but right then, he would've drunk hot dishwater.

"Are you injured?" Megan asked.

Wolfgang shook his head. "I'm good."

"Okay. What happened?"

Wolfgang ran his hand through his hair and sat forward, taking another sip of the coffee.

"There were Russians at the club, looking for Sparrow, I think. They got Sparrow and Edric."

"*Got* them? What do you mean *got* them?" Kevin said.

"I mean they arrested them!" Wolfgang glared at him. "What do you *think* I mean?"

Megan held up a hand. "Calm down, both of you. Wolf, start from the beginning."

Wolfgang rubbed his tired eyes. "There was a Russian . . . he recognized me from Paris."

Megan frowned. "From Paris?"

"You remember the guy I beat over the head with a toilet lid? At that hotel in Paris?"

Recognition dawned over Megan and Kevin.

"Yeah, well, he was at the nightclub. He recognized me, and I guess he assumed I was there because of Sparrow."

Lyle appeared from the next room, carrying a laptop. He flipped the laptop around. "This guy?"

Wolfgang peered at the screen, then snapped his fingers. "Yes! That's him. How did you know?"

Lyle smirked. "Your watch, dude. We saw the whole thing."

Wolfgang glanced down at the watch, suddenly remembering the camera mounted in its case. In the heat of the moment, he'd completely forgotten about that feature. "So, you saw me . . ."

"Toss his ass in the river?" Megan finished. "Yeah, we saw it. Hell of a thing to do to an SVR officer."

"SVR?"

Lyle tapped on the laptop, then spun the screen around again.

"Ivan Sidorov, Russian Foreign Intelligence Service."

"Wait, his name is *actually* Ivan?"

He scanned the screen. The document on view was some kind of personnel file, maybe from the CIA, boldly featuring Ivan's face at the top of the screen with details about his identity written beneath.

"Holy cow," Wolfgang muttered. "He's a senior officer. This guy is a big deal."

"Yep." Lyle flipped the computer shut, then sat down. "And I'm guessing he's not the president of your fan club."

Wolfgang winced, remembering the chunks of ice floating down the Moskva River.

Did I kill him?

"We're screwed," Kevin said, turning from the group and running both hands through his hair. "You guys realize that, right? The SVR has Edric. They have Sparrow. We're screwed!"

"Kevin." Megan snapped her fingers. "Sit. Now."

Kevin dropped to a chair like a cowering dog, ducking his head to avoid her gaze.

Megan's eyes blazed, then she turned back to Wolfgang. "Did you see where they took Edric?"

"No, Ivan had three guys with him, and they all went after Edric and Sparrow. There's no way they got out."

"So, they took them to the Ministry of Defense headquarters," Kevin muttered. "Then a freaking gulag!"

Megan snapped her fingers again, and Kevin actually flinched.

The powers of a big sister.

Wolfgang rubbed his temples, closing his eyes and trying to recall everything he could about the other three Russians with Ivan—the ones who took Edric and Sparrow. They were big, they were ugly, and they were Russian. Beyond that, he couldn't think of any distinguishing details.

"I'll phone it in," Lyle said. "We better pack up."

Wolfgang looked up. "What?"

Lyle picked up the computer and shuffled toward his bag. "I said I'll call it in to SPIRE headquarters. We'll need to leave the city until we hear back."

"Leave the city? Have you lost your mind? They have Edric!"

Megan held up a hand. "Calm down, Wolfgang. Lyle's right. It's protocol."

"Protocol? To hell with protocol!" Wolfgang stood up. "We're not leaving this city until Edric leaves with us."

"Bold words from the guy who lost him," Kevin said.

Megan started to interject, but Wolfgang spoke first. "You're right, Kevin. I *did* lose him. So now I'm gonna get him back, and the three of you are going to help me. Because that's your job. Understand? Lyle, unpack that computer."

Lyle hesitated, then everybody looked at Megan. She said nothing.

Wolfgang pinched his eyebrows together. "Seriously? How is this even a question? You want to quote protocol and—"

Megan held up a hand. "Wolfgang, chill. You're right . . . we're not leaving."

Wolfgang nodded a couple times, too wound up to calm himself down. "Damn right, I'm right! Lyle, hand me that computer."

He sat down again and fumbled in the pocket of Edric's coat, producing the flash drive a moment later and accepting the computer from Lyle.

"What's that?" Lyle asked. "It could have a virus! Don't put it in my—"

Wolfgang ignored him and jabbed the drive into the side of the laptop, then navigated to the files application while everybody else leaned in.

"Where did you get that?" Megan asked.

"Sparrow brought it for Edric. He left it behind. I guess he knew he was gonna get caught."

The group grew quiet as the files populated. There were over a dozen, all PDFs, all titled in Cyrillic. Wolfgang double-clicked on the first one, then expanded it to fit the screen. It was a diagram depicting what looked like a scuba diver's backpack. Wolfgang zoomed in on it, then panned from one end to the other. The schematics detailed pipes, wires, and various electronic components, but all the notes were in Russian. Wolfgang clicked out of the file and opened the next four. All the designs were similar to the first, detailing different types of machinery. Wolfgang couldn't make heads or tails of it. The sixth PDF, however, was a drawing he'd have recognized anywhere.

"Is that a football stadium?" Megan asked.

Wolfgang's blood turned cold. "It's Soldier Field, in Chicago."

"Oh shit . . ." Kevin said. "So, these drawings—"

"Are for a chemical weapon deployment system," Megan finished. "Big enough to take out sixty thousand people."

The room fell silent as they all processed what they were looking at. It took Wolfgang a minute to fully appreciate the gravity of the situation, but then his mind clicked into gear again, quickly unfolding the path of dominos that led into the future.

"The Bears are playing well this year," he said. "Imagine a playoff game. A full stadium. Thousands of tailgaters in the parking lot."

"But . . . why?" Lyle asked. "You can't seriously think the Russians want to bomb a football stadium. I mean, come on!"

Wolfgang clicked out of the drawing of Soldier Field, then navigated to the next document. This one featured pencil notes in the margins—rough English translations of more Cyrillic text. Seconds after scanning the page, he looked up. "They don't. The Russians know nothing about this."

Everybody crowded in around the screen, leaning down to read the compact document on view. It was blurry, probably photocopied multiple times, but the pencil notes were legible, alongside photographs in the main body.

Wolfgang set the laptop on the coffee table, then drained what remained of his lukewarm coffee. "The Russian Ministry of Defense has been infected by the same anarchist organization that we encountered in Paris. We asked ourselves before—why would the Russians develop illegal chemical weapons? They're a modern, civilized nation. The answer? They aren't developing them. A group of radical terrorists has infected the Russian government and is operating in secret in the heart of Moscow. They're the ones who recruited Koslov and forced him to design these weapons. The CIA has been tracking him for months, thinking the Russians are going rogue on the Chemical Weapons Convention, when in reality, the Russians don't have a clue."

"Or maybe they do," Megan said. "Maybe that's what this SVR guy—Ivan—is doing. He was in Paris, remember, sniffing out the same terrorists. Maybe he was at the club tonight because he thinks Sparrow, and now Edric, are part of the network. Maybe he's heading up an investigation into his own government."

Wolfgang made a noncommittal rock of his head. "Maybe, but Sparrow works for the CIA. Sparrow must have just found out about the Soldier Field attack, which is why she called the emergency meeting tonight and brought the flash drive to Edric. She's under pressure, probably from Ivan. She thinks Ivan is part of the terrorist ring."

"He could be," Lyle said. "Maybe that's why he wanted to stop Sparrow. How could we know?"

Wolfgang pictured Ivan in all his brutish glory—the look on his face when he saw Wolfgang—the delight and lust for blood. Then he remembered his conversation with Ivan back in the hotel bathroom in Paris, where they joked about beating each other to death.

Wolfgang opened his eyes and shook his head. "He's not one of the terrorists. If he was, his men would've shot Sparrow and Edric, not arrested them. As prisoners, they have the potential to talk—to tell stories he wouldn't want told if he were a terrorist. He's true SVR, and he arrested them because he's investigating them."

"This is huge," Kevin said. "We have to get this back to

corporate right away. They can use the files to uncover the whole thing."

"We can't do that," Wolfgang said.

"Why the hell not?"

"Because if we give them to corporate, they'll give them to the CIA. The CIA will use them for leverage against the Russians, which will inflame tensions. That's exactly what these anarchists want. My guess is, they planned to attack Soldier Field, then leave behind evidence that points to the Russians. For all we know, they're the ones who clued the CIA in on the chemical weapons program in the first place so that the Soldier Field attack would eventually lead to a war between the world's superpowers. It's an anarchist's dream. Meanwhile, Edric will spend days, if not weeks, in Russian custody. Remember, Ivan thinks Edric is a terrorist. What do you think he's doing to him right now? Cuddling? Edric doesn't have weeks, and he doesn't have days. We have to get him out, now."

"I follow your logic," Megan said. "But we can't just ignore a planned terrorist attack. We have to address that."

"We will," Wolfgang said. "We deal with the terrorists by giving the Russians a chance to clean up their own mess, thereby avoiding a standoff between our countries."

"So, we trade the flash drive for Edric?" Lyle asked.

"Ivan will never bite," Megan said. "If we show up with that flash drive, he'll be more convinced than ever that

Sparrow and Edric—and us, for that matter—are part of the organization."

Kevin tapped his knee with one hand. "There's got to be a way."

Wolfgang looked up from the laptop. "There is."

[7]

WOLFGANG LEANED over Lyle's shoulder, watching as his fingers flashed across the keyboard. Three laptops on the table were all linked by cables, and Lyle's attention turned from one to the next as he set up various programs, then waited for them to execute.

"What do you think?" Wolfgang asked.

Lyle shook his head, taking a sip of water before returning to the keyboard. "I don't know."

"Can you hack it?"

"I don't know."

"Isn't there, like, a back door or something?"

Lyle stopped tapping and looked up, his dark eyes blinking behind the ever-smudged glasses. Wolfgang took the hint and backed away as Megan walked into the room.

"I've got the tickets, and I coordinated with our pilots. Timing is tight, but he should be in Minsk on time."

"What about Kevin?" Wolfgang asked.

"Haven't heard back from him. Give him another few minutes before you call."

Wolfgang walked into the sitting room, leaning over the coffee table and the spread of maps that covered it. He picked up a pen and circled the headquarters for the Ministry of Defense, a giant block building on the bank of the Moskva River in the Khamovniki District. There was very little data about the structure available on the internet, but you didn't have to be a rocket scientist to know that it was probably one of the most secure structures in that part of the world. It was heavily guarded and littered with enough surveillance and security equipment to detect a mouse sneezing. Not ideal.

Megan leaned in next to him, lowering her voice. "Are you sure about this?"

"We can't break inside. It's impossible with the time and resources we have available. We have to be invited."

"I don't mean about the building. I mean the other thing . . . Ivan."

"Not really," Wolfgang said. "It's still possible he's a terrorist, or in league with the terrorists."

"And if he is, you'll never make it out. You understand that, right? You'll die."

Wolfgang met her gaze, surprised to see a new depth of

honesty there. Her usual wall opened for a moment, exposing a glimpse of genuine concern.

"We can't leave Moscow without exposing this plot," he said. "Too many lives are at stake. This is our best shot."

"Let me go with you, then," Megan said. "You'll need backup."

Wolfgang shook his head. "No, Ivan will get spooked. I have to do it myself. If anything goes wrong, I need you on the outside to clean up and get in touch with the CIA." He turned back to the map, tracing the outline of the streets leading away from the Ministry of Defense building. They were a complex maze of typical inner-city, two and four lanes, connected with roundabouts and traffic lights, with bridges leading across the river. It wouldn't be easy to navigate them under an emergency situation, but without an emergency, it would be impossible.

"Wolfgang?" Megan played with the end of her sleeve, then licked her lips and looked away.

"Yes?" The world slowed around him, and he couldn't hear Lyle's incessant typing anymore. The only person on the planet sat right in front of him.

"I thought I should say . . ."

The front door of the hotel blew open, and Kevin burst in, carrying two oversized duffel bags in one hand and a sack of carryout food in the other. Both items hit the floor, and Megan sat up, folding her arms and turning away from Wolfgang.

"Food? Really?" Megan said, not even trying to disguise the disgust in her tone.

"I'm hungry. Besides, if this harebrained plan of his ends like I think it will, I want a last meal."

Wolfgang pointed to the bags. "You find what we need?"

Kevin kicked the nearest bag, and the flap fell open, exposing the contents. Two heavy-duty firemen's uniforms, complete with helmets, boots, and face masks.

Wolfgang knelt and sifted through them, checking one jacket against his own torso. He nodded. "That'll do."

———

THE SUN BROKE OVER Moscow, bringing light but not much heat. A fresh snowfall had blanketed the city during the night, and snowplows ran up and down the streets, followed by salt trucks. Wolfgang's shoes crunched on the frozen sidewalks as he departed the hotel and turned north. He sucked in a deep breath of icy air, and his stomach growled. He'd skipped breakfast and also passed on Kevin's takeout. It was an uncomfortable decision, but probably best. Should things turn nasty, he didn't want to puke under torture.

He walked four blocks from the hotel, then slid his replacement earpiece into his right ear and adjusted it until it was comfortable. "Comm check. This is Sunshine."

Lyle said, "Charlie Eye, I've got you, Sunshine."

"Charlie One, online."

"Charlie Two, live and ready."

Wolfgang yawned twice, trying to clear the pressure in his ears. His heart thumped, and a strange tingling sensation ran up his fingers. Nervousness? Stress? Or a physiological warning that what he was doing equated to suicide? Probably the third option.

"What can you see, Charlie Eye?" Wolfgang asked.

"Your jacket," Lyle said.

Wolfgang looked down, realizing that after leaving the hotel, he'd put on Edric's coat, oblivious to the fact that it blocked the camera now built into the third button on his button-down shirt. The previous night, Lyle had removed the camera from Wolfgang's watch and fit the compact electronic unit into the thick folds of the flannel shirt. The camera now blended into the middle of an oversized black button, pointed outward only a couple inches above Wolfgang's belly button.

"Right," Wolfgang said. He unbuttoned the jacket and opened it, shivering as a fresh blast of wind ripped him straight to the bone. "How about now?"

"All clear, Sunshine."

Wolfgang steeled his mind against the next step. In his head, the night before, this seemed like such a good idea. Now it felt like volunteering to feed himself to a lion.

He stepped to the curb and held out his hand, waving

down a cab. The car squealed to the curb, and Wolfgang ducked into the back seat, then produced a notecard from his pocket and passed it to the driver. Charlie Team had copied the address, in Cyrillic, off of the internet, but Wolfgang wasn't sure how good his Russian penmanship was.

The cabby squinted at the card, then shot Wolfgang a look through the mirror that said he recognized the address. He rattled off a string of surprised Russian, but Wolfgang waved him down and pointed to the card. "Take me there. This address. Da. This address."

The driver shrugged, then shifted into gear and took a sip from a thermos. Wolfgang caught a whiff of something that wasn't coffee and rolled his eyes.

Starting out great.

"Charlie Eye, do you have me?" he whispered.

"Copy that, Sunshine. We have you en route."

Lyle had implanted a GPS tracker into Wolfgang's shoe, which would be helpful so long as he *kept* his shoes. He wasn't sure what the protocol was in Russian prisons, but he was pretty sure that at some point, you lost your shoes.

Wolfgang couldn't help but admire the Russian landscape under the blanket of fresh snow. Before the white turned to grey, and the grey turned to black, Moscow was actually a beautiful place. Still not the winter wonderland he hoped for, but in a way, it was more striking than that. It was real, with old brick buildings burdened by snowcapped roofs and icicle-lined eaves, frozen streets with occasional cars rolling in and out of them, and a parking lot covered in ice now populated by kids on skates. Parents stood next to the lot, taking pictures and calling out encouragement to struggling youngsters, then hurrying to pick them up when they crashed down.

Wolfgang recalled Sting's classic song about the Cold War, and it brought a whimsical smile to his face.

The Russians love their children, too.

He turned to face the front of the cab and drew a long breath. The Russians loved their children, and so did the Americans and the Parisians, and every parent scattered around this crazy world who wanted nothing more than to raise their offspring in peace and safety amid an ordered society—a society that these anarchists, by any means possible, wanted to rip down. Wolfgang closed his eyes, and for the first time in weeks, allowed himself to think of Collins— his bedridden sister back in New York. He saw her tiny body wracked with disease and the loneliness in her eyes as she clutched her teddy bear and watched SpongeBob on loop, with nobody but tired nurses to talk to. He remembered his own cowardice standing in front of that facility and not having the courage to go upstairs—not having the courage to look his own sister in the eye.

Instead, he ran. He waited by the phone for Edric's next assignment, even though the dust had barely settled over Cairo, and when that assignment didn't come for months,

Wolfgang went to Kansas City and bought a needlessly expensive car because the silence in his apartment and the guilt in his soul needed to be blocked by the loudest distraction he could find.

Are you sure about this?

The voice in his head pressed into his weary thoughts, and Wolfgang sank his fingers into the armrest, forcing himself to picture Collins again. Her beautiful, childish face, so full of life, and so crushed by the brokenness of her body.

Nobody cared about Collins. She was a disabled orphan girl. A forgotten inconvenience of society. Nobody cared about her dreams or her birthday or what her favorite color was. Nobody cared that she didn't have friends at school and couldn't remember her mother.

Nobody cared, but Wolfgang did, and he cursed himself for not being there. Yet, on the far side of the world, he was taking actions that were for Collins as much as any child who hoped to grow up in a peaceful, safe world. He may not be leaning next to her bed, but he was still there for her . . . wasn't he?

"Are you sure about this?"

Wolfgang opened his eyes. This time, Megan's voice rang through his earpiece. He looked out the window to see the cab pulling up in front of the headquarters of the Ministry of Defense, and the fear in his mind evaporated. Now, all he felt was anger and resolve.

"Copy that, Charlie One," Wolfgang said. "Never been more sure."

He paid the driver and stepped out of the cab, then looked down the sidewalk and up the steps toward the perimeter fence that encircled the giant block building directly ahead. Security cameras poked out from the top of the wall at regular intervals.

This is it.

"Okay, Charlie Team," Wolfgang said. "Sunshine going offline. Don't leave me hanging, guys."

Wolfgang pretended to run his hand through his hair as he flicked the earpiece out of his ear. It landed on the sidewalk, and he crushed it with his heel, then turned toward the guardhouse. The camera and the GPS unit were risks enough—the Russians would find the earpiece immediately, and that would wreck his entire plan.

As Wolfgang turned off the sidewalk and followed the concrete path to the guardhouse, he saw the two guards straighten, then one of them stepped out and held up a hand. He carried an assault rifle, and his face featured the hard lines of a man who wasn't in the mood for jokes.

"*Ostanovka!*"

Wolfgang offered his most disarming smile. "Good morning, gents. I'm here to see Ivan Sidorov. Can you tell him the Amerikos has arrived?"

[8]

WOLFGANG WASN'T sure if the guard recognized the name of Ivan Sidorov, but he shouted something at his companion, then placed both hands on his rifle and pointed it at Wolfgang.

"*Ruki vverkh!*"

Wolfgang didn't know what that meant but concluded that it was a safe bet to stick his hands up, so he did. The guard kept him at gunpoint while the second soldier made a phone call.

"Tell him it's urgent, if that helps," Wolfgang said. "And tell him I'm sorry about last night. I never go home with somebody on the second date, but I've reconsidered."

The muzzle of the rifle twitched. Wolfgang took his cue and shut up. The second man slammed down the phone and burst out of the shack, shouting at his companion and brandishing his rifle.

"*Opuskat'sya!*" Both men shouted, taking several steps forward and jabbing with the rifles.

"So you *do* know him!" Wolfgang laughed, dropping to his knees and placing both hands behind his head. "I thought you might. By the way . . . he's okay, right? No pneumonia or anything?"

Another chorus of shouts, then his hands were wrapped behind his back and cuffed in place. Five minutes later, he was blindfolded and being dragged through a side door into the massive building, one gun at his back and another jabbed into his side. Wolfgang stumbled along, trying to keep up with the bigger men as lights faded in and out through the blindfold and other footsteps rang around him.

Still got my shoes. Still got my shirt. Still got Lyle.

Wolfgang felt an elevator dropping beneath him, then he was yanked down a hallway that sounded like concrete beneath his shoes. A moment later, he was shoved into a sitting position and uncuffed. Powerful hands jerked his arms in front of him, then new cuffs snapped into place, and the blindfold was removed.

Wolfgang blinked in the bright light, but he didn't really need to see. He could feel the cold steel of an interrogation table beneath his palms and the rigid discomfort of a chair made of similar construction beneath his butt.

Outstanding. Glad we skipped the foreplay.

One guard stomped through the door and slammed it shut while the second retreated to a corner and kept his rifle trained on Wolfgang.

Wolfgang leaned down until he could reach his face with his hands, then rubbed his eyes. "Listen, Yuri. Ivan's not gonna keep me waiting, is he? I'm on a tight schedule." The guard said nothing, and Wolfgang smiled. "You guys love the stone-faced look, don't you? Is that something they teach you in Russian elementary school? 'Yuri! Stand here and look like statue!'" Wolfgang mimed his best stone-faced expression while adopting a Russian accent. The guard still said nothing, but the hint of a smile played at the corner of his lips.

He speaks some English.

Wolfgang prepared another probing jab, but before he could speak, the door burst open, and SVR Officer Ivan Sidorov barreled in like a charging rhinoceros. The door clapped shut as Ivan stood just behind the angled lights, glowering down at Wolfgang, then he jerked his head at the door and muttered something in Russian.

The guard nodded, then disappeared through the door. A second later, the bolt slid shut.

Hmm. I don't like that.

Ivan stood in the shadows a moment, still invisible thanks to the blast of light that glared down at Wolfgang. Then he placed both meaty hands on the table and slid in front of the light so his head blocked it, now haloed like a demented angel. Wolfgang faced him, unblinking. The Russian's hair was disheveled, and there was two days of stubble on his cheeks. His eyes were as cold and heartless as Wolfgang had ever seen them, glowering down with enough menace to fry an egg. So close that Wolfgang could smell the sour odor of Russian tea on Ivan's breath.

Wolfgang pictured the big man charging at him the night before. He saw him hurtling over the wall, frantically grabbing at thin air before crashing into the icy depths below. Even here, handcuffed to a table and probably about to be shot, he couldn't help feeling a little sorry about that.

"Glad you're okay, Ivan," Wolfgang said. "You really shouldn't go swimming this time of year."

Ivan's right hand shot out like a striking snake, and he slammed the table between Wolfgang's hands. The sound was as loud and sudden as a gunshot, reverberating off the walls and filling the room.

Wolfgang didn't move. He didn't so much as blink. He just stared at the Russian as his stomach flipped like a carnival ride.

Dear God, what was I thinking?

Ivan kept his hand only millimeters from Wolfgang's chest and continued to glower. Seconds ticked by, then a soft smile tugged at the corners of Ivan's mouth. After kicking back a second chair and settling into it, he reached into his pocket and produced a pack of cigarettes and a lighter. He lit a smoke and took a long drag, never taking his gaze off Wolfgang, then he blew smoke toward the ceiling and grunted. "You know something, Amerikos? I was wrong about you. You *do* have stones."

Wolfgang returned the smirk and turned both palms up. "How's your head, Ivan?"

Ivan sucked down the cigarette and grimaced. "Russian heads are made of iron, Amerikos. But a toilet seat . . . it hurt like a bitch."

"You treat those bruises with some vodka?"

"With vodka and good Russian women." Ivan held out the cigarette. "Smoke?"

Wolfgang nodded. "Da."

Ivan placed the smoke between Wolfgang's lips. Wolfgang took a slow drag, then coughed.

Ivan laughed, returning the cigarette to his own lips. "No such cigarettes in America, eh?"

Wolfgang shook his head, his eyes watering.

Ivan extinguished the smoke against the tabletop. "You should not have come, Amerikos. Now I must make example out of you."

"I understand," Wolfgang said. "Russian justice, da?"

"Da. Russian justice."

Wolfgang's heart thumped, but he resisted the urge to swallow.

Now or never.

"Whenever you catch those terrorists, I guess they'll also experience some Russian justice."

Ivan didn't move, but his left eyelid twitched.

Score.

"They gave you the slip in Paris, didn't they?" Wolfgang continued. "Me, too. But now you're on their trail again. Who would've thought hunting international terrorists would have led you right back to Moscow?"

Ivan ran his tongue across his lips, then spoke softly. "You're one of them. I know you are."

"Wrong. I'm hunting them, just like you."

Ivan snickered. "You expect me to believe this?"

"How else do you explain us crossing paths so many times?"

"Easy. You're one of them."

"What if I could prove I wasn't?"

"How would you do that?"

"With documents. The woman you arrested last night? She's CIA. She had in her possession certain files pertaining to an imminent terrorist attack. An attack involving chemical weapons."

Ivan stiffened.

Pay dirt.

"You work for CIA?"

"No."

"I think you do."

"I don't. I work for, let's call it, a third party. I came to Moscow to disrupt an illegal Russian chemical weapons program. Only, after I got here, I realized the program isn't

Russian." Wolfgang leaned forward now, only inches from Ivan. "You have a highly organized group of anarchy terrorists operating dangerously close to the heart of your government, and you know it. You just don't know who they are. That's something I can help with."

Ivan held his gaze. "If what you say is true, you would contact American CIA. They would pay you."

"Sure they would. And then they would leverage those documents against fragile American-Russian relations. They might use it as an excuse to develop their own chemical weapons program. Who could blame them? It's the right thing to do, defensively."

"You do not love your country?"

"Oh, I do. More than any place on Earth, which is why I would love to see these terrorists succumb to Russian justice."

Ivan smirked. "I don't know who you are, Amerikos. I don't know if you work for CIA or these imaginary terrorists, but—"

"They're not imaginary. They're very real, and you know it."

"How can you be sure?"

"Because you're still here, talking to me."

Ivan folded his arms, then finally stood up. "I almost believe you, Amerikos, but truth is proven in Russia. We shall see what stories you tell when you have no fingernails."

Ivan rapped on the door, then shouted an order in Russian. Boots thumped on the concrete, and Wolfgang stood up, exposing the button camera in his shirt to his cuffed hands. He held up both thumbs, then looked toward the ceiling.

Nothing happened.

The door opened, and two guards appeared. Ivan snapped an order and gestured toward Wolfgang. They both turned to the table, and Wolfgang held up his thumbs again, glancing down to make sure the camera caught the gesture.

Nothing happened.

The two guards unlocked his cuffs, then pressed him against the wall before re-cuffing his hands behind his back. Ivan led the way out of the interrogation room, then down a hallway to an elevator. He pressed the down arrow as Wolfgang's head throbbed.

Come on, Lyle. Where are you?

"Hey, Ivan," Wolfgang said. "Mind if I pee?"

Ivan chuckled. "Where we go, there is drain in floor. You can pee while you sit."

A drain in the floor. That's not good.

The elevator dinged, then the door rolled open. Wolfgang swallowed again, then glanced over his shoulder. There were no sounds and nobody in sight, but he could see alarm systems and cameras in the ceiling.

Now, Lyle. Now!

The guards stepped forward, shoving Wolfgang along with them. Wolfgang dipped his toe and tripped, hitting his knees with a grunt and stalling the guards just short of the elevator. Both men muttered curses and grabbed him by the elbows, hauling him toward the open elevator.

And then it happened.

A red light flashed from overhead, and a screaming alarm ripped down the hallway. Wolfgang blinked, disoriented by the noise as if it were from a flash-bang grenade. He stumbled again, and the guards let him drop as everyone looked to the ceiling. Again the alarms screamed, this time followed by a computerized voice calling commands in Russian.

"*Pozhar!*" Ivan shouted. He rushed past the guards and stuck his head around the corner of the hallway.

Wolfgang heard the beat of more boots on the ground, and he grinned.

Nice job, Lyle.

Ivan turned on his heel and shouted something at the guards. They grabbed Wolfgang by the elbows, then hauled him down an adjoining hallway and to a flight of stairs. Wolfgang walked willingly, keeping his camera lens exposed as he moved. The alarm continued to blare overhead, followed by computerized commands that now cycled through Russian, German, Eastern European languages, and then English.

"Fire, fire. Evacuate the building."

Wolfgang grinned as the guards unlocked a metal door and dragged him into some kind of detention facility with steel doors on either side. They rolled one door open and slung Wolfgang inside, then the door crashed shut, and the guards disappeared.

Wolfgang lay on the floor, his ribs and elbow throbbing from the crash landing. He coughed and blinked, then sat up and shook his head. The alarm was distant now but still way too loud.

A dry voice croaked from the corner of the room. "Wolfgang?"

The man lying on a cot was half-covered by a thin blanket, and his hands were cuffed to the bed.

"Edric!" Wolfgang fought his way to his feet, impeded by his hands still cuffed behind his back, and stumbled to the bed.

Edric lay on his side, hunched on one elbow. His face was a mottled mess of bruises, and he wheezed with each breath. "What the hell are you doing here?"

Wolfgang knelt beside the bed and gave Edric a reassuring smile. "Lie back, Edric. We're getting you out of here."

[9]

"DID YOU GET THE DRIVE?" Edric asked.

Wolfgang shuffled toward the door, peering down the hall through reinforced glass. It was empty, for the moment, but the siren continued to blare, and red lights flashed.

He retreated into the cell and sat down, bracing his back against the wall before kicking off his shoes.

"What the hell are you doing?" Edric asked, his voice cracked with exhaustion.

"Stay quiet, Edric. The cell is bugged."

Edric lay back, casting an involuntary look at the ceiling.

Wolfgang finished with his shoes, then wiggled his wrists until they passed beneath his butt and were trapped under his thighs. He winced at the strain on his muscles but slowly wiggled his cuffed hands forward, down his thighs, and toward his knees. Finally, he bent forward far enough to loop the cuffs past his feet, and then sat back with a relieved grunt.

"Come here," Edric hissed.

Wolfgang looked to the window again, then crawled next to Edric's bed.

"Did you get the drive?" Edric whispered.

"Yeah, Lyle has it. Do you know what's on it?"

"Sparrow said there were plans for a chemical attack, and details about a terrorist network. She said something about a football stadium."

"Soldier Field. The plans are for a chemical attack during a ball game."

"Shit." Edric closed his eyes and ran a dry tongue over his lips.

"Where is she?" Wolfgang asked.

"Sparrow? I'm not sure. Maybe in one of the other cells."

Wolfgang stared at the wall as he puzzled through the pieces at hand. Something was missing. Something still didn't fit. If the terrorists were now operating inside Moscow and Ivan was hunting them, how did Sparrow obtain the files? Who leaked them? "Where did Sparrow get the files?"

"Koslov. Sparrow said he stole them."

"Where's Koslov now?"

"Hiding in the city. The terrorists are looking for him.

Sparrow wouldn't disclose the location until we transmitted the drive contents to the CIA."

"She couldn't do that herself?"

"Apparently, she was communicating to the CIA via another agent—a handler, if you will. Two days ago, the handler disappeared."

Wolfgang leaned against the wall. "The CIA pulled him. Another effort to maintain plausible deniability, I'm sure. But how did she contact us last night?"

"The CIA left her with a phone number to call if she had an emergency. It rang to a dead-end answering machine —not something she could transmit the files with. They left her high and dry, honestly."

Wolfgang assimilated the news and wondered if it changed anything. He decided it didn't and turned back to Edric. "Can you walk?"

Edric nodded.

"Good. The team is on their way. We've got to get Koslov."

"Why? We need to extract immediately."

"No. This man risked everything to expose what he thought was state-sponsored illegal weaponry. When he discovered he was actually being used by a terrorist network, he risked his life to thwart them. We came here to get him out, and that's what we've got to do. Whatever it takes."

Edric sighed. "Damn you, Wolfgang. You're too good a man for this job."

Wolfgang grinned. "Tell Megan, won't you?" He walked to the door, peering out through the window again. From somewhere in the distance, Wolfgang heard the shouts of guards rushing down distant hallways. The voices grew louder, joined by the perpetual whine of the fire alarm.

"Get up!" Wolfgang said, motioning to Edric. "They're coming!"

Edric hauled himself into a sitting position and swung his feet off the bed, his hand still cuffed to the cot. In the pool of light spilling through the narrow window, his face looked even worse than before. A spiderweb of bruises ran across his cheeks, and his nose was stuffed with tissue paper.

Wolfgang winced. "Ivan really worked on you, didn't he?"

Edric grunted, and then something flashed on the other side of the window.

"Stand back!" Wolfgang ducked to the side, then the door shook violently.

A moment later, it crashed open, and a big man in full firefighter gear with a giant oxygen tank on his back stepped inside. He took off his helmet and flashed Edric a big grin. "'Sup, boss?"

Megan piled in behind Kevin, also dressed in firefighter

gear. Hers was designed for a woman but still much too big for her, gathering around her ankles and sliding around on her shoulders like a sleeping bag.

She flipped her visor up and motioned to Wolfgang. "Hands!"

Wolfgang held out his hands, and Megan produced a small set of bolt cutters from her pocket. She cut the chain between his wrists, then hurried to free Edric. "Kevin, get the smoke ready!" Megan snapped.

Kevin hurried out of the cell, sliding the tank off his back and setting it down in one corner. Wolfgang and Megan helped Edric up and guided him out of the cell to where Kevin's duffle bag waited.

"Dress-up time!" Megan said. She unzipped the bag and dumped out two more firefighter suits, complete with boots and helmets.

Wolfgang and Edric changed as shouts erupted down the hallway.

"That would be the *real* firefighters," Kevin said. "Let's go!"

Wolfgang pulled on a fireproof jacket. "Wait! We have to find Sparrow. Check the other cells."

Megan grabbed his sleeve and jerked him toward the door. "We don't have time. Kevin, start the smoke!"

Wolfgang jerked his arm free. "I don't have time to explain—we need Sparrow."

He broke into a run down the short hallway, glancing

into one detention cell after another. They were all empty, with stripped mattresses on metal cots. No prisoners. No sign of Sparrow.

"Wolfgang!" Megan shouted. "We have to go!"

The stomps in the hallway pounded louder now. Kevin hesitated over the bottle, one hand near the nozzle as he glanced between Wolfgang and Megan. Wolfgang continued to run, checking the last five cells one at a time and grinding to a halt at the fourth one.

"Here! She's here! Kevin, come on!"

Wolfgang wrestled with the lock. It was electronic, and the door wouldn't budge. Kevin appeared next to him a moment later, the bottle in hand. With one powerful heave, he slammed the base of the bottle downward, obliterating the electronic lock. The door clicked, and Wolfgang shoved it open, concluding that the cell was better designed to keep people in than out.

Before he crossed the threshold, he already knew she was dead. Sparrow lay on her back, foaming saliva trailing down one cheek and her empty eyes staring up at the ceiling. Wolfgang slid to his knees and grabbed her wrist out of habit, feeling her cold, thin skin under his touch. Her eyes were sunken in, and patchy blotches covered her neck.

"She's dead," Kevin said. "Can we go now?"

Wolfgang held up a hand, his mind still racing. The frailty of her body—the way her skin clung to her bones, and the look in her eyes—he'd seen it all before. He felt through her pockets, finding nothing but a worn photograph of her with a man he didn't recognize. He pocketed the picture, then saw something glistening beneath the edge of her neckline. He pulled the shirt down just a little and exposed a metal chain around her neck, disappearing beneath the shirt. A quick tug of the chain produced a metal tag, stamped with Russian writing on one side.

"Wolfgang!" Kevin bellowed.

Wolfgang snatched the tag, breaking the thin chain and jumping back to his feet. He gave Sparrow another long glance, feeling a sudden wave of sadness consume him as he stared into her forlorn eyes. He nodded. "Okay. Let's go!"

They barreled out of the cell, and Wolfgang scooped up a helmet. Megan waited by the door, supporting Edric with one arm as Kevin slammed the bottle down on the floor and twisted the knob next to the nozzle. Wolfgang heard a soft click, then a hiss as gas burst from the top. A moment later, dense white fog filled the room, clouding near the floor and spilling toward them.

Chlorosulfuric acid. A smoke screen.

"Let's roll!" Kevin said, pushing from behind.

The group crashed out of the dentition facility and into the hallway, immediately colliding with four Russian firefighters carrying axes and fire extinguishers. They paused in confusion as Megan and Wolfgang crashed ahead hauling Edric, his body limp and his shoes dragging.

"*Gaz! Gaz!*" Megan shouted.

The brigade of firefighters looked toward the clouds of white smoke billowing from the detention facility, and their eyes turned wide. They walked backward, shouting into radios as Megan, Wolfgang, Edric, and Kevin barreled through.

"Charlie Eye, which way?" Megan shouted, cupping her free hand over her ear. She nodded a couple times, then pointed to the left as they approached a T in the hallway. Wolfgang wheeled in that direction, dragging Edric with him. A small crowd of Russians dressed in business suits were being ushered down the hallway by another line of firefighters. Red lights now turned to blue overhead, and the siren continued as the computerized voice cycled through languages.

"Gas contamination detected. Obtain fresh air, immediately."

A panicked shout rose from the crowd while some of the firefighters looked to the ceiling and frowned.

Wolfgang grinned. *Nice one, Lyle.*

They merged with the crowd, charging around the corner and toward the nearest exit. Russian security guards stood at the door, holding out their palms in an effort to check the flood of humanity, but there was no stopping the stampede. Wolfgang caught sight of the bright Russian sky through the double exit doors as the fire alarm blended with the whine of fire engines parked on the street. People screamed, crashing forward like a tidal wave toward the exit.

Then Wolfgang saw Ivan. The Russian stood next to the door, shouting into a cell phone, his face a dark shade of red. Wolfgang ducked his face, twisting away and shielding Edric. His elbow slammed into Ivan's arm, but the Russian didn't give him a second glance as the four burst into fresh air and crashed down the hillside.

Russian soldiers in full biochemical gear stood near the wall, corralling the evacuees into a group away from the exit, where they could be contained, evaluated, and treated. Wolfgang steered his small brigade of pseudo-firefighters away from the rest of the crowd and toward the nearest gate, where the Russian State Fire Service had run hoses through the wall and were busy pulling them toward the building.

As they neared the gate, a Russian soldier stepped into their path and held out a gloved hand. His breath hissed through a gas mask, and he shook his head. "*Ostanovka!*" he ordered.

They slid to a stop, and Megan tore the helmet off Edric's head, exposing his purple and swollen face. Edric played the part, hanging limp with the tip of his tongue protruding between his lips.

"*Gaz!*" Megan said theatrically. "*Gaz!*"

It was probably the only Russian word she knew, but Wolfgang didn't need to speak Russian to get the message, and neither did the soldier. He stepped back and motioned them through the gate, panic flooding his eyes.

The team barreled onto the street outside, now a mess of parked fire engines and snaking hoses. Megan led the way, hopping over hoses and sidestepping firefighters. She jabbed her chin toward a parked ambulance twenty yards away. It was a Mercedes Sprinter, painted yellow with the word *скорая* stenciled on one side.

Wolfgang powered through the last stretch, hauling Edric to the back of the van as the doors burst open and Lyle appeared, a headset clamped over his ears, and his array of laptops scattered over the stretcher in the middle of the ambulance.

"Glad you could make it," he said. "Let's roll!"

They hauled Edric inside and set him in the nearest seat, then Kevin slammed the doors from the outside and rushed around to the front door. Wolfgang tossed his helmet to the floor and peeled the jacket off, surprised by the sweat streaming down his back.

I'm sweating in Moscow. Now, there's a story for the grandkids.

Edric leaned against the wall, wiping his face and casting a glance around his team. Then he let loose with a quick chuckle. "You guys are idiots, you know that?"

Megan patted him on the shoulder, then sat down and fastened her seatbelt in one of the EMT seats. "Don't laugh yet, boss. We're still in Moscow. Kevin, let's move!"

Wolfgang hurried to sit next to Megan. "Do you have it?"

Megan opened a drawer beneath the stretcher and produced a padded envelope with a small lump inside. Wolfgang opened the end of the envelope and saw Sparrow's flash drive resting inside.

"Pen," Wolfgang said.

Megan handed him a Sharpie, and Wolfgang tore a strip of paper from a clipboard hanging on the wall. He uncapped the marker with his teeth and scrawled a brief note on the paper as the van began to move.

Dear Ivan,

Hope this helps. Sorry about the fire.

Until next time,

Amerikos

Wolfgang stuffed the note inside the envelope and sealed it, then flipped it over and jotted down Ivan's name, along with an address. It was in English, but somebody would translate it, and it would eventually find its way to his desk.

"You sure about this?" Megan asked. "He could be one of them. He could be playing you."

Wolfgang smiled. "He's not."

"How do you know?"

Wolfgang turned to Edric. His boss leaned against the

wall, flinching as Lyle slid an IV needle into his arm.

Wolfgang tucked the envelope into his shirt. "I just know."

"Train station?" Kevin called from the driver's seat.

"No," Wolfgang said. "We've got one more job to do."

Kevin frowned through the rearview mirror. "Huh?"

"Are you crazy?" Megan said. "We've got to get out of here. Now."

"Not without Koslov. He's put his life on the line for this mission. We're not leaving him behind."

"We don't have time," she objected. "We don't know where he is!"

Wolfgang looked at Edric, and his boss nodded.

Wolfgang said, "I know where he is."

WOLFGANG TORE another strip off the clipboard and scratched down an address, then passed it to Lyle.

"Translate that into English, and give Kevin the directions."

Lyle squinted at the paper, then punched the address into one of his computers and waited a moment while the browser loaded. His head snapped up. "You've got to be kidding."

Megan pushed past Wolfgang and leaned over the computer, then looked up, already shaking her head. "No, no, no. Are you out of your mind? We're leaving. Right now! Kevin, take us to the train station."

She pushed toward the front of the ambulance, but Wolfgang caught her arm. "Megan, listen to me. Koslov was a private scientist. The terrorists recruited him to build a chemical weapon, leading him to think they were Russian authorities. But why did he take the job, Megan? Have you ever asked yourself that?"

Megan jerked her hand away. "I don't *care* why! It doesn't matter."

"It *does* matter. It matters because Pascha Koslov is a good man. A man in love with a woman who was dying and needed very expensive treatment."

Megan frowned. "What the hell are you talking about?"

"I'm talking about Sparrow, Megan. Sparrow was Koslov's girlfriend."

The ambulance fell silent.

Kevin stomped on the brakes and pulled them into a parking spot next to the curb. "Edric!" he said. "Can you be in charge again?"

All eyes turned to Edric, who wheezed between busted lips.

Wolfgang held up a hand and kept talking, more quickly now. "Sparrow wasn't a professional spy. She was just a go-between. The CIA couldn't interact directly with Koslov without the Russians being alerted, right? So how did Sparrow manage it? She managed it because Sparrow knew Koslov personally. The terrorists weren't alarmed by her presence because they knew who she was."

Kevin started to object, but Edric held up a hand and nodded at Wolfgang. "Keep going."

"Koslov believed he was working for the Russian

government, designing illegal weapons. He fed the CIA information for a while, but then he suddenly demanded extraction. Why?"

Megan shook her head. "Because he chickened out? It doesn't matter. Wolfgang, we need—"

Wolfgang dug the metal tag he'd taken from Sparrow's neck out of his pocket and flung it onto the stretcher. "He wanted to leave because his girlfriend, Sparrow, was dying. She had advanced cystic fibrosis. That tag is a medical tag used to identify her condition to emergency medical services, and when I found her in the detention cell, all the symptoms of CF were there. That's how she died. Koslov probably went to work for the terrorists in order to pay for additional treatments that state-sponsored medical care wouldn't cover, but when he discovered what sort of weapons they were building, he sold the information to the United States instead. Koslov needed money to cover Sparrow's advanced medical treatment, and he wanted to stop the Russians. So, for a while, he sold secrets to the CIA, but then Koslov discovered that the people he was working for weren't the Russians at all. They were terrorists planning an actual attack. That's when he reached out to the CIA demanding immediate extraction."

"He didn't tell the CIA about the terrorists, though," Edric said. "He withheld that."

"He withheld it because he wanted bargaining power to get Sparrow out, also. The CIA probably planned to abandon Sparrow, proven by the fact that they pulled her handler two days ago. That's when Koslov panicked and sent Sparrow to meet with Edric to arrange a deal. He didn't know Ivan would follow her to Bar Gypsy."

In the distance, sirens grew louder, and Kevin shoved the ambulance into drive again. "Edric, we've got to move."

"Just drive west," Wolfgang said. "Let me finish."

"Why was Ivan following Sparrow?" Megan asked.

Wolfgang could hear the engagement in her voice. The buy-in.

"Because Ivan has been working leads to track down these terrorists for months, and somehow those leads led him to Sparrow," he said. "Maybe he found the paper trail Koslov was feeding the CIA. I don't know. Regardless, Ivan raided Bar Gypsy to take Sparrow, and his men took Edric because he was with her. I guess they didn't check Sparrow's tag, and the stress was too much for her. Cystic fibrosis reduces your lung capacity and cripples your ability to breathe. My guess is she had a panic attack and suffocated."

"Tragic, really," Kevin said. "What does that have to do with us?"

"It has everything to do with us," Wolfgang said. "Koslov risked everything to protect the woman he loved, and when he learned about the Soldier Field attack, he risked even her to stop it. When the people he's working for find out what happened, they'll hunt him down and kill him. Ivan will deal with the terrorists, but we need to do what we came here to do. We need to save Pascha Koslov."

"Where is he?" Edric said.

"Where he's always been. At Sparrow's apartment." Wolfgang reached into his pocket and withdrew the photograph. It was worn and stained, just as he found it in Sparrow's pocket. The washed-out color image depicted Sparrow and a tall man in wire-rimmed glasses holding each other outside an apartment building. In the distance, the Kremlin rose out of the cityscape, bathed in the blaze of a setting sun. They smiled into the camera, their warm eyes full of love and laughter, but Sparrow's cheeks were hollow, and her body was frail, wracked by illness.

Wolfgang passed the photo to Edric. "That's Koslov standing next to her, isn't it?"

Edric gazed at the photo, then nodded.

"You can see the landmark in the background," Wolfgang continued. "Neither Koslov nor Sparrow were professional spies. They didn't have safe houses or know how to disappear in a crowded city. When they realized his life would be in danger, they hid him in the only place they could think of—her apartment. And that's where he is right now, waiting for her, and for us, to come get him."

Edric examined the photo, then passed it to Megan.

She gave it a quick glance, already shaking her head. "This is crazy. You're connecting dots a mile apart. And this *landmark* is the Kremlin. The *Kremlin*. Does that name mean anything to you?"

Wolfgang ignored her. "I'm right, Edric. I know I am."

Edric turned to Megan. She shook her head but didn't comment, so he turned to Kevin. "When does the train leave?"

Kevin rolled his eyes. "Two hours."

"Then we have time?"

Megan started to speak, but Edric held up his hand. "Do we have time?"

Kevin nodded reluctantly.

"Okay, then. Let's roll. Wolfgang, this better be quick."

———

SPARROW'S APARTMENT building was easily recognizable from the photograph. It was built of dirty brown bricks, with trash tubes dangling from chutes down into dumpsters and windows smudged with years of filth. Kevin drove back and forth down narrow city streets east of the Kremlin for only ten minutes before Wolfgang pointed.

"There! That's it!"

Kevin stared up at the building rising six stories out of Moscow's concrete jungle. "Which unit? We have no way to know."

"Just get me to the building," Wolfgang said. He turned back to Edric. "This is it. Give me ten minutes."

Edric turned to Lyle, and the tech shook his head. "It's not a good idea. Ambulances don't wander around like this. We're drawing attention."

"Ten minutes," Wolfgang repeated, throwing the back door open and jumping out before anybody could stop him. He broke into a run toward the apartment tower, then heard softer footsteps pounding behind him. Megan appeared next to him, her ponytail bouncing as they closed in on the building and rushed through the glass doors of the main entrance.

The grimy lobby of the complex featured scuffed walls and a yellow light that flickered overhead. An oil heater burned in one corner, with soot gathered on the wall behind it. Everything smelled hot and dirty, like the inside of a machine shop.

They approached the front desk, where a clerk's wide eyes switched between them and the oil heater. Wolfgang remembered that he and Megan still wore firefighter gear, and he connected the dots quickly. The oil heater was probably a fire hazard and illegal.

Megan produced the photograph of Sparrow and Koslov from her pocket and held it up. "Which apartment?" she said in English. The clerk shook his head, still glancing impulsively at the heater. Megan repeated the demand, then paused and cupped her hand over her earpiece.

Lyle. Thank God.

Megan looked up again. *"Kakaya kvartira?"*

Again, the clerk looked confused. Megan repeated the question, jabbing the photo closer to the clerk's nose. Recognition dawned on his face, and he rattled off something in Russian.

Megan snapped, "I don't speak Russian, pal. Which apartment?"

The clerk held up four fingers, closed his hand, then held up three.

"Forty-three!" Wolfgang said, turning toward the stairwell. Megan followed, the two of them barreling up the steps two at a time. The fourth-floor landing was littered with garbage, and the stairwell door hung on one hinge. Wolfgang kicked it open and twisted down the hall, checking each of the doors as they passed. The brass numeral plates that adorned each door were all written in Cyrillic.

Wolfgang cursed and scanned the doors again, then took a chance. He counted three doors from the end of the hallway, then tried the knob, but it was locked. He drove his foot into the door, and it blasted back on its hinges. They rushed inside, clearing the hallway and turning into the main living space, where Pascha Koslov sat on a couch with panic-filled eyes.

Wolfgang recognized him immediately from the photograph.

Koslov bolted to his feet and held out both hands.

"Pascha Koslov?" Wolfgang asked.

Koslov hesitated, seemingly confused by the uniforms, and Wolfgang decided to throw all his cards on the table. "Mr. Koslov, we're the Americans. We're here to get you out."

A tear slid down Koslov's face. "America?"

"Da. America." Wolfgang held out a hand, feeling his own eyes sting. There was something about the pain in this man's face that was so deep and lonely. A man who loved. A man who just wanted to be free, and for the one he loved to be saved.

"Come with us, Mr. Koslov. You're safe now."

"I wouldn't be sure of that," Megan said. She stood next to the window, looking down at the parking lot, then cursed under her breath.

"What is it?" Wolfgang said.

"Your buddy's here."

Wolfgang ran to the window.

Ivan Sidorov climbed out of a car in front of the apartment building, a small army of Russian soldiers close behind.

[11]

WOLFGANG HESITATED NEAR THE DOOR. He wanted to look back out the window and check Ivan's progress, but it was a pointless maneuver. Somehow, Ivan had found out about Koslov's association with Sparrow and then tracked down Sparrow's address. It was quick math and brought with it enough SVR agents to bring down the house.

"What's the play?" Megan said.

Wolfgang shifted, realizing he'd subconsciously expected her to take the lead.

But no. This is my mess. I've got to clean it up.

"We've got to get Koslov to the train. Ivan will expect us to take a plane. We'll be in Belarus before he realizes what happened."

"What about the others?"

Wolfgang shrugged, hurriedly stripping out of his baggy

firefighters's overalls and gesturing for Megan to do the same. "Edric knows the plan. They'll meet us in Minsk."

Voices boomed from the stairwell, and Wolfgang looked to the door. His mind spun, searching for an option. He could pull the fire alarm, but Ivan wouldn't be fooled by the same trick twice. Alternatively, he could charge into the hallway and leverage the element of surprise, but surprise was a poor substitute for firepower in the face of half a dozen armed SVR agents.

The trash chutes.

Wolfgang remembered the dangling tubes that ran from chutes, down the sides of the building, and into dumpsters outside—a cheap and grimy disposal system.

"This way! I've got an idea."

Megan grabbed Koslov by the hand, and the three of them ran to the door, throwing it open and hurrying through without waiting to see if Ivan's crew had reached the fourth floor. Wolfgang turned to the left, dragging Koslov by the hand as angry Russian voices filled the stairwell behind them.

If Ivan has a rage problem, it's probably my fault.

Wolfgang slid around a corner to the east hallway and immediately saw the uncovered mouth of the trash chute gaping at them like a black hole. It was about eighteen inches wide and framed with sharp, dirty metal.

Terrific. I'll need a tetanus shot.

Wolfgang slid to a stop at the mouth of the chute and

beckoned Koslov forward. "Come on, Pascha. Down you go!"

Koslov's eyes widened, but then Ivan's crew reached the fourth floor, and the door to the stairwell blew back on its hinges as they rushed through. That was enough for him, and Koslov allowed Megan and Wolfgang to lift him by the arms and shove him feet-first into the chute. A moment later, he slid out of sight into the dark tube, leaving behind him nothing but the stench of household garbage.

Wolfgang grabbed Megan by the hand and steadied her as she wrinkled her nose and poked one foot into the chute, then the other. Around the corner, a fist pounded on a door —Sparrow's door, no doubt—then Wolfgang recognized Ivan's pissed-off tone demanding entry.

"Go!" he said.

Megan wiggled her hips into the chute, then crossed both arms over her chest as though she were a kid at the top of a water slide. Wolfgang gave her a little push, and then she was gone. He lifted one foot and stuck his leg in, then contemplated for the first time exactly what he was about to do. He thought about the mucky inside of the tube, coated with rotting garbage and maybe broken glass. At the bottom —assuming the tube wasn't jammed and Koslov and Megan weren't already stuck halfway down—there would be more garbage, and maybe more glass. Maybe a broken bicycle with its handlebars jammed upward, ready to slide between his legs and—

Sparrow's door exploded open, and Russians shouted. Wolfgang threw his other leg into the tube and wriggled inside. At six one and a buck eighty, Wolfgang wasn't a big guy, but he was bigger than Koslov and a lot bigger than Megan. He felt his hips grind into the edges of the chute, and momentary panic clouded his mind. He wriggled farther in, wincing as sharp metal scraped against his pants as it moved across his hip bones.

Wolfgang pushed and grunted, grabbing the inside of the chute and pulling himself until his hips slid inside. Both of his feet were in the clear now, kicking against the inside of the chute, but the metal mouth now ground against his elbows.

His eyes watered, and he twisted. Then he heard another shout and looked to his left to see Ivan burst around the corner.

The big Russian paused mid-step as their gazes met. Ivan's eyes blazed with fury, and his face flushed red, then he shouted something in Russian and lunged forward, reaching for his gun.

Wolfgang grinned and winked, then jammed his elbows against his ribcage and dropped through the chute. The dirty inside of the tube smacked against his sides, but there wasn't time to worry about glass or tetanus or whether Megan was trapped beneath him. He hurtled downward like a bullet, his butt riding along the bottom of the tube and only partially slowing his descent. The sound of shouting

Russians faded away, and then his feet hit something soft and bright light flashed in his eyes.

Wolfgang crumpled into the dumpster, where black trash bags surrounded him on all sides. Megan clambered over the bags and held out a hand, shouting something about guns.

Pistol shots rang from overhead, and Wolfgang scrambled over the trash. He climbed to the top of the mound, then rolled over the side of the dumpster and landed on concrete as bullets smacked into the dumpster, ringing like cowbells. His knees hit first, then his hands. Megan yanked him up by the collar and pushed him forward, then the three of them broke out across the parking lot in a mad dash for life.

He ran like he hadn't run since he was a kid, blasting through the hills and trees of West Virginia. He imagined his bare feet pounding over rocks and sticks without pause, the thick callouses on his soles protecting him. As a kid, he'd often imagined he was running for his life—not in West Virginia, but in the Amazon jungle or the deserts of South Africa.

Or the streets of a big city, someplace far away.

Be careful what you wish for, fool.

The team hurtled through the parking lot and didn't bother looking for the ambulance. Edric and the others were either long gone or already in Russian Federal custody. Either way, Wolfgang had to get Koslov out of the country.

"How far to the train station?" he shouted.

"Two miles. Let's move!" Megan led the way around another corner and across a narrow Russian street. Koslov ran between them, already panting and glancing over his shoulder every few seconds as if a pack of wolves was right on his heels.

Not far from the truth.

"Katya?" Koslov managed between pants. "Katya?"

Wolfgang felt a strange weight descend on his chest. He saw Sparrow again, lying on her back in the Russian detention cell, choking for air as her deteriorated lungs finally gave out. He wondered what her final thoughts were and if she thought of Pascha the way he thought of her now.

"Run, Koslov!" Wolfgang said, placing a hand on his shoulder and urging him forward. Each step against the concrete shot waves of pain up his knees, and his head throbbed, but he didn't dare look over his shoulder. He just followed Megan, winding in and out of alleyways and backstreets.

Wolfgang didn't hear the wail of Russian sirens behind him, but the SVR wouldn't use police cars or helicopters. They would use generic black sedans and silenced pistols, ready to assassinate them as presumed terrorists.

He stole a glance at the passing rooftops, recalling the first time he'd encountered Ivan in an apartment building in Paris when Ivan was armed with a silenced sniper rifle. Did he have a rifle now? Had he somehow circled ahead of them and was even now sighting down the barrel of his weapon, watching as his targets crashed toward him in single file?

An ideal setup for a sniper. Three quick presses of the trigger, and we all bite the dust.

"Left turn!" Megan snapped, jerking them suddenly into an alley.

Wolfgang smelled grease and fried pork and felt a sudden craving for egg rolls. As they crashed forward, he realized they were passing behind a Chinese restaurant, and Russian shouts reverberated through the open back door.

They're close.

Koslov flagged, leaning forward and holding his side.

Wolfgang pushed him, feeling his own irresistible desire to cave to the pain in his legs and the burning in his chest. "Keep going, Koslov!"

They reached the end of the alley, and Megan held up a fist. They all ground to a halt, and Wolfgang panted for air as Megan stepped out of the alley and cast a quick glance each way. Then she beckoned for them to follow her to the right.

The blocks faded into a pounding mixture of pedestrians and muddy snow. They dashed across one street after another, narrowly avoiding collisions with cars as horns blared and Russians shouted. Wolfgang wanted to count his steps and speculate on how much farther they had to run, but he couldn't spare the energy. Ivan could be a mile behind, or only a few yards, and Wolfgang doubted that his fourth encounter with the irate SVR officer would go as favorably as the first three.

"There!" Megan pointed to a tall, square building with a glass face, only two hundred yards distant.

Pedestrians milled about outside as taxicabs pulled to and from the curb. Wolfgang couldn't read the Cyrillic lettering mounted to the top of the building, but he prayed Megan was right.

Wolfgang patted Koslov on the back. "Almost there, Koslov. Keep moving!"

The exhausted scientist stumbled and coughed, and Megan slowed a little. They couldn't simply barge into the train station without drawing attention, and Wolfgang wondered suddenly if there would be customs or security to process through. He knew that many European countries, specifically those in the European Union, allowed for open travel between countries without the fuss of immigration or customs, but Russia wasn't a member of the EU, and neither was Belarus.

No time to worry about it now.

Megan held the door, and they slid inside, Koslov still panting like a winded elephant. The train station's main lobby was immense, crowded with pedestrians and rolling suitcases, and noisy enough to drown out both Koslov's gasping and Wolfgang's quiet remarks.

"You have the tickets?"

Megan nodded. "The train for Minsk leaves in ten minutes. Make Koslov hurry."

She hurried across the room to the ticket counter and presented her phone with three digital tickets queued up and ready to go. There was a brief hesitation from the ticket clerk, and he glanced toward Wolfgang and Koslov, then motioned toward a rail line and resumed staring at his cell phone.

Megan beckoned them on, and they wound their way across the lobby, down an escalator, through a set of glass doors, and onto the main platform of the station. The warmth of the train lobby vanished as the air filled with the screech of metal on metal and a chorus of shouts from conductors and travelers. Trains sat at random on multiple tracks, sheltered by a giant glass dome laden with snow. Megan glanced at her ticket, then scanned the trains. She pointed at one, and they hurried forward again. Koslov held his side, and Wolfgang glanced over his shoulder.

There was no sign of Ivan. Not yet.

Megan slid to a stop at the entrance of a car, where a disheveled conductor dressed in a thick woolen coat was busy scanning digital tickets with a plastic gun. Megan presented her phone again, then motioned to Koslov and Wolfgang. The conductor shrugged.

"Stay here," Wolfgang whispered.

Koslov looked up, panic shining in his eyes. Wolfgang gave his arm a squeeze, then hurried across the platform.

Mounted against the wall twenty yards away was a small, blue metal box emblazoned with the gold emblem of the *Pochta Rossii*—the Russian mail service.

Wolfgang dug the envelope out of his pocket and felt to ensure that the flash drive was inside. He hesitated a moment.

What if Ivan is one of them?

He held the envelope and rubbed the bulge of the thumb drive.

He's not. I just know.

Wolfgang slid the envelope into the mailbox, then ran back to the train. The conductor waved him in with an impatient grunt, and Wolfgang hurried down the aisle. Megan sat in the back of the car, holding a newspaper over her face while Koslov sat next to her, chewing his fingernails. He saw Wolfgang and started to speak, but Megan grabbed his arm and shot Wolfgang a frantic look over the top of the paper. Wolfgang turned to his right and looked through the train window.

Ivan Sidorov barreled down the platform toward the train.

Without stopping to think, Wolfgang sat down on a bench seat and turned his back to the window, bending down and pretending to tie his shoe. Shouts rang out from the platform as the train's doors slid shut. Wolfgang heard Ivan's now-familiar voice demanding answers from a transit employee on the platform. He looked over his shoulder and saw Ivan holding out an iPad with photos of Wolfgang displayed on the screen. The employee gave it only a casual glance, then shrugged and walked away as the train lurched forward.

Wolfgang grinned and looked away, leaning back against the glass. A moment later, the wheels of the train caught on the tracks, and they slid out of the station in a rush. Wolfgang's last view of Ivan was of the big Russian throwing the iPad at one of his companions, then turning toward the escalator like a raging bull, once again thwarted.

The train shook as it gained speed, and Wolfgang turned to Megan. She lowered the paper over her lap and glanced at the fading train station, then turned to Wolfgang. Megan grinned, then broke into a soft chuckle. Wolfgang joined her and leaned back in the seat. For a moment, they just laughed as though they were swapping some sort of old inside joke. Wolfgang still felt cold from the bite of the Russian wind, but in the warmth of Megan's laugh, his numb fingers and aching legs didn't matter anymore. For the moment . . . all was well.

And then Koslov leaned forward, his eyes wide and strained, and whispered the word that brought that moment to an end. "Katya?"

IT TOOK nine hours to reach Minsk. Most of those hours were traveled in silence as Koslov held his face in his hands and cried. He didn't shake, and he didn't make a sound, but tears streamed down his face as Wolfgang and Megan sat in heavy silence, each avoiding the other's gaze.

Wolfgang wondered if he could have saved Katya. Maybe if they had bumped their timeline up and he reached the detention facility sooner. Maybe if he spent less time talking with Ivan, or less time arguing with the team back in the hotel. If he could've gotten to Katya sooner, before the stress and panic overwhelmed her weakened body . . .

There was no way to know, and there never would be. Katya was a casualty of war—not a war against Russia, or even a war against the anarchist terrorist—Katya was a casualty of war against the darker side of life. The side of life that brought curses like diseases and illness and bad hospitals and no money. That was a war as old as humanity, and it would take many more casualties in Wolfgang's life alone.

But that didn't make her loss any easier to bear.

At Minsk, a CIA contact waited for Koslov. The man wore jeans and tennis shoes with a Tampa Bay Lightning hat and a college kid's backpack. He beckoned to Koslov at the edge of the platform, and the broken scientist turned to Wolfgang. His eyes were bloodshot, framed by dark bags. There was no spirit left in his body. No desire for life. But he nodded at Wolfgang once and said again, "America?"

Wolfgang nodded. "America."

Koslov looked up at the sky, visible from the roofless outdoor platform. He nodded again, and to Wolfgang's surprise, he said in broken English, "Katya would have liked America."

Then Pascha Koslov followed the kid with the backpack, never looking back.

———

A TAXI CAB waited for Megan and Wolfgang at the train station, as they expected it to. Edric knew what time the train from Moscow would arrive, and he would have dispatched the cab to pick them up and bring them to whatever private airfield SPIRE's Gulfstream G550 waited at.

They climbed into the back of the worn car, relieved to find it warm, and sat in silence as the driver wound them through the darkened city, then turned toward the outskirts. Wolfgang stared down at his hands, feeling suddenly exhausted and sad. He could still see the haunted loneliness in Koslov's eyes. It was a look he would never forget.

What must that feel like . . .

Megan's gaze was fixated out the window, staring up at the starlit sky with bright eyes that were tired but so alive. So bright.

She has to know. I can't risk losing her without her knowing how I feel.

Wolfgang ran his tongue across his lips, searching for the words, but he couldn't think of any.

How do you tell a person that they keep you awake at night? That you wonder what their favorite color is, and that you want to dance with them in some quiet place, far away, under a sky that isn't so cold and dark? How do you tell a person . . . everything?

"How did you know?" Megan said.

Wolfgang looked up. "Know what?"

"You said Sparrow had cystic fibrosis, and the tag proved it. But the tag was printed in Russian, and we didn't translate it until later. How did you know?"

Wolfgang winced and looked back at his hands. He wished he'd spoken a little sooner—asked her what her favorite color was, or where she was from, or how she liked her coffee.

"I'm sorry," she said. "I shouldn't have asked."

Wolfgang swallowed. "My sister has it."

"You have a sister?"

Wolfgang hesitated and then decided to just tell her. It was a secret he was weary of bearing alone.

"Her name is Collins. She's ten now and lives in Buffalo." Wolfgang met Megan's gaze, fully aware that his eyes were red. "She's had it since she was a kid. My family . . . well, my parents died. It was kind of a mess. Edric was there, and he offered to help. He told me I could take care of Collins, and get her good medical care, all while having some adventures. I guess that's how it all started. Me and SPIRE."

It all just bubbled out before he could stop it. The words tumbled over themselves in a rush. Wolfgang cursed himself, but it was too late now. The lid was off, and he was exposed.

"When was that?" Megan said softly.

Wolfgang sighed. He saw West Virginia again, green and hot in the grip of summer. He saw his mother lying in a corner of their beat-up single-wide, bleeding and bruised. Not moving. He heard Collins crying from the couch, screaming for her mommy. Then he saw the New River Gorge Bridge stretching out over the churning New River, far below. He saw his father standing there in the dark, drunk and screaming.

"I was fifteen. It was six years ago."

He was at once embarrassed and relieved. He'd told no one the details of that night—he hadn't even discussed it with Edric, even though Edric was there. He'd not even said the words out loud to himself, and he never would. But maybe telling Megan where he was from and that he had a family once . . . maybe that was enough.

It was enough to ease the pain, at least for now.

Megan put a hand on his, giving it a soft squeeze, and then she smiled.

———

"WONDERBOY, BACK AGAIN!"

Megan and Wolfgang piled into the plane as Edric appeared from the aft cabin. He stood next to the minibar, his face still bruised and battered, but a light in his eyes that Wolfgang hadn't seen in a while. The interior of the jet was warm, with soft yellow lights and inviting leather seats so comfortable that Wolfgang wanted to crash down and fall asleep right away.

The door shut behind him, and almost immediately the plane taxied to the runway. Wolfgang and Megan settled into seats and strapped themselves in as Edric poured himself a bourbon and turned a megawatt smile on the two.

"Well done. Both of you. Damn good job."

Lyle sniffed from a back seat, and Kevin muttered a curse. Edric turned the grin toward them and lifted the glass. "Calm down, guys. I haven't forgotten you." Edric settled into a seat as the plane's engines spun up and the aircraft gained speed on the runway. He took a sip, then faced each of them, one at a time. "You guys broke protocol. You took some shitty risks. You put the entire mission on the line."

Kevin snorted. "And right about now, I'm wondering . . . why?"

Edric laughed. "I owe you one. All of you. Here's to Charlie Team!"

Everybody with a drink raised it, then sloshed liquor over themselves as the plane's nose reached for the sky. Wolfgang felt the ground disappear beneath them, and he settled back in the seat. He looked at Megan across from him and thought again about words unsaid.

Those words he would keep, he decided. For a little longer.

Kevin and Lyle started shot-gunning questions about Koslov to Wolfgang and Megan. Mercifully, Megan offered the answers, allowing Wolfgang to lie back and relax for the first time in days. He didn't pay attention as Edric stiffened in his chair, glancing down at his phone. He didn't turn his head as Edric stood up suddenly and walked to the cockpit, the smile vanishing from his face. But he sat up when Edric burst back into the cabin and placed his hand on Wolf-gang's seat.

"Somebody just attacked SPIRE. The director's daughter has been kidnapped."

The plane fell into stunned silence as they all turned toward Edric. Then he answered their question before anybody could ask. "We're going to Rio."

WOLFGANG RETURNS IN...

Visit LoganRyles.com for details.

ABOUT THE AUTHOR

Logan Ryles is the author of the Reed Montgomery thriller series, and the Wolfgang Pierce espionage series. You can learn more about Logan's books, sign up for email updates, and connect with him directly by visiting LoganRyles.com.

ALSO BY LOGAN RYLES

THE WOLFGANG PIERCE ESPIONAGE SERIES

Prequel: *That Time in Appalachia* (read for free at LoganRyles.com)

Book 1: *That Time in Paris*

Book 2: *That Time in Cairo*

Book 3: *That Time in Moscow*

Book 4: *That Time in Rio*

Book 5: *That Time in Tokyo*

Book 6: *That Time in Sydney*

THE REED MONTGOMERY THRILLER SERIES

Prequel: *Sandbox*, a short story (read for free at LoganRyles.com)

Book 1: *Overwatch*

Book 2: *Hunt to Kill*

Book 3: *Total War*

Book 4: *Smoke & Mirrors*

Book 5: *Survivor*

Book 6: *Death Cycle*

Book 7: *Sundown*

LoganRyles.com

Made in the USA
Coppell, TX
15 March 2022

75005957R00246